DEDICATION

– As Always,
For my favorite Ks

{ PROLOGUE }

Ignoring the blood dripping from his hand and the uncontrollable tremble that held his fingers hostage, Logan sank to his knees and reached down.

Down into the embers.

Down into the ashes.

Bone.

Shreds of a dress. Scorched hair, the smell burning his nostrils.

A tiny glimmer.

The ring.

Clutched in the bent crook of her finger bones.

Clutched until the very end.

His wife's ring.

The ribbon she'd always wrapped around the band to make it fit snug on her delicate finger had burned away, leaving nothing but a gaping, empty hole within the scorched gold. He'd offered to have a goldsmith resize it a hundred times, but she'd always refused. She'd wanted it exactly as he had given it to her.

His hand shaking, he plucked the ring from her charred grasp, ashes clinging to his skin.

It was what he deserved.

Choosing his soulmate over his men.

He knew this would happen. Knew she would die. Leave him alone on this earth. He'd known it from the start. Known it since she was three and he was five.

One did not grow old in the world they existed in.

For death followed him.

It always had.

That he'd gotten away with loving her for as long as he did—a mere trick he had played on fate.

Fate had finally caught up to him.

Fate knew he wasn't worthy of her love.

Just the same as he did.

His head jerked up at the rifle shots thundering into the air outside the cottage. Steel clanging against steel. Yelling. Shrieks.

Boney's forces were rampaging, dealing death.

He pushed himself to his feet and grabbed his sword from the smoking embers.

Let them. He was ready.

{ CHAPTER 1 }

Logan gasped a breath, the air freezing in his lungs as his body seized upon itself, stilling his motion. Stopping his feet.

He'd followed the woman from the village. Followed her as she walked past the rows of cottages lining the dirt path that ran at a cross direction to the main road though the village of Sandfell.

That he had even seen her, even been in this part of Yorkshire had been happenstance. Torrential rains had turned the roads along his usual eastern route into a hoof-sucking, muddy mess so he'd travelled inward.

He had just stepped outside of the coaching inn where he'd spent the night, eager to get to his horse and be on his way when he spied her. For as much as he'd needed a break from London and the Revelry's Tempest—a break from the three proprietresses of the gaming house flitting about in wedded bliss and the bi-weekly drama that ensued from the gaming nights—visiting his estate in Northumberland hadn't given him the respite he'd hoped for.

Once a year, obligation forced him to make the journey north to meet with Hunter, his steward of the lands and his Northumberland interests. Whereas he usually enjoyed his time in the north, in the clean air that didn't fill his lungs with muck day after day, this particular trip had found him itching to escape the area.

Itching to escape the happiness that his friend was flush with.

Hunter's three young children—two boys and one girl—were all healthy, curious, and enamored with their "Uncle" Logan. Logan hadn't sat without a child on his lap for a week. Hunter's wife, a surgeon and bone setter by luck of her father passing down his skills, had served Logan's lands as their healer, midwife, and general scourge upon any traveling apothecary that dared to set foot in her domain. Beyond her many assets, the woman still looked at Hunter as though he was the only man in the world.

Bliss, all around. Too much of it.

Envy was not an emotion Logan was familiar with.

But staying with Hunter, staying with his family— watching the smiles on their faces and the simple pleasure they took in being together, laughing with one another— had sparked a jealousy that had crept out of nowhere and settled upon his shoulders.

He didn't begrudge Hunter any of the happiness he'd found in life. It was an odd thing, to be proud of his friend for finding happiness, yet deeply envious of him at the same time.

Logan had suffered through it for days. Then he'd finally cut his trip short, the prickly need to escape the realm of their happiness forcing him to leave without even manifesting a half-witted excuse to leave early.

His abrupt absence at the estate was sure to worry his friend and Logan had almost turned back to explain his hastily written note that merely said he was needed back in London.

Yet he couldn't turn back. Explaining was weakness. Envy was weakness.

And he was not weak.

But he was slightly insane.

Logan's rooted stance next to a low, dry-stone border fence allowed him to stare—truly stare—at the back of the woman he had followed. A fair distance in front of him, she carried a basket with two loaves of bread sticking tall from the top, bumping into the back of her light blue muslin dress with every other step.

Just exiting the coaching inn, he'd seen her across the street as she stepped out from the baker's cottage. She'd been a distance away, but Logan was close enough to see her delicate profile and the swing of her long reddish-blond hair under her crisp blue poke bonnet as she spun away from him. The bonnet, trimmed with a simple white ribbon, had obscured the top half of her face, her eyes, but the tip of the nose, the chin and the lips were hers.

His wife's.

So he followed her.

He'd done this before.

Seen a woman that looked like Sienna and trailed her. Drawn to memories he could not escape. The pull of her still so strong after more than ten years that he would stalk a stranger just for a few precious moments of fantasy— moments of hope.

The heels of his boots ground into the dirt of the path and he shook his head to himself. This was where he needed to turn around. Get back to his horse. Be on his way.

He had just walked a good mile from the village in an inane pursuit of this woman.

His gaze centered on the line of the woman's proud shoulders, mesmerized by her graceful gait. A forest to her right, open field to her left, she moved up a small incline and then disappeared over the crest of a low hill.

The sudden absence of her made him jerk into motion, his feet flying forward even as his mind reminded him it was beyond madness to follow a strange woman into the countryside. It was, in fact, bordering on menacing.

Just a few more moments.

He moved to the crest of the hill, fully intending one last glance at her before turning back to the village. Instead, what he saw stopped him in his tracks.

At the base of the hill the woman had moved off the path to an apple tree draping over the dry-stone wall and was cutting free a late-blooming cluster of blossoms from the end of a long branch with a small knife. She slipped the bonnet back from her head to let it dangle from the ribbon about her neck and then pulled her hair back on the side to tuck the stem of the white blossoms behind her ear.

A motion he'd seen a hundred times before. How she twisted her hair to get it out of the way. How she tilted her head as she tucked the twig to her ear. How she closed her eyes, her chest rising in a deep inhale.

The soft smile on her face as the scent filled her.

A smile he knew.

A smile that had once been the center of his world.

His head shaking, swiveling, he looked around. It was a trap. A mirage. An elaborate ruse upon him. He was seeing things.

Seeing things he *wanted* to see. *Needed* to see.

Plucking a single star-shaped blossom from the stem, her fingers lifted it to lightly drag it along the bridge of her nose. Her face tilted upward, her eyes closed as she held the petals to the tip of her nose with just her forefinger.

Hell.

He'd only seen one person in the world ever do that.

His wife.

His legs were running, blasting him down the hill in a frenzied blur before he could think.

She didn't see him coming, didn't open her eyes until the last second, her mouth flying open with a squeak.

He grabbed her arm, twisting her fully to him, and the blossom fell from her nose, drifting downward.

Wide blue eyes—shock filling them.

Sienna.

His wife.

His dead wife. Dead for ten years.

There was no doubt.

He grabbed her other arm, staring down at her, searching—searching for some small defect, some small dissimilarity that would prove she wasn't Sienna.

Her mouth agape, the woman looked up at him.

No recognition in her blue eyes—not the slightest glint.

She stared at him, her wide eyes rapidly blinking as she gently tried to tug her arms away from his grasp. "Do I know you, sir?"

His knees weakened, almost sending him to the ground.

Her voice was unmistakable.

"Sienna." Her name came out awkward, rushed, his tongue not able to believe the possibility that it was her. He hadn't uttered her name once since she had died.

Her mouth snapped shut, her lips stretching to a thin line as her eyebrows drew together. "Sir—"

"Sienna." He shook her.

Her eyes widened, sudden fear taking root in the dark azure streaks in her irises. She attempted to jerk free from his grasp.

"Sienna, it's me."

"Sir, no, no. You are mistaken on who I am."

"Sienna, just stop and listen to me. You know me." He ignored her wrenching and shook her again.

"Please, sir—"

"Sienna." He paused, then shook her again, his fingers digging into the flesh on her upper arms.

"Please, sir, you're scaring me." She twisted viciously, trying to escape.

His clamp tightened on her arms, shaking her. He would damn well shake her until she recognized him. He had to.

Pain.

Searing pain attacking his middle from nowhere.

He looked down. The tip of a blade was in his flesh, digging into his gut before he realized Sienna still held the knife. She lunged forward at him with her feet, putting all her weight and both hands behind the blade piercing his belly.

His fingers dropped away from her arms, going to her wrists to rip her hands and the blade free from impaling his belly. Blade removed, his hands clasped over the wound in his gut.

Horror crossed her face and she stumbled backward, the basket still hanging from her arm swinging wildly. The bread tumbled from the basket as the handle slipped off her arm, thudding to the ground.

He lifted his right hand from his belly, stretching it out to her. "Please, Sienna—no—stop, Sienna." He staggered three steps toward her, his left hand holding against his bleeding gut.

Her face twisted in terror and a small yelp squeaked from her mouth as she spun and ran. Ran so fast, her blue skirts flew out behind her. She veered to the right, scrambling over the dry-stone wall and then raced into the woods that offered obstacles, if not protection from him.

"Sienna." His yell trailed, his desperate voice giving out to the pain in his gut tearing him in two.

She jumped to the left, disappearing behind a clump of oaks.

The world went still, silent. Logan staggered to his right, falling along the low stone fence for support, his fingers digging into the rough rock.

He stared at the woods, willing her to reappear. To run to him. To throw her arms around him.

He stared for far too long, his belly oozing blood.

But he couldn't move, couldn't leave. Could only stare at the oak she'd disappeared behind.

Hell.

His wife didn't recognize him.

And she had just stuck a dagger into him.

If he wasn't convinced before it was her, the blade in his gut told him all he needed to know.

He had made sure of it long ago—Sienna knew well how to protect herself.

His wife was alive.

~ ~ ~

She made it to her room, clicking the door closed behind her as quietly as she could manage, then collapsed back against it.

Her breath sped and she curled over, holding her stomach, her chest, trying to calm her thundering lungs, her gasps for air.

Gasp after gasp. No air finding its way past her tight throat, her tongue, her mouth that no longer felt like part of her body.

Her mind wild, terrified notions flew in all directions and she attempted to find one sane thought to grasp onto.

The man hadn't followed her. That was it. She had to hold onto that.

He hadn't followed her.

She'd run with her head craned back over her shoulder, searching the trail, searching the woods, searching the front walk of her grandmother's estate. Even glancing over her shoulder as she tore through the house, rushing up the stairs.

Safe. She was safe.

She was safe in her home. Safe in Roselawn.

Except he knew her name. She didn't know the man, so how in the heavens above did he know her name?

She pulled up slightly, her chin dropping to her chest and she caught sight of the knife still gripped in her hand. Blood streaked across the silver of the blade.

No. Please, no.

An image exploded in her mind, consuming her whole, the sensation of being thrown through the air and slamming into a wall. The pain in her mind manifested throughout her body. Pain everywhere.

Hitting the wall. Blackness.

~ ~ ~

Sienna jerked, her head hitting the door behind her.

She blinked the grogginess from her eyes, her room coming into focus.

She had fainted.

But she *never* fainted. She wasn't delicate. She didn't swoon. Even though her grandmother liked to tell her she was fragile, she didn't faint.

Yet there she was, shifting her hand onto her head on the floor, trying to right her mind to the here and now.

She swallowed hard and turned her face to the side only to be greeted by the blade.

Red streaks still smeared the steel.

The blade had done this to her. Why?

She had looked at it and then felt overwhelming pain. Nothing but pain. She tried to draw the memory to the front of her mind again. But the dark recesses of her brain sank away, shriveling away from her consciousness, scurrying to hide that memory away in the depths.

She stared at the blade, focusing on the streaks of crimson, now dried on the steel.

She had stuck a man.

Sank a blade into his belly.

Yes, the man had accosted her out of nowhere. Yes, a desperation like she had never seen had been in his dark silver eyes. It was what had terrified her.

But to gut him? To thrust a blade into his belly?

Her stomach churned.

Where had that come from? She didn't know how to stab a man. How to hurt another person.

She'd never held a blade to anything but an apple, but she knew—knew how to press it into his skin. How to thrust. She'd never hurt anything in her life. But she knew how to stab that man.

Her eyes shut against the thought, and the man's stunned face when he realized what she'd done filled her mind.

His face.

She jerked upright from the floor, scrambling to her feet. Stumbling to her secretary along the wall lined with windows, she flipped open the top rosewood cabinet. Pushing aside her charcoals, she pulled free a stack of vellum that she had set aside deep on the high shelf. The pile of sketches she kept for no reason other than she was unable to toss them into the fire.

Her fingers shaking, she flipped through the stack of vellum, sending sheets of paper flying in all directions, the edges fluttering to the ground until countless pages surrounded her.

She sank to her knees in the middle of the mess, her gaze flickering from one sketch to another. And another. And another.

Charcoal and pencil on the vellum sheets. Each from a different angle. Each capturing something new her imagination had conjured up.

She gasped, sinking down onto her heels. Her hand stretched out, her fingers trembling as she touched the sheet directly in front of her.

All the sketches were of the same man.

The man on the road.

He was the man her fingers sketched again and again. Years of sketching him.

And he had just appeared out of nowhere, grabbing her. This very same man.

She shook her head. She'd always believed he was an imaginary figment—for she knew she had never met him. At least as far as her memory went back. She had lived here at Roselawn her entire life. Her grandmother had assured her of that fact long ago after she had fallen from her horse and knocked all the memories from her head. It had been nine, maybe ten years, since the riding accident.

But the man said he knew her. Preposterous. After her accident, her grandmother had kept her safe, for her head was far too delicate to put out into the world with balls and parties and dinners where she would have met a man like him. And then she had reached the age of spinsterhood, and she hadn't even considered attending balls and parties to meet new people in years.

But that didn't mean she didn't dream.

Sienna picked up a sketch in front of her knees, her fingers still trembling as she studied it. It was of his eyes, just the top of his face. His dark grey eyes—not so dark they frightened, but they held just enough hidden depths to haunt her. To make her want to sketch those eyes too many times to count during the years.

She closed her eyes, picturing him in front of her. Seeing his dark silver eyes again. Eyes that lifted slightly at the edges, his dark lashes pinpointing his gaze. Eyes that were unmistakable.

She could almost feel his fingers still digging into her arms—how he had latched onto her. There had been something so undeniably primal in how he grabbed her. Like he owned her. Like he could do anything he wanted to her, because she belonged to him.

He was an utter stranger.

She had to remember that.

Her eyes drifted down to the sheets of paper scattered about her legs.

And she had to forget that she had just seen the one man she had fixated on her whole life in real, living, breathing person.

{ CHAPTER 2 }

"He is in the fourth room to the right on the third level?" Sienna's eyebrows arched as she looked at Mrs. Wilson, the innkeeper's wife.

If the man was on the third level, that meant either there were a lot of travelers staying here at the moment, or that the man was planning on staying in the village for a spell. The lack of horses in the coaching inn's stable told her it was most likely the latter. The thought sent a heavy rock of foreboding into her gut.

Mrs. Wilson nodded, juggling tankards and glasses as she moved away from Sienna and her maid as quickly as she could, weaving her way through the tables in the inn's dining room.

Sienna watched Mrs. Wilson for a moment before her eyes flickered to the stairwell on the far side of the inn's large dining room, then to her maid next to her. "Don't look at me like that, Bea."

"Like what, Miss Ponstance?"

"Like you know my grandmother would have your hide if she knew you accompanied me here. You don't need to worry. She won't know we stopped here at the coaching inn."

"That woman sees everything, even with her failing eyesight and you know it, miss." Bea shook her head. "I don't see why you need to check on the man. He attacked you and you stuck a knife into his belly. Seems right justice to me."

"Again, Bea, he didn't so much attack me, as to…stop me on my way." Mrs. Wilson exited the dining room into the kitchens and Sienna reached over and took the basket Bea was carrying, draping it onto her arm before starting toward the stairwell. "Or maybe he did attack me. I don't know. Anything is possible. That is why I brought you with me. I'm not a complete fool."

"I've never stuck a blade into a man, Miss Ponstance," Bea said. "Don't know what help you think me to be in that situation, a man attacking you and all."

Sienna paused at the entry to the stairwell and met Bea's wary look. "You can yell, can you not?"

Bea sighed, following Sienna up the stairs, every heavy step an argument against what Sienna was set on doing.

"And your presence will keep my reputation intact—or at least with a thread of respectability. It would not do with the village gossips, going up to a man's chambers here at the inn by myself—even in the most innocent of circumstances."

Bea snorted. "My presence isn't about to keep the yapping traps of the town's gadflies closed."

"No, but it will lessen my direct affront to the bounds of propriety, at the least. Between your presence and my spinsterhood, that is all I ask."

They trudged up the last flight of stairs in silence and then Sienna walked the long hallway, counting the rooms. Dark shadows abounded even though it was the middle of the day. At the fourth door, she stopped, squaring her shoulders to the door before taking a deep breath.

With questions of idiocy on her actions brimming in her mind, she knocked.

A muffled, "Enter," came from the bowels of the room.

Sienna kept her eyes straight ahead. If she looked at Bea again, she knew her maid's face would be all it would take to make her toss aside this plan and turn to run down the stairs.

But she had to know.

Know that he had survived her knife well enough.

And more importantly, she needed to know *who* he was.

Opening the door, she stepped quickly into the room before she lost her nerve. Bea followed so close she bumped into Sienna's back before turning to close the door.

The man was lying on the bed in the tastefully appointed room—dark green linens lined the bed and coordinating drapes adorned the window. The matching green damask coverlet was shoved to the side of the bed next to his legs. This chamber was larger than the rooms below it for guests that stayed in the area for a longer stretch of time.

His eyes met hers and she had to instantly gulp back another gasp.

She hadn't seen it in the flurry of the day before—in his grabbing her and her panicked attempt to free herself—she hadn't seen how atrociously handsome the man was. Her sketches of him had captured his eyes, the strong line of his chin, his jaw, his straight nose and cheekbones that were bred from an ancient refinement.

But nothing she had ever sketched compared to the reality of the man now staring at her with blazes of fire in his steel grey eyes.

Bea saw it instantly, her gasp not choked back. "Oh, good heaven above that is beautiful," she muttered under her breath, but loud enough for Sienna to hear.

If the man heard Bea, he didn't acknowledge it, his stare fixated on Sienna. "You." The one word came out rough from his chest, almost pained.

Sienna forced a smile onto her face. "Me. Yes. Me. I am here to apologize to you, sir, and see that your wound was appropriately taken care of."

He shifted on the bed, moving to sit upright with slow arms. Clad only in a white linen shirt and trousers, his boots were oddly on for a man recovering in bed. He shuffled his body backward, leaning against the wide walnut headboard of the bed.

His dark grey eyes sliced into her. "Who are you to judge if it was taken care of appropriately?"

"I—I—" She looked around the room, her eyes landing on Bea. Bea just raised an eyebrow at her. Her look travelled back to the man. "I have rudimentary knowledge of knife wounds. I would like to examine yours to make sure it is on the path to recovery."

Now his eyebrow lifted.

She had no such skill and every person in that room knew it, but now that she had uttered it, she was sticking with the lie. She turned back to Bea. "Will you wait outside, Bea? I shall not be too long."

For a long second, she thought Bea would fight her on this, but then her maid inclined her head and spun back to the door, exiting out into the hallway.

"So?"

He asked the question before she had a chance to turn around toward him.

"So what?" she asked, her lips drawing inward as she faced him.

"So are you truly going to look at the wound, Sienna?"

"Of course." She moved across the room, stopping beside the bed as she looked at his torso. He was tall, wide, and judging by how he moved, she imagined there was little fat on his body. Probably none at all, if his face was an indication.

She set the basket of meats, cheeses and a mutton pie that Cook had made this morning on a wooden chair next to the bed and then stood frozen, staring at the bandage wrapping his torso that she could see through the white linen of the shirt covering his stomach. A wave of apprehension swept through her as she realized how close she was to him. It wasn't a fear that he would harm her, but an unease she couldn't name.

"I am at a disadvantage, sir, as it appears you know my name, but I do not know yours."

"Lipinstein. Logan Lipinstein." His grey eyes pierced her, so expectant with his words that it almost made her take a step backward. Did he expect her to suddenly recognize his name? Recognize him?

She offered a slight nod, looking to the black granite fireplace on the far side of the room.

He cleared his throat. "Truly?"

Her eyebrow lifted as she looked back to him. The man liked to speak one vague word at a time. "Truly what?"

"You truly intend to look at my wound?" The rumble of his deep baritone voice wrapped around her.

She forced an apologetic smile. "Yes. I am the cause, so I must also be the reaction."

He winced at her words. Visibly in pain.

The cut had to be deeper than she'd thought.

She took a quick step forward as her eyes dipped down, unable to meet his look. "Yes. Your shirt, please. It won't take but a moment to assure me the wound was tended to in a satisfactory way."

For a long breath, he didn't move. But she could feel his eyes boring into her. Feel him assessing her.

She focused on his waist, the rumple of his shirt as it met his trousers, nothing else.

With a sigh, he shifted, tugging his shirt up and free of his trousers and exposing his midsection.

No fat. No fat at all. Just lines of muscles disappearing under the white bandage wrapped around his waist. Scars. Many of them, white ragged lines along his skin. The man was no stranger to pain—to knives and bullets piercing his skin.

He tucked the bulk of his shirt under his upper arms and then slid his thumbs behind the bandage, his stomach sucking in as he pulled the white cloth downward to expose the wound. Whether the bandage was tight and he had to suck in, or the pain of the movement made him suck in, she wasn't sure. If she could brave a look at his face, she would probably know, but she couldn't bring herself to lift her eyes.

His wound came into view and she instantly leaned forward, bending over the bed to get a look at the jagged skin. A scab had crusted around the opening.

The taste of bile chased up her throat and she had to swallow it back. That she had done this—cut into another person—it curdled her stomach. "I—I am sorry—I did not mean…"

Her words trailed and she shook her head, trying to clear it before truly studying the stitches holding the wound closed. She took in the crooked cross lines of the thread, the tugging of the ragged skin.

Her eyes finally lifted to his face. "These stitches are horrible. Tell me you didn't let Doctor Miller see to it—he probably left a leech inside you, he is so blind."

His grey eyes narrowed at her. "I did them."

"You did?"

"The wound wasn't that deep."

"Oh." She snapped upright, giving a curt nod as she took a small step backward. "Then the stitches are admirable, what with the pain you must have worked through."

His look stayed upon her as he shrugged, and then he tugged the bandage upward before letting his shirt fall back into place.

"You have seen what you needed to?"

She nodded. For as much as his curt words insinuated it was time for her to exit his room, her feet stayed rooted in place.

She needed to ask him. Ask him now before she never got another chance.

Her lips parted, and it took a long moment to gather the strength to utter the most difficult words of her life.

Her voice dipped low so Bea couldn't hear her through the thin wood of the door. "I do know you, don't I, sir?"

Except for flashes of pain, his grey eyes had stayed neutral, placid since the moment she had walked into his room. Wary, if anything, and rightly so. He probably thought she was there to stab him again.

But then a sudden burst of the same desperation she'd seen the day before cut across his eyes.

His mouth opened, offering her only one word. "Yes."

She nodded, her brow crinkling. "Do you know my grandmother? Have you worked for her? Is that how you know me?" She remembered nothing of the time before the riding accident, but this man could have very well been part of her grandmother's staff when she was young.

"No." The room, the very air around him stilled with his answer.

Sienna's arms lifted, wrapping around her middle as the rock that had been in her stomach expanded tenfold. She looked to the window in the room, staring for a long moment at the rays of sunlight bending in through the glass.

She had long ago come to peace with the fact that she would never remember her past. Not that it was much to remember her grandmother had always said. She'd had the usual childhood, full of governesses and tutors, and needlepoint, music, reading, riding lessons, and sketching. Of all those things, sketching was the only thing that had come natural to her after the accident. All the other pastimes seemed foreign, her body awkward with the motions of them. But never the charcoal on paper. That had always been easy.

The sense of foreboding crept up from her stomach to wrap heavily onto her shoulders. She was treading too deeply into something she knew nothing of. Into something she shouldn't question.

Yet she couldn't control her tongue.

Her gaze shifted to him. He was still staring at her, his dark grey eyes cutting into her.

She met his look straight on. "Tell me who you are."

For a long breath he was still, his eyes not blinking.

Then his arm lifted slowly, his fingers landing on the back of his neck. His forefinger dipped below the back of his linen shirt, fishing. Hidden deep, he pulled a golden chain from below his shirt, bringing it into the daylight.

Dangling from the end of the chain, a ring.

Blue stones dotted the gold band that he held up to her. "I'm your husband, Sienna."

The ring, his words, stole her breath. Stole it and would not return it.

She stood, still and staring, at a loss to move or say anything.

A sudden knock on the door made her jump, sending her heart into a pounding flurry.

"Miss Ponstance, your grandmother will be most upset with me." Bea's shrill voice cut through the door. "This has gone on long enough."

Her look still locked with the man's stare, Sienna's head started to shake. "No."

Her feet shuffled backward toward the door. "No. You are sorely mistaken, sir. I have no husband. I am a spinster. Grandmother explained it to me—she said it would be better this way." Her back bumped into the door and she spun to it, her fingers fumbling on the doorknob. For the quickest second she paused and looked back to him.

"No. No. No." Her head shook harder, her fingers finally clasping onto the brass knob and yanking the door open.

She ran into the hallway, slamming the door behind her as she gasped for breath and then nearly toppled over Bea.

Bea caught her forearms, stopping Sienna's charge down the hallway. "Is the man well?"

Sienna swallowed, attempting to calm her voice. "The man will recover. My blade didn't sink too deeply."

"We are done here?"

Sienna nodded. "We are done."

{ CHAPTER 3 }

Sienna kept her eyes averted from the coaching inn as she walked past the weathered yellow and orange bricks of the sandstone exterior. She hadn't wanted to come into Sandfell today—hadn't wanted to walk into the village at all in the last four days.

But her supply of charcoal had dwindled and every time she sent Bea to pick up more from Mr. Simmons, Bea came home with compressed charcoal made with the weakest wax binders, no matter how many times she chided the man for pawning his sloppy scraps upon her. If she didn't pick up her supply of charcoals herself, she would be making the trek into the village in another day regardless.

Sienna hadn't seen or heard anything of Mr. Lipinstein since the day she'd visited his room at the inn. Not that she had been brave enough to inquire after his whereabouts with Mrs. Wilson—or even to ask Bea to make some delicate inquiries around the village on his presence.

For all she knew, the man had left Sandfell the same day she had seen him.

It was both a comforting and unnerving thought, and she wasn't sure which emotion was winning over the other.

Her latest bundle of charcoals secured in the canvas pouch she had strapped across her body, she made her way down the main lane of the village, turning on the lane next to the butcher's cottage that led to her grandmother's estate.

Waving at Mrs. Hart, the weaver's wife, beating a rug outside her door, Sienna was just to the end of the line of the cottages that spread out from the main thoroughfare when she heard heavy steps echoing behind her.

"Sienna—Sienna." Her name, bellowed in the deep baritone voice that had engraved its way deep into her mind, came from the main road.

She took three more steps, undecided, before her feet shuffled to a stop in the dust of the lane. Well aware Mrs. Hart would be watching the unfolding scene, Sienna debated. Ignoring a man chasing after her was probably far more egregious than just turning around to say a few dismissive words to Mr. Lipinstein. Mrs. Hart was too far away to hear their conversation, so her gossip on the matter could only go so far.

Bracing herself, Sienna turned around.

He was fast—not in a full run, but not dawdling in his long strides. His short dark hair sat slightly ruffled along his brow and his fingers were quickly attempting to button the front of his black waistcoat.

She *knew* she shouldn't have walked in front of the coaching inn. Yet she'd done it anyway.

A smile that barely lifted the corners of her tight lips fell into place. "Mr. Lipinstein. I assumed you had travelled on from Sandfell."

He took the last steps toward her, coming to a stop an arm's length away. "I have not been able to leave."

"Oh." Her eyes dipped down to his stomach, guilt flooding her. "Has your injury not healed well?"

The edges of his grey eyes crinkled slightly. "No. The cut is fine. Nothing but a nuisance." He took a slight step toward her. "I think you know exactly why I haven't left the village."

She took a quick step backward, keeping the swath of space between them as wide as possible.

His hand flew up, palm to her. "Stop, Sienna. I have been waiting. I didn't want to scare you again—I wanted to intercept you while you were in the village so you would feel safe."

"Safe?"

His hand dropped to his side. "Safe from me. So you wouldn't stab me again."

"Oh—I…" Her words trailed as she looked at him, her head cocking to the side. Funny, the thought of her being in danger from him had never occurred to her past their initial meeting. The side of her mouth lifted in a grin. "Or is it that you would like to feel safe from me?"

It took him a long moment to realize she was teasing, and he blinked hard, a cautious smile creeping onto his well-formed lips—not too thin, not too thick. "I would prefer not to have another knife in my belly, yes."

"You are in luck. I have no blade with me today." Her thumb went under the strap of her pouch, readjusting it along her shoulder as she tried not to stare at the crook of his mouth—how it turned his face into a lightness that scattered away the serious lines she thought were permanent on his face. "Just my charcoals."

He looked down to the canvas pouch. "You still draw?"

Her lips parted in a tiny gasp. "I—I do." But what did *he* know of it? She rushed on. "Why are you still in town, Mr. Lipinstein?"

"I thought with a few days' time…"

"Yes?"

The smile had vanished from his face and hard lines took over his countenance. "I thought you would remember…remember something."

Her eyebrows lifted at him.

"You still don't remember me?"

"No."

He nodded, his jaw shifting to the side as his gaze slid off her, his look going to the far off distance past her shoulder. The consistent thwacking of Mrs. Hart on her rug filled the early summer air. After a moment, he sighed, his steely eyes shifting to her. "Do you know the name Bournestein?"

"You know my uncle?"

His left eye twitched, his head snapping slightly backward. The man was an expert at keeping his thoughts concealed. But that—that had almost been a flinch. A flinch about her uncle? Clearly Mr. Lipinstein knew him, or he wouldn't have inquired on the name.

"Bournestein is your uncle?" he asked.

"Yes. My mother's brother."

"I see."

The thwacking of the rug ceased, and Sienna looked down the lane to Mrs. Hart. Now the woman stood, rug clutched under her arm as she leaned against her doorway, brazenly watching the two of them.

She had talked to Mr. Lipinstein long enough.

Sienna's head tilted as her gaze went back to him. "I do not know what to make of you, sir. Why you would come here? Lie to me so about our association? You must have me confused with another woman, as I would most certainly know if I had a husband. My grandmother would know."

He nodded slowly, pretending to at least ponder her words for a long moment. Then his head stilled, his grey eyes skewering her. "Have you considered, Sienna, the possibility that I'm not lying?"

She stared at him, stared at the way his dark eyes sank into her, like they cut her in two and dove straight to her soul.

What man would look at her like that?

For as much as she didn't remember him, she had to admit the undeniable fact that she was drawn to him like nothing else.

But that didn't mean he was her husband.

She shook her head. "No. I have not considered it."

He exhaled a long breath and for a second she thought he was going to grab her arms again. Shake her. Demand what he thought was the past from her.

But his mouth stayed clamped shut, his feet in place. Unspeakable agony flickered across his eyes, disappearing as quickly as it appeared, his face turning hard.

For a second her heart stilled at the sight, a sharp pang of pain shooting through it. For as much as she didn't know him—didn't know what he wanted of her—she couldn't bear to see the misery she had just seen in his face.

It was enough—enough to spur her mouth open when she knew she should keep it shut. "Though I have remembered something, Mr. Lipinstein—well, not remembered so much—as it is more of a recognition."

"What did you recognize?"

"I draw you." The words blurted out of her mouth.

"You what?"

"I sketch you—or I have. Again and again throughout the years. Or someone who looks very similar to you. I searched all my drawings from the years and the likeness is unmistakable. It is uncanny and I would be dishonest if I didn't admit to it."

For how hard his face had turned, it softened in that second. Abated and sparked, like hope had suddenly been set aflame.

She didn't want to give him hope, but she also didn't want to have to witness the pain he was moored in.

Her eyes flicked to Mrs. Hart and then back to him. "I will be riding on the east side of my grandmother's estate tomorrow, into Baron Valsper's lands, as he graciously offers me full use of his trails." She glanced up at the long grey clouds gathering in the sky to the northwest. "That is, if the next bout of rain holds off."

"Is that an invitation, Sienna?"

"It is a possibility of a chance meeting." A hesitant smile came to her lips. "I will be out early on the lane, at the junction of the lands."

He inclined his head to her. "To possibilities, then."

She nodded and turned, starting down the lane. Only by the grace of Mrs. Hart still watching at her doorway, did Sienna manage to walk away without glancing back at Mr. Lipinstein.

~ ~ ~

The scream—so high in pitch he thought a pig was being slaughtered—had him running into Sienna's room.

She stood next to her tiny bed, shrieking, tears falling fast and furious down her chubby red cheeks as she stared at her hand.

Sure she'd lost a finger somehow and he'd have the devil to pay for it, Logan raced to her, snatching the hand she was looking and screeching at.

No blood.

But a butterfly wing. Orange with big blue and yellow dots on it gripped in her tiny fingers.

"Sienny—stop—stop—are you hurt?"

Another screech.

"Sienny, are you hurt?" He had to yell to be heard over her wails.

Her mouth closed, her watery blue eyes stunned wide. She had to swallow a sob before she pointed with her free hand to the corner. "Robby."

Logan glanced over his shoulder. His brother was skulking in the corner, the other half of the butterfly on the floor by his feet.

Sienna screamed, fury filling her face. "I didn't want to let it go. It was mine—mine and you broke it," she shouted with all the power her six-year-old lungs could produce. "You broke it, Robby, you bully. You're awful—I hate you. I hate, hate, hate you."

"Shhhhh, Sienny, shhhhh." Logan jumped in front of her, blocking Robby from her view as he grabbed her shoulders. "Don't wake my mama—if she knows you were at the gardens she'll be mad and you know how she is when she's mad."

Sienna's huge blue eyes went wider, tears quickly refilling the rims. She nodded. Logan's mother hadn't always been angry—she had once been so very kind—but not now.

Sienna lifted the wing she still clutched in her tiny fingers. "Can you fix it, Logan?"

He shook his head. "It's a butterfly, Sienny. It's dead."

"But no." Fat tears rolled out of her eyes. She leaned to the side, daggers shooting at Robby. "I hate you, I hate you, Robby. It was mine and you broke it."

"You broke it, Sienny. You wouldn't let go."

Logan's head snapped back. "Go, Robby, leave."

Robby's face twisted and he stepped on the wing on the floor before stomping out of the room.

"I hate him. He broke it, Logan. He breaks everything. Everything." She looked down at her hand, her fingers rolling around the wing, crushing it. Her tears fell fast, heavy sobs starting.

Logan loosened his hold on her shoulders and pulled her into a hug, more to quiet her than comfort her. If his mother woke and found her this distraught, there would be hell to pay and he was the only one in the room to pay it.

"I just couldn't let it go, Logan. I couldn't. I loved it too much. It was too pretty and I loved it." Her voice squealed high into his body.

"You just found it, Sienny."

"But I loved it. I loved it more than anything and I didn't want Robby to touch it. I knew he would break it and he did."

Logan sighed, pulling back slightly so he could see her face, still red with anger and tears. "You're a fighter, you know what's yours, but sometimes you have to let things go or they get broken, Sienny. Sometimes, it's all you can do to save something."

She wedged herself further back from him, fire replacing the sadness in her eyes. "But it's not fair. I lose everything I love.

Everything." She shoved at him with all the strength her skinny arms held and spun, running toward the door.

Three steps and he caught her with ease. He was at least two heads taller than her now. His fingers wrapped around her forearm, stopping her escape. "You won't lose me, Sienny."

Her feet stopped and she looked back at him. "You could get broke, too. Just like my mama."

Logan shook his head, his eyes solemn. "You will always have me, Sienny. I will be your always."

The orange peacock butterfly that had floated by her head, landing for a moment on the front edge of her blue bonnet and sending him deep into the past, flittered high and away as Sienna spurred her horse onward with a laugh.

He had to shake himself. Shake the memory before he nudged his horse into a full gallop next to hers.

As much as he tried to avert his eyes from her, he couldn't.

Sienna rode next to him, racing across a field dotted with sheep bleating at the intrusion.

At least if she was flying, the wind sending her loose red-blond hair trailing behind her in the wind, she wasn't peppering him with questions.

He tugged on his reins, keeping his horse at an even clip with her mare. He didn't want to get ahead. Didn't want to lose her from his sight.

Even if he knew this was a mistake. Knew it an hour into their ride.

She'd had a thousand questions for him and he had no answers to give her.

When did they get married?

What was their first kiss like?

Where did they first meet?

He knew the answers to each and every question, but he refused to answer any of her inquiries, much to her annoyance.

Instead, he held fast to the rule he'd made for himself after she visited him in his room at the coaching inn. If she couldn't remember herself, then any answers he gave her of their past were moot. Answers wouldn't change a thing. Answers wouldn't get him his wife back. Answers wouldn't put the love—the burning heat—back into her eyes.

They were strangers until she remembered him. Until she remembered their life together.

That rule had forced him to evade her questions of the past all day long, while continually steering their conversations to his own questions about the present—to what she'd been doing for the past ten years.

Until he knew what had happened to her, what trauma she'd suffered to take away all her memories, he didn't dare revisit the past with her.

Not with Bournestein lurking about her life.

It wouldn't be safe to tell her anything until he knew what happened to her years ago in Spain. How her ring ended up charred with another woman's body.

Nothing was safe until she remembered.

Her laugh exploded into the air as she drove her speckled mare forward, cutting Logan off just as she reached the line of trees and the trail that led through the woods back to her grandmother's land.

His head snapped up, and he latched onto her laugh, onto the glee on her face.

Just this one moment. He needed it. This one moment when he could revel in her spirit that had never changed.

He needed this moment to hold in his heart. A moment just for him to feel like the man he once was.

Just as they reached the woods, mist started to dapple his face.

Their horses slowed and he nudged his stallion forward to fall into adjacent step with her horse.

She looked to him, a smile so wide on her flush face he thought she might collapse in a fit of laughter. "That was glorious—pure heaven. I never get to race and it is"—a laugh cut into her words—"it is delicious fire in my veins."

He chuckled. "You've never shied from competition, Sienna. That I will tell you."

She eyed him, her smile tempering. "But nothing more—I understand. You have been most canny all day long in avoiding my questions."

"Can I continue to be so?"

"Why would you stop at this juncture?" She waved her leather-gloved hand in the air. "Never mind that, as I have a question of you that I think you can answer."

He inclined his head at the mirth in her voice, his eyebrow cocked. "Do give it a go."

"Do you limp?"

His shoulders stiffened, his look going ahead to the trail. "I do."

"Forgive my rudeness, but I wasn't positive. Sometimes I see it and sometimes I don't when you walk. So the times I have seen it, it is either a pesky rock that keeps appearing in your boot, or a limp. Regardless, you hide it well. It was only by careful study that I saw it."

His gaze went to her. "You studied me?"

A flush touched her cheeks. "I did. Unabashedly so, I'm afraid. At the edge of town. When we stopped earlier by the brook for the cheese and bread you brought." Her head tilted to the side as her blue eyes ran along his chest and up to his face. "You are a handsome man and it is a beautiful thing to watch your body move. Even with the slight hiccup of a limp. That flaw makes you interesting—real."

The flush that had been on Sienna's cheeks jumped onto the back of his neck. He knew he drew the eye of women, always had. But from Sienna's mouth, the way her lips said she watched him, studied him—he felt like a young buck just noticed by the most beautiful girl in London.

The horses took several strides. "If it is not too presumptive to ask—" The side of her face lifted in a slight cringe—she wanted to ask him something, but didn't know how to do so.

"You're my wife, Sienna. Nothing is too presumptive."

She blinked, startled, then offered a nod. "Well then, why? Why do you limp? Have you always done so?"

"It happened in the war. The last battle I was in on the continent. My heel caught the full fire of a bullet, and they had to remove the bone fragments if there was a chance to walk half to normal again."

Her lips pulled inward, her eyes scrunching. "It sounds horribly painful."

He shrugged. "I survived. I can walk. It is more than many of the men that met Boney's forces can say. Many of my guards."

"Your guards?"

He nodded. "It is what I do in London. I was hired long ago to be the head guard at the Revelry's Tempest, a gaming house that is run by three of the most unusual titled ladies one will ever meet."

"Ladies running a gaming house? That sounds delightful—and deliciously wrong." She smiled, excitement twinkling in her blue eyes. "Tell me of your guards."

"I had free rein to hire the other guards as I saw fit." He pulled his horse to the side to veer around the stump of a fallen tree on the trail. "And I chose men that had been injured during the war and needed gainful employment. All had been maimed as I was during the war, and all were finding honest work hard to come by. But I have on call the most talented cobbler in London, and with specially crafted boots, it takes a keen eye to notice the limps." He looked at Sienna. "I am surprised you noticed mine."

A grin lifted her lips. "As I said. There was a bit of scrutiny afoot."

He chuckled. It was a relief to finally be able to tell her something genuine of his life. Something he could talk about and not worry it would spark memories for her. Aside from Sienna, nothing was closer to his heart than the Revelry's Tempest and his guards.

The horses turned a curve in the trail, and Logan glanced at Sienna's profile. She looked as though she was still turning over again and again in her mind the idea of ladies running a gaming hall, there was so much mischief in her eyes.

He interrupted her thoughts. "Now I have another question for you."

She nodded, her bright eyes moving from the trail to him. "What do you want to ask me now?"

"Your uncle, Mr. Bournestein, do you know what his business is?"

"I know he owns several shops in London." She shrugged, the question not tempering her good-natured patience at his many inquiries. "For his generosity in how he supports me, grandmother and the estate, I imagine his shops do quite well. Is that where you know him from? His business?"

Logan's tongue pressed into his cheek. "Yes, our paths have crossed numerous times."

Not exactly a lie.

He wasn't about to tell her of Bournestein's sins. Of his brutality. That the man owned a wide swath of St. Giles—every gaming hell, every brothel, every pocket that was picked in his area, he had his fingers in deep. That too many of Logan's guards had tangled with Bournestein and his brutes—and Logan had spent far too much time extracting his men from Bournestein's clutches.

That the man was the devil incarnate.

And his wife would always be in grave danger with Bournestein in her life.

All that was information for another time. *If* she remembered.

If she didn't, he needed to leave well enough alone.

His wife was content, generally happy, even. Even if it wasn't with him, it was all he had ever wanted for her. To see her face light and free from worry. Free from their past.

He needed to not hold on so tightly that he broke her.

His breath lodged deep in his neck below a lump that had formed as he looked at her. Her cheeks flush with the exertion of racing across the field, her full pink lips still held the smile that came so easily to her face.

She had never been like this. Smiles that appeared effortlessly. She'd always had to consider her smiles carefully, lest they reveal too much.

Except with him. When they were alone, just the two of them, those smiles had come easy, even though it was hard for her to let go. For him, she had done it.

The mist turning, a fat droplet of water splashed past the rim of his hat and into his eye. "Rain has started."

She nodded. "It has. And it's wonderful."

Her head swiveled to him, rain collecting on the brim of her bonnet. Sparks flew in her blue eyes as she watched him, the smile still dancing on her face.

She was falling in love with him. But what did he expect? Their attraction spanned lost memories. This guttural, unspeakable need for each other. She felt it just the same as he knew it. And now she was free—open where once she was not. Open to meeting a strange man for a ride. Her caution had disappeared, replaced by a blind trust he couldn't fathom her ever possessing. Meeting him—effectively, a stranger to her—was something she never would have even considered ten years ago.

She was free. Free of the past that haunted her. The past that curbed her smiles. The past that made her suspicious of everything around her.

He needed to leave. Leave her to her freedom. For all she smiled at him, for all she found him and who he claimed to be curious, she didn't remember him. He'd thought there would be a chance for them if they spent time together and it sparked a memory.

But nothing. All day, and nothing. Not a glimmer of recognition.

It was too much to be near her like this.

All he wanted to do was grab her and bury his face in her neck, tug down her dress, hear her laugh when his knuckles brushed along her ribcage under her breast.

All he wanted was his body sinking onto hers.

His look jerked away from her, his gaze fixed to the passing trees. "We will part ways at the split in the trail ahead. You need to get back to your grandmother's home so you don't catch a chill."

She chuckled. "Though it is kind of you to worry upon me, I am hardly a child that will catch my death in a spot of rain."

His mouth went terse at her light voice.

Resist. Resist at all cost.

He needed to leave Sandfell. Needed to gather his belongings and leave this village, leave this land and forget he ever stumbled upon this place.

A moth to the blaze, he couldn't stop himself from looking at her and a rage he could barely control swept through him.

He wanted his damn wife back. He wanted her looking at him like he was the one person in the world she needed. Just as he needed her.

But she sat there on her horse, entertained—intrigued—by him and what he told her, but nothing more. What had he thought would happen—a day riding together and she would fall in love with him again? Regain all her memories?

She still had no inkling of their love. Of the life they once led.

And it was killing him, for he'd never been able to resist her—she'd always been a flame that would burn him to a crisp, time and again, and still he would be driven back to her.

He tore his gaze away from Sienna's profile. He couldn't look at her and bring himself to be the man he needed to be.

If her memory of him came back to her, so would all the memories. Memories that were better left forgotten.

She was content, so what kind of a monster would he be to trade her current peace and happiness away for memories that would only ravage her mind? Memories that needed to stay buried.

He had to give her this. No matter what it cost him.

He had to get out of Yorkshire.

{ CHAPTER 4 }

Five miles out of Sandfell, Logan passed by the abandoned gamekeeper's cottage at the edge of Baron Valsper's lands. Mostly hidden in woods, Sienna had pointed out the decaying thatched-roof cottage as they rode past the day before.

The rain had poured thick after he parted ways with Sienna the evening before and he'd had no choice but to give himself one last night in Sandfell. One last night wavering—his selfishness waging a vicious battle with his integrity. That he'd had a bottle of brandy delivered to his room hadn't helped the matter and he had awoken with heavy eyelids, slow muscles, and muddled thoughts.

Muddled, except for one overriding decision. He needed to leave Sandfell. Needed to leave Sienna to her peace.

Peace she would never know again if she remembered all that had happened.

He would get back to London and send two of his guards to watch over her—a necessity until he knew what Bournestein's true strategy was with Sienna.

The edge of the forest cleared in front of Logan and he could see the intersection that marked the crossroad to London. The road still thick with muck, he'd passed no other traffic on the road that morn. He pulled the front of his black, broad-brimmed hat further down his brow. The rain had dwindled to a drizzle that he'd been shielded from by the trees, but now in open land he realized it would be a slow, wet slog to London.

He heard it before he saw it, in the same moment he turned south on the crossroad. A horse and rider galloping through the woods behind him at full speed.

He turned to the sound just as the horse broke free of the line of trees.

Sienna.

Her brown mare heaving, its long legs stretching with every stride.

He didn't stop his horse, even though it nickered at him, watching Sienna and her mare just as intently as Logan was.

Five more steps on the road to London, and she caught up to him, pulling her horse to a stop directly in his path.

He had to hide a smile. She was bold. She hadn't lost that when she'd lost her memories.

Her hand flat on her chest, she panted a few hard breaths before swallowing hard, her blue eyes piercing him. "You said you were going back to the village last evening."

"I did. And now I am leaving Sandfell."

Her lips pursed as her eyes narrowed at him. "You're not leaving Sandfell, you're leaving me."

He paused, and for one second in time, he almost gave in. With a shake of his head, his mouth clamped shut and he set his heel into his horse's flank, moving it forward.

Sienna's mare danced a step away and she flicked on the leather reins, moving to block his path once more. She waited until his horse stopped, then scrutinized him. "Why are you leaving me after what you told me?"

"That you're my wife?" Logan sighed, looking out across a hayfield soaking in the drizzle. "You don't remember me, Sienna. Let us leave it at that. Your life will be immeasurably better as it is now."

"I disagree—I may not remember you—"

"And that is the point, Sienna—you don't remember me."

"No—you were the one that approached me." Her voice pitched higher, filling the thick air. "You were the one with these wild claims of being my husband. And now what? You are just going to leave? Without telling me?"

His jawline hardened. "Exactly." He nudged his horse to the right to pass her. For a moment, he thought he would clear his way around her. But his wife was never one to back down.

Facing the opposite direction, her horse alongside his, she reached out just as he passed, shifting her weight into the stirrup of her sidesaddle. The stretch of her arm committed—if she missed him, she would fall off her horse.

Her fingers snagged the backside of his overcoat at the last instant, stopping her momentum toward a long fall to the ground.

He yanked up on his reins, looking back at her balanced precariously between their horses.

"My mind may not remember you, Logan." Her blue eyes were wide, fight still firing in the azure depths. "But my body remembers you. My hands. They can do nothing but draw you. Years of drawing you. Your eyes. The line of your jaw. You."

Damn her. Damn that the first time he'd heard his name from her lips in ten years was in this moment.

All caution to the wind, she released her hand from the pommel of her sidesaddle and reached out to grab his forearm, committing herself to stopping him, no matter the consequences of her mare moving.

Her fingers squeezed his arm as her eyes centered on him. "And my body...when you are near me...I cannot breathe..." She paused, her head dipping down as she swallowed. She looked up at him. "I cannot stop the whirlwind that tears through my insides, the aching. I have never felt this—never looked at another man and even considered it, but with you, it is...it is a need for you that demands to be satiated but is never satisfied."

His hands frozen on his reins, he shook his head. "But you don't know me, Sienna."

"I do. You say I do." She shook his arm. "You are the one that asked me to consider you were telling the truth. And I have considered it."

"Sienna—"

"I have considered it—considered you. And my mind may not recognize you, but my body—my body knows you, Logan. I don't know how, but it does. My body needs yours in a way I've never imagined."

His name again.

She said it with such ease, such familiarity that it made his gut sink in horror that he hadn't left her soon enough— he hadn't left before he could do more damage than good.

Her hand clutching the back of his overcoat shifted, grabbing the edge of his saddle and she pulled herself upward, so far he wondered if her toes were even still on her stirrup. Her blue eyes almost eye level with his, she leaned in, her lips brushing against his, the gentlest touch.

Of all the things he could deny, kissing his wife was not one of them. His hand instantly lifted, his fingers curving around the back of her neck, holding her lips to him. Kissing her. Full and hard with no question as to who she belonged to. Who he belonged to.

Her lips molded under his, her body leaning into him. The smallest mewl came from her throat.

The sound of it reached through the fog enveloping his head and he panicked, yanking his head away.

What was he doing? Doing to her? Doing to him?

Her head snapped back, confusion rolling across her face. "You—you don't want to stay. You don't want me."

Words so rough they were barely understandable ripped from his throat. "I cannot love you again, Sienna."

"Why not?" She leaned away from him, shifting her weight back down to the stirrup of her sidesaddle. The movement pushed on her horse and her mare skittered several steps away. Sienna slipped, her hands dragging from Logan and flailing for a moment in midair.

His heart stopped, her fall head first into the ground already in his mind. But then she twisted, untangling her foot from the stirrup just before she fell to the road. She landed sideways, one foot and one hand sinking into the wet muck of the road and catching all of her weight.

Before he was down and off his horse to help her, she had shoved herself upright with a grunt. She glanced over her shoulder as she stood, checking her horse. It had stopped at the edge of the road next to a low stone fence, happily munching on sprigs of bright green summer grass.

Logan reached out to help Sienna steady her balance, but she whipped her look back toward him and the glare she shot him stopped his movement.

"Why not?" The two words hissed through her gritted teeth.

His hands dropped to his sides as his shoulders lifted in a heavy sigh. "You mistake what I want to do with what I have to do, Sienna. I cannot love you because you are at peace. You are safe here. No matter how I want you, I cannot take that away from you."

"I am at peace?" A caustic chuckle left her lips as she slapped her muddied hand against the skirts of her dark blue riding habit. "I haven't been at peace since the moment you grabbed me on the lane and I stuck you, Logan."

He winced, turning from her and looking back into the woods he travelled from, his fingers running through his hair. "Then because I am death, Sienna—how about that? I am death when I am with you. If I love you, death will follow. It always does. And I won't do that again."

"Death?" She stepped in front of him, confusion thick in her eyes. "What madness is this?"

She planted herself before him, a demanding ball of fire, and all he could do was look away.

She grabbed his forearm. "Logan, you cannot charge into my life, upend it, and then keep everything you know and I don't hidden from me. It's not right. It's cruel." Her fingers curled hard into his muscles. "And I don't think you're a cruel man—in fact—I'm fairly positive you're the farthest thing there is from cruel."

He stifled a sigh. He couldn't defend against it. It wasn't fair to keep her from the past she had every right to remember. He knew that. But the burden of the last time his love for her had caused death was his alone to suffer.

Her fingers loosened and went gently to his upper arm, and she angled herself close so she could look up at him from under the brim of her bonnet. "Tell me what haunts your face, Logan."

He found her eyes, the azure depths of the blue making him waver. She wanted so much to touch this past that she could not grasp.

She believed.

He had gotten her to believe they had a past. And now all he wanted to do was protect her from remembering it.

She wouldn't give up fighting for an answer. He knew that of her spirit. She would always fight.

Maybe…maybe if he told her, she would understand. Understand how life in Sandfell—far away from him—was exactly what she needed. Was exactly why he had to leave this place.

His body tensed and he braced himself as he met her look. "I chose you over my men, Sienna."

"What?"

"On the continent against Boney's forces."

Her forehead scrunched. "Boney's forces? How— where—how could you do that?"

"You were there during the war."

"I was on the continent?"

He nodded. "In Spain—you followed me into the damn war. I had you safe in a village far from the fighting, but then…"

"Then what?"

"Then the French swept the countryside. When I learned where they were coming, what they were doing along the way…" He stopped, his eyes closing as his head shook at the barbarity of the memory. "They were burning everything in their path."

He opened his eyes to her, his voice vehement. "You were in their path."

"Logan…"

His head dropped, his eyes hiding from her. "So I gathered my men and instead of joining the other forces at Arapiles I marched my men toward your village. It was suicide and I knew it. They knew it. Yet I made them march into that village. All of us. Not one of them questioned me."

Her fingers tightened on his arm, a gasp fluttering from her lips.

He rushed on before she could question him—question his stupidity—for it was nothing he hadn't played over again and again in his own mind. "Their eyes—I saw it in there, the betrayal. Yet their feet kept moving. Straight into the devil's flames. My men died because I was weak—because I chose you—I had to. I had to save you."

Her fingers dropped from his arm, her voice choked. "You…you shouldn't have…didn't need…"

"I damn well know that now, Sienna. For the whole of it—it didn't matter. You were dead. When I got to your house it had just been swept with flames and your body was charred in the ruins. But your hand—you still clutched your ring. That is how I knew you were dead."

"But it couldn't have been me."

"No." His head shook, his voice bitter at his own idiocy. "And my men died because I was weak. If we had saved you…then maybe…maybe it would have been justified, what I sacrificed to save you." He paused for a long moment, his words going to a choked whisper. "A man does not consider failure when he needs to save his wife. But it was a failure. I didn't save you. And then I couldn't save them. And it has been my burden to bear ever since."

Achingly slow, he lifted his eyes to her.

Her face had blanched, her arms wrapping around her stomach. For a long second, she looked as though she were about to retch.

As much as he wanted to say words to ease the truth of the past for her, he steeled himself. He needed to leave and he was going to be as brutal as he needed to be for her to let him go.

"Your mother always saw it in me, Sienna. She told me to my face when I was young. 'Death is about you, boy,' she said. 'It always will be.'"

"My mother said that?" Her arms unfolded from her waist. "You knew my mother? But Grandmother said she died when I was young—before I could even speak."

Logan's mouth clamped shut. He hadn't meant to mention her mother.

"What are you not telling me, Logan?"

He drew in a deep breath and swallowed a sigh. "You are at peace, Sienna. Please, let us leave it at that. Go home to your grandmother and Roselawn. Go home to your life. Forget I ever came through this town."

He turned from her and walked toward his horse.

Her steps were quick behind him. Her fingers snatching his forearm were even quicker. "No. I am your wife."

His wife? Now she said it?

He spun around, fury flying. "This is killing me, Sienna. Can you not see that?"

"Is it? From where I stand, this isn't killing you at all. You know everything and I know nothing."

"I'm trying to do the right thing." His voice went into a yell, thundering into the surrounding trees and fields. "I'm doing this for you, Sienna."

"Are you positive on that fact?" Her hand jerked away from his arm. "Because from my vantage, this is all about you. What you want. What you think I need. I am your bloody wife, Logan, and you're the one now refusing that."

She stomped around him, reaching her horse and snapping the reins into her hands. Without bothering to mount her horse, she led her mare past him, moving back along the road into the forest.

Every step a blow to the ground, every step a blow to his will.

{ CHAPTER 5 }

Blasted man.

Humiliation still wrapping her neck in hot fury, Sienna slowed her pace, glancing back at the white nose of her mare.

Maybe now she was close to being able to ride without panicking her horse. She had stomped away from Logan knowing she couldn't trust herself on her sidesaddle.

She had walked for twenty minutes and still had not been able to shake the humiliation that had enveloped her.

He didn't want her. Didn't want his wife.

He had made that abundantly clear.

He had convinced her of it—that she was his wife— and it had taken such bravery to finally admit to herself she believed him.

To chase after him.

And then he rejected her. Coldly.

Telling her of the deaths she'd caused.

Her shoulders shook in a shiver that skipped down her spine.

What it had taken for her to come after him, to offer herself to him, had tested her like nothing ever had. She'd had to draw upon courage she didn't know she possessed. Take a leap of faith so frightening that she had turned her horse around three times after she set out after him.

He had rejected her.

She wasn't the same person she'd been before she lost her memories of him. She wasn't the person he wanted as his wife.

The blow of that fact wasn't lessened by what he had told her about the war. Not only was she not enough for him now—she had been the cause of numerous deaths. Indirect or not, he had come after her. For what? Maybe he was right. Maybe death did follow him and she was better off without her husband.

Her husband. She had just brought herself to believe those words. That she had a partner in life that she never knew. That the missing piece of her could be filled.

She never should have tried.

She lifted her left hand, rubbing the softness of her worn glove along her neck. The heat of her skin seeped through the leather to warm her hand.

If only she could remember. Remember who she was. Remember who he was. Maybe then.

Maybe then, what?

It didn't matter. He had rejected her. He didn't want her. She had to scrape together some dignity—what little she could at this juncture.

Warm orange rays of sun cut through the grey clouds as they moved low into the sky, the light filtering through the trees from an open field ahead. It would be an excruciatingly long slog home if she walked the rest of the way. She hoped her anger had dissipated enough she wouldn't make her mare skittish—but for that to happen, she had to stop thinking about Logan. Put him out of her mind.

Sienna spotted the small, thatched roof of the
abandoned gamekeeper's cottage nestled into the woods
ahead. Why had she chosen this horse when she had raced
to the stable? This mare was particularly tall—not to
mention skittish. Good timing in that there was a block
outside the gamekeeper's cottage to help her up onto her
sidesaddle.

She veered right onto the overgrown trail that led
to the cottage, trying to control her breathing that still
seethed despite her best efforts. She didn't want to aggravate
the skittishness of the horse. She was always conscious of
the fact that she'd fallen off of one horse and lost all her
memories—her life and everything she knew of it. She
wasn't looking for it to happen again.

Almost to the cottage, branches behind her crunched
and speeding hooves on the mossy ground vibrated the dirt
below her boots. She spun, and barreling toward her was
Logan on his horse. Logan coming at her far too fast to slow
down on the narrow path.

She jumped to the side of the trail, her hand yanking
on her mare's reins to move off the path. Logan and his
horse brushed past her, his boot almost skimming her chin.

Five steps beyond her into the clearing around the
cottage, his horse reared high, spinning in a circle on its
hind legs.

Her breath held, she watched him grip his pommel.
Hold on. Hold on. Hold on.

The front hooves of the horse dropped to the ground,
the steed dancing at the abrupt halt. Logan stayed seated
firmly in the saddle.

She exhaled.

He managed a full stop without falling. Ten steps too late. But a full stop.

What did the idiot think he was about?

She stomped forward, yanking the reins of her horse behind her. "What of you, Logan? You could have trampled me."

He stared down at her. "I lost you, I couldn't see you through the woods and…" His mouth clamped shut and he looked to the side, his jaw flexing. "I cannot let you go, Sienna. Not even for six hours. Not for a half hour." His head shook, his eyes closing for a long breath. His steel grey eyes opened to her, the tormented depths of hell reflecting both in the dark flecks and in the vicious tremble of his voice. "I *cannot* let you go."

He exhaled, his lips parting as his teeth gritted, and a low whistle escaped his lips. A whistle so low, so distinct, she'd never heard anything like it.

Never, except that she remembered it.

Remembered the distinct pitch. The set line of his lips, as though he was exhaling every bit of anger and frustration filling his chest.

A spark ignited somewhere deep in the recesses of her brain and she remembered the sound.

Remembered the first time she had ever heard it.

Flashes of the memory tunneled forward in her mind. Blurred faces. Anger. Arms flying in a fight. She swayed, her eyes closing, trying to reach out and touch the memory— grab the snippets of the fuzzy scene in her mind.

She opened her eyes, her look slowly traveling upward to Logan, high on his horse. "You hated me."

His head snapped back, his forehead crinkling.
"Sienna?"

"You hated me." She exhaled the words in a wispy
breath, the reality of the scene taking root in her mind. She
gasped air, swallowing, trying to create moisture in her dry
mouth. "You hated me. Your face, I can see it clearly. Except
you were little and you hated me. You whistled just as you
did now. Just as…just as…"

Her voice trailed off, words floating away from her
head as if they were no longer hers. No longer her tongue,
no longer her sight.

The sway of her body went wide and blackness
swallowed her whole.

~ ~ ~

Cold. Wet.

On her brow, seeping down into the crevices about her
eyes.

Cold water.

Her eyes cracked open. She was upright. On the
ground, but upright. Her arms tucked into her sides.
Something hard behind her. The cottage. She sat propped
upright against the wooden boards on the outside of the
cottage.

The cold splashed across her forehead again.

A blurry figure in front of her came into focus. Logan
bent over in front of her. Concern furrowing his brow, his
mouth pulled to a tight line. A dripping wet cloth in his
hand.

"You fainted." His words were gruff, sinking slowly into her head.

She shifted, her palms going to the ground on either side of her to steady herself against the side of the cottage. "I don't faint."

"I agree." He eased slightly away from her, giving her space to breathe. "But you just did. A rock dropping to the dirt."

She sighed as she tugged off her gloves. Her fingers went to her wet forehead. Her bonnet was gone. She rubbed her eyes. "I did the other day as well."

"You fainted? When?" The concern etched in his forehead deepened.

"After you accosted me on the lane to my home. I made it to my room and I couldn't breathe and I found myself in a crumpled ball on the floor."

"Sienna—"

"Prove it to me." Her hand slipped away from her eyes and she focused on his face. On his mouth. "Whistle for me again."

"What? That is ridiculous, Sienna."

"No. Please. I need to hear the sound again. Just as you did when you were on your horse. Please."

He stared at her, his grey eyes assessing her.

Walking her hands up the side of the cottage for support, she pushed herself to her feet. His hands at the ready, Logan watched her, his hawk-eyes scrutinizing every movement as though she were china ready to break and he would need to swoop in.

She ground the heels of her boots into the ground until she was solid and she lifted her gaze to meet his stare. "I am not mad, Logan. Please."

He took a step back from her and drew a deep breath. With one long exhale, he whistled.

"No. Not like that, Logan."

His eyebrow cocked. "My whistle did not please?"

"Do it as you did earlier—angry—when you were furious and you whistled."

"I wasn't furious."

Her hand waved through the air. "You weren't furious with me—you were furious with yourself—I saw that. But I need you to whistle as you did."

His chest lifted in a deep sigh, and he exhaled the same low, teeth-gritted whistle.

Her legs gave out and she collapsed backward to the side of the cottage, sliding down toward the ground. Jelly in her legs, but at least she didn't faint.

His hands were instantly under her arms, breaking the fall and setting her backside gently down onto the dirt.

"I—I remember." A mere whisper left her lips as her eyes lifted to him. "I remember. There was a golden penknife I had hidden in my skirts. I stole it and I was so scared. And you hated me because I took the pen knife and he thought it was you." Her head shook. "He? Who is he? Who was I terrified of? It wasn't you."

Kneeling in front of her, Logan's hands moved to her elbows and tightened to an iron clasp. His head dropped, his eyes hiding from her as his breaths came fast and hard.

Her face crumpled as memories flashed forward in her mind. Flashed in snippets, in random bits and pieces, in surges of emotion, of pain. "The war…" She gasped against the pain flooding her with each horrid image—gasped again and again, trying to send air into her barren lungs.

She grabbed his forearms, gripping with all her might. Gripping so she didn't faint, didn't leave the world for the pain that was coursing through her body. "The—the war— the man—you—you—Spain—I followed you and you were going to send me home and then—oh, hell, Logan—the fire—Boney's men—the wall—he threw me into a wall—"

He lifted his head to look at her. "You remember? You remember what happened in Spain?" He shook her. "How did that woman—the charred one—get your ring? How did you get out of there? Back to England?"

Her hand lifted from his arm, and she held it up feebly between them. "Slow—I—I am trying." Her eyes squinted shut, her head swinging back and forth as she fought to find a thread of continuity in the flashes firing in her brain.

"The ring." A whisper more to himself than to Sienna, and Logan's hand jerked away from her arm and dove under his loose cravat, pulling free the ring on a chain. With a snapping tug, he yanked it off his neck, breaking the chain and thrusting the ring in front of her.

She looked at the gold. At the blue sapphires circling the band, evenly embedded in the smooth surface of the gold. Her ring. It belonged on her finger. Ribbon. Ribbon should have been on it. Wrapped to hold it tight to her finger.

"I knew—I knew they were coming, and I knew I wouldn't get away so I asked Mrs.—Mrs.—Mrs. Clavel to hide me in her larder and she was so afraid. There was so much confusion and she was yelling. So I begged her and begged her and then I was desperate so I offered her the one thing I had of value—my ring."

Sienna reached out, her fingertips shaking as she grasped the ring, slowly, almost as though it would burn her, burn away her memories if she touched it.

Her forefinger and thumb clasped it, taking it from Logan's grip and she lifted it close to her eyes. "She took my ring. She grabbed it from me. And then just when it left my hand a man—"

A gasp swallowed back her words.

"A man?"

Her eyes clamped shut as she attempted to conjure the scene in her mind. It took her long, heavy breaths before she could continue. "A man came—he came for me—me, not her, because he pushed Mrs. Clavel aside and came after me. But he wasn't wearing a uniform. No. He was different. An Englishman."

Logan's hands moved down to wrap the sides of her ribcage and they tightened, near to cracking her bones. "Who was he?"

Her eyelids fluttered open, and she found Logan's face. Something steady, steady against all the madness in her mind. "I—I don't know. That man—he grabbed me, and then Mrs. Clavel jumped on him—fought him." Her eyes squinted shut. "He hit her, yanked her to the ground and kicked her head. And then he—he grabbed my hair and then the wall—the wall was coming at my face."

Her head dropped, her chin to her chest as she tried to still the fear rolling through her body. She was safe. Safe in the woods. Safe with Logan directly in front of her.

She didn't know how long she sat there crumpled into herself, trying to calm her thundering heart.

Logan's voice, low and calm, broke into the rustling of the forest. "What happened next?"

Her head shook slightly, her chin rubbing on the lace bodice trim of her riding habit. "I don't remember anything after that. I woke up on—" Her eyes squinted shut and her head tilted to the side as she searched the dark recesses of her mind. "On a boat, maybe, it was rocking— or a wagon—" She shook her head. "And then I was at grandmother's home. And she told me what happened, that I fell off a horse and hit my head and I have been at Roselawn ever since."

Her eyes flew open to escape the chaos of her mind and she stared at Logan's steel grey eyes. "Except, except, Grandmother—she's not my grandmother. Or is she? And I didn't fall off a horse. Or did I?" She shoved her ring onto her pointer finger and lifted her hand, gripping her forehead. "None of this makes sense, Logan. It's all a jumble." Her head started to shake, her eyes closing again as her breathing sped. "I don't know—none of it makes sense and it's all just snippets, images that don't make any sense. And blasts of pain running through my gut, my chest, again and again."

"Pain?"

"As the snippets flash." She nodded, bringing her other hand to her head, trying to hold the images from flashing and retreating. "But then the opposite, also."

"Opposite of the pain?"

Her fingers tightened on her scalp. "No one is who I think they are. You hated me. Hated me, but then…" Her eyes opened and she looked up at him as her hands fell away from her head. "Except you. You are…" She stopped, gasping for breath and looking away, staring at the horses at the edge of the clearing.

"I am what, Sienna?" Logan's voice went hard, his fingers digging into her ribs. "What?"

She dragged her look back to his face, overwhelmed by what she was seeing in her mind, even as unsure as she was of it. "Every snippet I see of you. It is the opposite of pain. It is…love…this brutal sense of staggering love every time I see you in my mind. Love that cannot be touched—cannot be denied it is so powerful."

He let loose an audible exhale, his hands lifting from her to catch himself on the cottage wall. In one harsh move, he shoved himself up to his feet and away from the wall, staggering backward away from her.

His feet planted, his shoulders heaved with every breath as he stared at her.

She saw it instantly. He stood, unable to be near her, to touch her, not until she was certain. Not until she knew it in her soul just as deeply as he did.

She set her hands onto the outer wall of the cottage, pushing herself to her feet. But she couldn't step toward him—couldn't step away from the support of the wall.

Her look dragged from his boots upward, scrutinizing every whit of his being. Every muscle in his body resisted. Trembled with the sheer power it took for him to stay three steps from her. Every breath he drew, ragged, brutal.

Her gaze travelled up his body until her eyes locked with his. She managed one unsupported step away from the wall, her chest splintering at both the horror and beauty of the reality she knew in her heart. Horror that she had just lived without this man for ten years. Beauty that he was before her now, still as desperate for her as she was for him.

Her lips parted, her voice cracking. "For all I don't remember, Logan, there is one thing that is undeniable—you are my always, my true everything. That, I remember."

He launched himself at her in that breath, his body ramming into her in one swoop, wrapping her to him. Her shoulders slammed against the cottage wall. Every shred of self-denial he'd suffered during the past week released in a raging, crushing hold.

His body shaking around hers, he encapsulated her fully, not giving her air to breathe, room to move.

She didn't care.

This was right. This was what had haunted her dreams for years. This man holding her like it was always meant to be.

A moment of eternity passed and he loosened his hold slightly, enough for her to wedge her arms free from their bodies. She reached up and wrapped her fingers around the back of his neck.

All the invitation he needed.

His lips came down on her in a hard kiss that sank into her, shaking her to her bones. The heat, the woodsy scent of him, his lips demanding on hers, his tongue finding way to plunge into her and send sharp pangs running through her core—all of it intoxicating. How had he managed to hold it back this past week? Had their positions been reversed, she would have kissed him like this that first day—ripped his clothes off whether he remembered her or not.

He pulled from her lips suddenly and it took several breaths before her eyelashes fluttered and she could find his face through the pounding haze that had enveloped her body.

His steely grey eyes, darker, more dangerous than ever, pierced her. "Are you really back to me, Sienna?"

"Yes."

He didn't move, didn't reply. It was deep in his eyes, the disbelief. He thought she was lying.

Her hands came forward, clasping his face between her palms. "You don't believe me. It's either that or I died to you ten years ago and your love for me died then as well. Which is it, Logan?"

His eyes darkened. "Death could never stop my love for you, Sienna."

"Then you don't believe me. You don't believe I remember."

"It's all I've wanted for the past week, Sienna, for you to remember. And now that you say it...I just...I just want it to be true so badly that I cannot trust it—you—myself."

Her fingertips curled along his cheekbones. "The feeling in my soul—that you are my world—that my heart is beating so furiously just because I am near you, kissing you. I may not have all the memories, but I have the feeling. It's something I couldn't deny even if I wanted to, Logan."

"Do you want to deny it?"

"No. Heavens no. But I don't know what I can do to make you believe me."

His head dropped forward, his eyes hidden for a long moment before he lifted his chin, his heated gaze meeting hers, the low rumble of his voice vibrating against her body.

"That moment when I part your legs and the air reaches you. That moment when you are bared to the world, trusting that I will take care of you. Your eyes. How you look at me in that one moment. How you've always looked at me in that moment. That's when I know I have you. When you will always be mine and only mine."

She shifted to press her face close to his, her lips brushing his with her breathless words. "Then remove my dress, Logan."

His last kiss curled her toes—every wicked thought of what she could do to a naked man taking hold in her mind.

This kiss left the last in shame, searing her from head to toe. His body pressing against hers, his member already hard and long, nudging into her abdomen through their clothes, his tongue thrusting, exploring, pulsating into her mouth. Her folds went wet, begging for him, for their clothes to cease their barrier.

His hands were quick.

While his kiss was sending her body into a mad frenzy, his fingers worked far too many buttons to count. Her skirt and petticoat fell, the jacket of her riding habit ripped back off her arms, her chemise and stays slid down her body.

The stockings and boots he left.

He knew exactly how to undress her. His fingers trailing along her curves, sending ripples of carnal fury to every nerve in her body. And all she wanted was more. Him. Him deep inside her.

Her hands dove between them, unbuttoning the fall front of his trousers and setting his cock free. No hesitation, she grabbed him. She'd never touched a man before— except she had. The second her fingers wrapped the length of his member, felt the silky cords that ran along his shaft, the ridge of the head, she knew it. Knew she'd done this a thousand times before.

That his body was hers.

His mouth had moved down her neck and a growl shot from him, rumbling into her skin as her fingers tightened around his length.

"Damn, Sienna. Damn your hand."

Her hand stilled. "I shouldn't touch you?"

"Yes. Hell, yes. It's just been so long since you've…since your fingers have wrapped around me."

She smiled into the top of his head and squeezed harder.

His face jerked up, a wicked gleam in his eye burning bright. "You've never been patient. I wanted you inside this cottage, at the least, lying down where I could see your body that has haunted my dreams for so long. Where I could worship it."

Her left hand ran through his dark hair, gripping a swath of it at his neck. She kissed him, her lips parting his, her tongue delving into his mouth, tasting. "We don't have time for that, Logan. I want you. Now. Here."

She wedged her hands upward, stealing away his overcoat, waistcoat, and linen shirt. Her fingers ran along the skin of his chest, trailed along the ridges of muscles low on his stomach, avoiding the scab where she had gutted him. She looked at him, a breathless smile on her face. "Now."

"You are a demanding one."

"Yes? I do want what I want, I guess."

He chuckled and his right hand came down in between them, teasing down her stomach, lower and lower until his fingers slipped into her folds.

Nerves aflame, an instant wave of need swept through her with the motion, sending her mouth dry, her tongue begging for more. He plied her folds, her nubbin, her soft screams at every swipe of his fingers sending him faster, sending her own hand downward to stroke his cock.

Her breath flew into madness, scream after scream tumbling from her mouth. Through the pounding in her head, the building waves she couldn't control, her body lifted. Logan's arm had gone under her backside, lifting her and positioning her against the outside of the cottage.

Lifting her right leg, she slipped her right thigh up his body, resting heavy on his hip bone as she pulled her left leg up the other side of him. Bared, open to him, she wrapped her legs around his backside as his dark grey eyes searched her face, her soul. She met his look, not hiding the slightest bit of what she was feeling in that moment.

She was his. She would always be his. And she knew it.

It flickered in his eyes. The recognition. The belief.

He plunged into her. No word, no warning, and it was the most delicious thing she'd ever felt. The length of him filling her, so wide she didn't know how her body stretched to accommodate him.

His other hand went under her backside, supporting her fully as he withdrew and slammed back into her.

This was no longer exploring. No longer caressing. This was hard and fast—a brutal need that had been ten years in the making. He needed to be crashing into her just as much as she needed it.

Stroke after stroke, her back slammed against the wall of the cottage, the pain of it only heightening the fire in her nerves. Every time he slid out, her breath stopped, the savage desperation for him to be back inside of her swallowing her. The building in her core pitched higher, her nonsensical screams filling her head, filling the air around them.

He withdrew, this time for a long moment, the thick tip of him poised just inside her entrance. He held it. Held it until she was clawing at him, her legs around him tightening, kicking.

He drove into her. Drove her body over the edge, sending her splintering into a million stars with one final scream, his name on her lips.

His body shuddered at her scream, a ferocious growl escaping his throat to twist with her cry.

His body collapsed against hers, smothering her to the wall.

She was back.

At least in this, she was back.

And they both knew it.

{ CHAPTER 6 }

"You're shaking."

"I am not." Her voice, soft and muffled into his chest, warmed his heart.

"You are." His fingers stroked down the length of her red-blond hair, twining along a russet strand. He had forgotten how much that one little motion meant to him—her hair long down her bared back where he could twist it in silent contemplation for hours. He didn't care that splinters from the rough wood of the cottage were digging into his back, not while she straddled him, spent, her naked body entwined with his.

He ran his fingertips along her shoulder blades, checking for any splinters that may have embedded into her skin. He hadn't meant to take her that fiercely, her body slamming into the wall. But they had always been a force he couldn't control—merely manage, at best—when they were naked together.

When he'd spun them and sat, he'd needed to collapse to the ground just as much as her limp body did.

Wrapping her hair along his palm, Logan tugged her head back so she had to look up at him. "You're trembling and I want to know why."

She grinned. "You can't just let me revel in our bodies being meshed like this for a few more minutes?"

He could see right through the smile she had conjured to cover up whatever her quaking was about. "Not when I'm worried about why you're shaking. Tell me."

She shrugged, her shoulders bumping into his upper arms. "It was nothing, just another image that suddenly appeared in my mind that didn't make any sense."

"What was the image?"

She sighed. "You aren't going to stop your insistence, are you?"

"No."

"The name, Bournestein, how you said it the other day—it popped into my mind. I never met my uncle in all these years, my grand—" she shook her head, looking at his chest "—the woman that *claimed* she was my grandmother and was taking care of me at Roselawn, she said Bournestein was my uncle, my mother's brother, and that he was the one that supported the estate. She said he was very generous."

She craned her neck to look up at his face. "Is that true? You must know him? Who is he? I get an image of a man a half head shorter than you with half a head of hair and a barrel chest descending down into a belly. And purple flashes. Why do I see purple flashes? Is he wearing purple? It sounds bizarre, I know, but the name Bournestein—it's so familiar and my mind keeps going back to it."

Logan's body started to stiffen and he had to force his muscles to relax. He kissed her forehead. "I would prefer you remember on your own, Sienna. I don't want to confuse your memories."

She shifted in his arms, her index and middle finger poking at his chest. "Tell me who he is. The emotions I feel flash so distinctly with the other snippets of memories I've had—fear, love, danger, hatred—even if I can't place the fragments into actual, full memories. But the purple—with the name Bournestein and those purple flashes—I cannot figure it. The emotions I sense are all in a jumble and such drastic opposites that there is no clear overriding emotion attached to the name."

His hand stilled in her hair. That was the last thing he wanted to hear.

He wanted to hear her say hatred. Pure hatred. Only hatred for the name Bournestein.

He leveled his voice. "I think these snippets of memories are ones that you need to allow your own mind to work out for you, to expand into full—"

"Why? Why not just tell me, Logan? You obviously know what I'm talking about. Who is Bournestein?"

Logan looked away from her, staring for a long moment at his horse on the edge of the clearing around the cottage. "It…it is complicated, Sienna. And if you don't remember who Bournestein is, you are better off without the complications."

"That isn't fair, Logan." She grabbed his face in her hands and dragged his attention back to her. "You know everything and you're just being cruel by holding it back."

"I'm not being cruel, Sienna. I'm attempting kindness."

Her hands dropped from his face. "But you don't know what this is like—the gaping holes in my head that are all mysteries, nothing more. I lost my life—I lost you—and if I had only remembered…"

"But you did. You do remember me now. At least your heart does. That is what's important."

His fingers lifted to tuck a stray lock of red hair behind her ear. As selfish as it was, she remembered *him*, and if she never had another memory of the past surface, that would suit him well. But he did sympathize with her frustration.

"And you're correct—I don't know what it's like. But maybe your mind is doing exactly what it needs to in order to keep you sane."

"Keep me sane?" She leaned away from him. "I won't be sane if I know who Bournestein is?"

Logan stifled a sigh, his palms coming up to rub his eyes. His hands sank and he centered his gaze on her. "Do you trust me, Sienna?"

"Yes." Her answer was immediate, no reservations in her blue eyes. That, at least, was to his favor.

"Then believe me when I tell you, whatever you have in your mind about Bournestein, it is better left at rest—a forgotten memory."

Her face fell, her mouth clamping shut.

His hands settled on her upper arms, rubbing. "Sienna, I can't imagine what is going through your mind, or how frustrating it must be to not understand all those memories in your head. But I think your brain is only trying to protect you—to not overwhelm you with years of forgotten memories. I think you need to wait. Be patient and your mind will tell you what it needs to when it needs to."

It took her a long moment before her eyes lifted to him. "Why do I suspect I'm not the patient type?"

He chuckled. "As verified a few minutes ago, you aren't. You want what you want when you want it."

"Oh. I thought that was maybe just because I had this in front of me." She motioned with her fingertips to his bare chest. Sudden worry cut across her brow and her eyebrows lifted. "Am I a harpy?"

He grinned. "Nothing of the sort. You are a very determined person, that is all."

She shook her head. "I don't feel like I've been that way for the last ten years. I suddenly feel like I was in a very placid dream—a bubble—that replayed the same unperturbed scene day after day. I would sketch. Go to the village. Grandmother would make me practice my stitches, since apparently, I had forgotten how to sew."

"You sew now?"

"Yes, of course—wait—" Her eyes widened. "Am I so terrible at it because I never knew how to do it?"

Logan nodded, a slight grin on his face. "You were determined to never learn how. I used to have to stitch my own buttons."

Her hand went down in between them, her fingertips gentle atop the crooked stitches holding together the wound in his gut. "And you're terrible at it as well."

He laughed.

Her fingertips left his healing wound, lightly skipping from one scar to the next on his chest and belly. "These scars, are they from the war?"

"Many of them."

Her lips pursed into a frown. "I don't like seeing them, seeing them mar your skin, seeing the pain you must have endured."

He wrapped his hand over her fingers on his chest. "There's no need for your eyes to darken—the pain of them is long past."

Her head twisted around, looking toward his feet. He'd kicked off his left boot and pant leg, but his right boot was still in place, his trousers bunched around the leather.

"Your right foot is the one that was maimed? I haven't even thought on it since you mentioned it, you hide the limp so well. But that pain hasn't stopped in all these years, has it?"

"It is manageable."

"Can I see it? I don't want any of you hidden from me, Logan."

He inclined his head toward his boot.

She extracted herself from his arms, her naked body moving down his limbs. She didn't turn from him—stayed facing him as she crouched in the grass by his feet. A silent cue she wasn't about to hide anything from him. His heart swelled—a trait she'd never lost.

Her hands wrapped around his boot, wedging it from his foot. She spun it in her hands, reaching in to feel the extra support ingrained into the boot that let him stand normal.

Her arm elbow deep in his boot, she glanced at him. "The padding and the shape—this boot is a marvel."

"It is."

Her look went down to the boot as her hand nosed around the inside of it. "Does it have springs under the wood?"

"It does. It's the eleventh rendition of the design."

"Your shoemaker is a wonder." She extracted her hand from the boot.

"He is. And he does the same for all my guards."

Setting the boot aside, she tugged off his trousers and moved to sit on her calves.

In spite of himself, his breath caught, lodging in his lungs. He was facing the only person in the world whose opinion on his injury he cared about.

Her hands soft, her fingers traced up along his foot from his toes, slow, almost sensual as though she meant to seduce it. She lifted his foot to her lap, turning it over and back and forth, her fingers exploring the wide sunken dip along his heel where bone was removed. Her fingers trailed again and again along the lines of long-healed scars.

She didn't flinch once. Didn't hesitate in where her fingers travelled. And they touched all of his ragged, mangled foot. Her blue eyes lifted to him, wide with unshed tears. "I wasn't there."

He exhaled his held breath. "Sienna—"

"I wasn't there." Her head shook. "I'm just so heartbroken you suffered this alone—the pain it must have taken to maul your flesh so. And I wasn't there for you."

Her look dropped down to his foot, her forefinger following the zigzagged stripes of scars along his heel— where all the skin had torn away and had been painstakingly sewn back together.

A sad smile came to her face. "The scars of these stitches—now these are beautiful—straight and even. Whoever the surgeon was, was a marvel."

"He—they—were."

"Do you know my grandmother liked to tell me I used to have wonderful, straight stitches before my accident?" Her look lifted to him, confusion still clouding her blue eyes. A flash sparked in her face, and her eyes narrowed. "Which wasn't an accident and she had to have known that. She had to have known I was thrown against a wall in Spain. So who is she? She's not my grandmother—I feel very certain of that."

She lifted his foot from her lap and set it to the ground, moving up to crawl onto him again. Curling into him, she settled her head along the crook of his chest. "Is that true, do I have a living grandmother, Logan?" She craned her neck to look up at him. "Do you know who the woman at Roselawn is?"

Logan shrugged. "She's a mystery to me as well—she's the woman that's been taking care of you for the last ten years. That is all I know of her—what you've told me." His eyes shifted from her face to the grasses growing along the edge of the woods. He didn't want to start telling her about family she didn't have. That was something he never wanted to have to broach with her. But she would demand at least this answer from him.

He sighed, cheating on his promise to himself not to tell her anything of the past. "And no, you have no living grandparents."

She nodded, a frown taking over her face. "I don't want to go back there, Logan."

"What?"

"Back to Roselawn. I want to leave. Leave with you right now. Were you on your way to London?"

"Yes." His eyebrow cocked. "But you don't want to go back there to pack anything? To tell her—or ask her anything? I want to know the answers of who she is just as much as you do, Sienna. And I will be at your side the entire time."

"No. I don't want that woman and I don't need her." She shook her head. "That woman—as kind as she's been—has been lying to me for ten years, so I am done. Done." Her hands splayed on his chest as she paused. Drawing a deep breath, she pushed away from him to meet his eyes straight on. "You were out there, and I didn't know. I didn't know you existed. She must have known of you and she kept me from you."

His mouth set to a frown. "But if we don't go back to Roselawn, to that woman, we may never have any answers about your time here. Answers I need to know."

"I don't care. I have a horse, you have a horse, and we can leave." Her fingertips pressed into the muscles of his chest, imploring. "I know what happened these last ten years, and it was much of nothing. Of me being told I was fragile. But I'm not fragile, am I?"

The corners of his mouth twitched. "No."

She shook her head, her eyes going to the sky. "And I was convinced that I shouldn't stress myself with friendships or dalliances or anything normal."

He leaned forward to kiss the tip of her delicate nose. "Well I, for one, am happy about the curbing of the dalliances."

She swatted his chest. "Of course you are." She grinned. "Me too. This would be horribly awkward if I had another husband waiting for me."

His hands tightened around her backside. "Don't even utter such words."

She laughed. "You're the jealous type—I think I'm recalling that now."

"I am. Unabashedly so. I am nothing but the you-are-mine-and-I-will-skewer-any-man-that-dares-to-look-at-you-crooked type." He leaned to the left and nipped her ear, sending her squealing. "And I don't apologize for it."

She squirmed, laughing, until he pulled away and she could see his eyes. "I also think I remember that I always adored that in you."

"Good. Then you're remembering well." His face went serious. "But you are sure you would like to leave here without confronting the woman at Roselawn? There may not be another chance."

"I need to go back to London, Logan. With you. There is a pull to it and I feel as though I might remember more there." She wrapped her hands behind his neck. "I want to come with you. Now. Today. This moment. Because I belong with you, Logan. Nowhere else."

{ CHAPTER 7 }

His little brother came crashing into the room, all floppy legs and arms flailing in madcap fashion. Dirt from the tussle in the muck on the street was still caked on his face.

Dirt…and blood?

For eight years old, Robby looked at least twelve. People demanded more out of him because they thought he was older. Logan knew exactly what that was like. Bournestein had treated him like a grown man for a long time already, and he was only ten. Or at least Logan thought he was ten. He may have lost count and his mother didn't remember.

Logan pushed his voice low, hissing, not wanting to believe what Freddie Joe had run in and told him. "Dammit, Robby." He snatched his brother's arm, dragging him past two of Bournestein's brutes and out the side door of the room and into Mable's room. Mable was downstairs. They had a few minutes of it being empty.

Logan spun Robby into the room, sending him tumbling. "Dammit, Robby, I told you to whistle—the whistle works— you do it when you're angry or scared or huffy or irked and you just want to attack and beat something and it takes all the heat out of it. It—"

"It don't work, Logan. It don't work none." Robby spit into the corner, not even aiming for the chamber pot. Blood strung along with the spittle. "I tried and I can't even whistle like you. Nothin' bothers you and everything bothers me and that's just the way we are."

He grabbed his little brother's upper arm, shaking it. "You gotta figure something out, Robby. I don't care if it's whistling or digging a poker into your leg or crossing your arms and squeezing your chest, but you gotta find something that works. You can't just attack everything you see—you're gonna get stuck by a beast like Wally if you can't stop going screwy all the time."

"Or I stick him first."

Logan stepped back from Robby, stilling, his eyes boring into his little brother. "What do you mean, you stick him first?"

Robby's eyes dipped, his look going to the lower corner of the room like a beaten dog.

"What the hell did you do, Robby?"

His steel grey eyes, a perfect match to Logan's, flickered up for a second, then his look dropped back to the floor. "I did it. I stuck him. He wouldn't stop and he tried to grab the coin I stole from the drunk on Thompson's stoop."

Logan jumped forward, grabbing his little brother's arms and shaking him. "What did you do, Robby?"

"I stuck him, Logan. I stuck him and he bled and bled and bled in front of me."

"He's dead?" Logan's shaking hands ceased, his fingers gripping into Robby's arms.

It took an eternity for Robby to lift his look to Logan, and his little brother's eyes hardened, aging a thousand years directly in front of him. "It was easy, Logan. He was going to kill me. So I killed him first."

For the shortest of moments, Robby's eyes turned terrified, the little child he truly was both horrified and frightened.

"It went in easy, Logan. Too easy."

"Bournestein."

Logan's head swiveled to his wife, breaking him out of the past. She sat atop of her horse, her eyes widening as he looked to her.

"Wait—what were you thinking of, Logan? Your face is ashen."

He shook his head. "Nothing of note. I was thinking of the whistle that I did—the one that brought you back to me. It was from a different time—I haven't whistled like that in years, but by the grace of the fates, I did it and you heard it."

He managed a half smile.

He wasn't about to tell her the story of the moment he lost his little brother. She already knew it—or at least she knew it long ago. She had snuck into Mable's room after them, hiding along the purple velvet curtains and had heard the whole thing.

With any luck, she would never recall the story.

With any more luck, she would never recall anything of their childhood. Wouldn't recall how he'd failed Robby. How he'd failed her.

She hadn't remembered much more in the two days that they had travelled on horseback towards London. And for that, he'd been grateful.

He gave himself a shake and adjusted himself in his saddle as he attempted to widen his smile. "What about Bournestein, Sienna?"

She had mentioned the name several times during the past two days, and he'd deflected all her questions. And not only the questions about Bournestein, but all her inquiries about what happened before she got slammed into a wall and injured her head. He'd protect her from recalling the painful memories for as long as he could.

"I think...no...it's just..." She shook her head, interrupting her own ramblings. "I don't know what memory I just had, but I need to just speak it out loud—Bournestein—he—he's not my uncle, is he?"

Logan shook his head, careful to keep his mouth sealed tight.

A cringe crept onto her face. "He's my father, isn't he?" *Hell.*

His heart thumped hard in his chest. The one thing he prayed she wouldn't remember. The one thing, the one man he'd been trying to—needed to—protect her from their whole lives.

But he couldn't protect her from the truth and he knew it. He swallowed the lump in his throat. "Yes."

She took his answer stoically, not flinching. "Who is my mother?"

Logan looked away from her, searching the road ahead. The next village with a coaching inn was within sight. If he could stall her long enough, he could get her eating and into bed. That had been the best way to curtail her ravenous mind during the past two days—get her fed and into bed where he would wear out her body, satiating her again and again until she murmured herself to sleep, wrapped in his arms.

She'd more than enjoyed it—rediscovering what their bodies could do together. The heights they could push each other to. But that wasn't the peace that she was searching for—she was desperate to regain her memories.

It would do by him, his current practice of evading her during the day and distracting her at night. But his wife was too canny for the routine to work indefinitely. The only hope he held onto was that the roads had been fairly busy, so that had curtailed many of her questions during the days—and they would only get busier the closer they got to London.

Logan looked about them. That the road was void of other traffic at the moment was an uncommon occurrence and of little help to him.

He glanced at her. "Have you remembered something of your mother?"

"Possibly. I have an image, but I don't know if it is of a random woman or not."

He offered a quick nod, looking forward as he adjusted his hand around the leather of his reins. He had to give her something. "Her name was Vivian and your mother was beautiful. She had red hair—it is where you get the russet locks in your hair. She had flawless skin and her eyes were a match to yours. That clear, exquisite blue, except your eyes have more dark azure strands shining through than she did."

"That sounds like the image I have in my head, but it is fuzzy." Her mouth tugged to the side. "Why do you remember her so well but I only have a vague picture of her?"

Logan looked to her, meeting her blue eyes and bracing himself. "She died when you were five, so while you loved her, I imagine the image of her may have faded over time."

"I loved her? She was a good mother?"

"You did." He set his gaze forward, hoping that would be enough. He wasn't about to tell her that her mother was a horrid person—wasn't anything like a mother to Sienna. She didn't need to know that. Didn't need to know she was unwanted.

The horses took a few more steps before her voice broke through the silence. "But you didn't say she was a good mother, Logan."

He glanced at her. Her eyes had narrowed at him.

"And you didn't say how she died."

Hell. Logan shifted his focus straight ahead, his mouth clamped shut. His horse kept moving. Sienna's did not.

He kept forward until he was convinced she wasn't going to set forth again. He stopped his horse, turning it sideways on the road so he could look back to her.

She sat, motionless, glaring at him.

"Sienna, is something amiss with your horse?"

"No. There is something amiss with me and you are refusing to help."

"Sienna—"

"No, Logan. You have put me off with half-mumbled answers for days now and I can see the village ahead of us. You plan to shut my mouth with food and sex and sleep again instead of answering my questions."

He cringed. So he hadn't been covert about it.

He nudged his horse back to hers and stopped it, facing her. "Sienna, it is as I said it was when you first started remembering things. Our past is not kind. If you remember things, fine—but if you don't, you will be better for it."

"Or will you be better for it?"

"Yes, I will, and I happily admit to it." His voice dropped to a hard timbre. "I'll be protecting you from things better left forgotten."

"And you get to make that decision for me?"

"Yes."

"No." Her mouth pulled back in a terse line. "If there's one thing I have realized about myself in the past few days, it is that I don't think I ever would have allowed you to browbeat a decision like this upon me."

"And I never thought I would have to, Sienna." His voice took on a cold edge he couldn't control. "But here we are. I am protecting you."

"You are controlling me."

"Protecting."

"Controlling." She lifted the reins in her hands. "And I'm not letting this mare take another step until you tell me what happened to my mother."

He took a deep breath, a low whistle bubbling from his chest.

"Stop." Her hand flew up, her voice pitching high. "You don't get to whistle—you don't get to calm—you get to damn well tell me what happened to my mother, Logan, or I swear—"

"She died in a whorehouse from too much laudanum, Sienna. Is that what you want to hear?" he yelled. "She died in the whorehouse where we all lived. How desperately do you need to know that?" His mouth clamped shut, horrified.

Dammit. She was the one person that could get him to do that. To push him so far past his control that he exploded in a raging mess.

Her jaw dropped, the horrification he felt reflected on her face. "She…we…she…" Her head shook—trying to recall or trying to strike his words from her mind, he couldn't tell.

Her head suddenly stilled, her eyes half closed as she looked at him in a slight daze. "Logan, we grew up in a whorehouse? I am a by-blow?"

{ CHAPTER 8 }

His look pained, Logan nodded.

She was the daughter of a whore.

For all she'd expected Logan to tell her, this was not something that would have ever occurred to her. Her grandmother—her fake grandmother—had said they were of the gentry. A wealthy merchant family that went back ages. Her great-great-grandmother the daughter of an earl. That was why Sienna had been so skilled at needlepoint and Latin and the pianoforte.

Except she wasn't skilled at needlepoint and Latin and the pianoforte. She was horrible at those things.

She was skilled at drawing—and gutting a man. Those things she knew how to do. Those things her hands were born with.

But to be the daughter of a *whore*. To grow up in a *whorehouse*.

Her skill with a blade suddenly made much more sense.

Her gaze flew up to Logan. The concern in his eyes was heartbreaking, stealing her breath. He didn't want to tell her anymore, she could see that, but she needed to know.

"This…" She had to stop, swallowing a breath before she could form words. "This Bournestein that I keep seeing images of—the man in purple—he is truly my father—you know that? For if my mother was a whore…"

Logan exhaled a long sigh, almost to a whistle.

"There is no turning back from this now, Logan, you have to tell me."

His lips pulled inward, gritting for a moment, and then his head tilted to the side, acquiescing. "He owns the whorehouse, Sienna. Your mother was his favorite—his exclusive woman for a long period of time. You are his child."

Her fingers went to her forehead and she rubbed it for several long breaths. Her hand dropped and she looked at him. "Then who are your parents, Logan? Is your mother a whore as well?"

"Not exactly."

"Then why did you grow up in a whorehouse with me?"

"Unfortunate circumstances."

"Which were?"

Logan looked around, searching. There was no one on the road to overhear—or save him from this conversation. His gaze settled back on her. "My father was wealthy, but my mother was his second wife and he married her when he was rather old. I had three older half-brothers that resented—strike that—hated my mother, and in turn, hated me and my younger brother, Robby, when we were born."

"Robby?" She blinked hard. "I know that name—I know him, don't I?"

"You do." His horse nickered, sidestepping and he tugged on his reins to still it.

Her gut started to sink, as she could already guess how things turned for his mother. "I assume your father died?"

"He did. And my half-brothers couldn't wait to get rid of us after the funeral. My mother hadn't even recovered from the shock of my father's death when they tossed us, penniless, into the gutter. She was the despised second wife—younger than the older two sons—and the only thing that kept my half-brothers in line was my father."

"She didn't try to fight them?"

He shook his head. "If she hadn't been in shock… things might have been different. She might have thought it through properly, the power she didn't realize she had."

"But she didn't?"

"No. She had no family, so she went straight to Bournestein in London with my brother and me in tow. Bournestein had been deeply in love with her when they were young, but he was destitute and she left him to marry my father—she needed the security he could afford."

"And Bournestein still took her in? Even though she left him?"

"He made her crawl." The words were steady, even though they came through gritted teeth. "But yes, he did. By then he had taken over the brothel. So that is where we lived. With you."

Sienna nodded, her sinking gut now turned into a hard, bitter rock.

No wonder Logan hadn't wanted to tell her. And to see his eyes when he talked of his mother. He'd held a facade on his face that was impenetrable, imparting the tale with no emotion. But to her eye it was flimsy and she could see right through it. Even if she couldn't remember most of their past—she knew him. Knew this man so intimately that she could see the wounds from long ago deep in his silver eyes.

"How old were you when you came to London?"

"I was five, Robby was three—the same age as you."

"Logan, what—"

The four horses of a coach crested the upcoming hill, their thundering hooves interrupting her question.

Logan looked over his shoulder and the relief on his face was instant.

He quickly nudged his horse to turn around and move in front of Sienna, leading her mare to the side of the road so the coach could pass.

He didn't stop his horse's gait as the coach passed, instead moving quickly toward the village.

She stared at his back.

He thought he'd just been delivered from her inquiries, but all he had done was create a whirlwind of questions in her mind.

More questions without answers.

She wasn't done with him just yet.

~ ~ ~

Logan walked into the room at the carriage inn carrying a silver tray holding two platters piled high with beef, breads, asparagus and parsnips, and large cuts of grapes nestled along the edges.

For as ravenous as she was, the heavenly soak of water around her body took precedence over her empty belly. After three days of the muddy roads and the early summer heat, she had begged Logan to convince the landlady of the coaching inn to have a bath brought up for her.

She had left Yorkshire with the clothes on her back, and her body was now just as much a sticky, dirty mess as her skirts.

The room they had been shown to was stifling hot until the breeze had found its way inward. The third level chamber was spacious, bedecked in airy peaches and mauves layered over white wainscoting that belied the heat it captured. Yet once the windows were opened, the room caught most of the evening winds.

Wedged deep into the bathing tub that had been brought up and filled with tepid water, Sienna peeked at her husband over the rim of the basin, the comb she was pulling through her wet hair stilling.

Logan stood with his back to her, setting the tray down on the small round table by the open window. He moved the platters, along with the teapot and cups and the small decanter of brandy onto the table, then fiddled with the utensils. She caught glimpses of his profile as he set the table. The dark scruff of a beard that had started along his face had grown quickly in three days. It made him look older, like the weight of the world was on his shoulders.

An image flashed in her mind—an image of that same dark scruff on his face. Of him in uniform. Of him striding away from her, angry. Furious.

The memory of him stomping away reached into her chest and squeezed her heart, constricting it so painfully in her chest it made her gasp.

He spun around. "What is it?"

The comb dropped into the water as her fingers dug into the skin above her left breast, trying to ease the sharp pang that had just swallowed her heart. "I wasn't supposed to be there, was I?"

"Where?"

"In Spain." Her eyes closed, her head shaking as she tried to conjure the memory. "I followed you...you left me in England and I followed you and it took months for me to find you. And then I did." Her eyes popped open to him.

He had moved across the room to stand next to the tub. His fingertips started tapping the rim. "Yes."

"And you were raging—raging—that I had come. And I only wanted you, but you turned and you left—you left me." Her eyes closed again and her head dropped forward, her face scrunching as she tried to hold onto the memory.

It was gone.

For minutes, she tried, tried to conjure the feel of it. To live the pain again so fully she had no choice but to remember more of it—all of it.

Nothing.

"I came back." His fingertips brushed across her furrowed brow, his soft words breaking her futile concentration.

She opened her eyes, looking up at him. "You did?"

"I could never leave you for long. That was the hardest thing I had ever done, leaving you in England for the war, Sienna." His voice low, achingly gentle, he reached behind him to grab a simple wooden chair and pulled it next to the tub, sitting down.

He leaned forward, settling his arms on his thighs and clasping his hands together. "And then when you showed up in that village in Spain, you scared me to Hades and back. So yes, I was raging. Yes, you were beyond headstrong to come after me. But at the core of it, as much as I didn't want you there, I couldn't deny my need to be with you. There was supposed to be a channel of deep water separating us—that was how I was going to deny myself of you for the years."

Her head softly bobbed. "I wasn't supposed to be there, and I knew it. I knew it was a mistake to follow you. But I was just so…so…I needed you, Logan. I needed to be near you in case…in case…"

"In case I died." His lips pulled inward for a moment before he continued. "You came because you wanted the last thing I saw to be you, if I died."

She drew a deep breath, her chest rising out of the water as she nodded. "I couldn't stand the thought that you would die alone, that the last thing you would see would be a bloody battlefield. And I didn't care about anything but that." She drew in a wavering breath to choke back a sob. "I had to come, but I shouldn't have."

"No. You shouldn't have. And I shouldn't have let you stay—not even for those five nights. But I understand why you came. "

His head bowed for a long moment, the knuckles of his clasped hands turning white. "When I thought you were dead, when I saw your body charred in the rubble." His look lifted to her, his grey eyes glistening. "All I could think of was that I wasn't there. That you died alone. Alone, struggling to live, wondering where I was, desperate for me. Struggling. That your eyes closed without me there to hold you."

He drew a ragged breath. "I swore I would always be there—till the end. Nothing devastated me more than that moment, that thought. That you died without me. To this day it haunts me, even with you here before me—alive—I cannot think of it without my soul shattering."

He inhaled a deep breath, his head shaking. His right cheek pulled up into a half smile full of regrets. "We both made mistakes, Sienna. But you were young. I was young. And we weren't always wise."

Her hand lifted from the water, sending ripples along the surface. She rubbed her eyes, the bathwater mixing with tears that had filled her eyes. Her fingertips dropped from her face. "And then you brought your men—how many men died because of me?"

"No, you do not get to do that, Sienna." The deep rumble of his voice was vehement. "My men died because of a choice I made. Me. I marched them into that village."

"But you did it for me. Because I was stupid. Because I wasn't the one strong enough to be apart from you. You did it for me."

"And I would do it again because I would sacrifice anything—anything to keep you safe." His voice notched lower. "I told you before, Sienna, this is my burden to bear. Not yours. And I have been attempting to atone for my sins ever since."

"How?"

"By making sure every soldier I can find that has lost his way discovers a path back to the land of the living. By helping them move past what they lost in the war."

"Your guards at the Revelry's Tempest?"

Logan nodded. "My guards. All of them have worth they did not see in themselves, and most have found their path in life again. But there are always more to help."

"Which is why going back to London and the Revelry's Tempest is so important to you. Why didn't you tell me this?"

"It's complicated, Sienna—everything is complicated until you remember things. I didn't want the guilt I now see in your eyes to manifest, as I knew it would. What happened was never your intention. Never my intention."

"So why do you get to carry the burden of the past while I escape it free and clear?"

He shrugged.

"You don't have an answer for that, do you?"

"I don't."

She nodded, somewhat mollified by his honesty. "I will own the guilt as I need to, Logan. It is a hard thing to learn that I have been selfish at the cost of others."

A crooked grin crossed his face. "You think you've always been a saint, Sienna?"

She looked at him, unable to resist his half-cocked smile. "Of course I have been." She splashed water at him and it landed about his face. "I have no evidence to the contrary, so I'll just believe what I choose to believe, thank you very much."

He smacked his lips, the water dripping from them. "I was wondering if the water had turned cold yet."

"It is getting chilly. Why?"

He dipped one of his hands fully into the water, his fingers stretching to tickle her side.

She giggled, grabbing his hand to stop him.

His fingers on her side stilled. "I want a turn in there before you dunk your muddy skirt into the water to clean it. But I only want cold water."

"Cold?"

He paused, drawing his hand from the water, all levity from his face gone. "I prefer it when it is this warm outside, the cold water." He stood and turned from her, moving away from the tub toward the table. The set of his shoulders had gone stiff. His walk, wooden.

She stared at his back. "I used to know that, didn't I?"

He stopped halfway to the table. For several long breaths he was silent. "Yes." He didn't turn around to her.

She pushed herself up in the tub, water sloshing along the sides. "Logan, look at me."

For a moment, she questioned if he would, but then he slowly turned to face her.

She met his silver grey eyes, her look penetrating. "I know you, Logan."

She moved to stand in the tub, then stepped out of it and walked to him, a pool of water trailing behind her. She stopped in front of him, the breeze sending chilled bumps across her skin. It didn't matter.

What mattered was this man in front of her. This man that she knew to the bottom of her soul she loved, she needed, and would never let go of again.

"I know you, Logan, like I know my own breath, my own flesh. Don't doubt that, just because I don't remember a detail like whether you like your baths cold. I can relearn all of that about you. All of it. Me not knowing something like that in this moment doesn't mean a thing—not when I know in my heart and in my soul that you are mine and I am yours."

"Sienna—"

She lifted her hands, wrapping them around his neck and pressing her wet body into him, soaking his clothes. "You believe me the most when I am parted for you, trusting you with everything I am." Her fingers moved downward, working off his waistcoat and linen shirt. "And I know all sorts of things you like, Logan."

She dragged his linen shirt up over his head. "I know you like it when I strip you."

Silently, she removed him of his trousers, going to her knees to pull off his boots, one by one. His erection too hard, too pulsating to ignore, she grabbed him, setting her lips to the head of his cock.

Her eyes lifted upward. "I know you like this." With brutal slowness, she took him into her mouth, her tongue sliding along the ridges lining his smooth skin. His cock fought her, going impossibly hard under her tongue.

She withdrew, taking him in four more agonizingly slow times before he clutched the back of her wet hair, dragging her upward.

She stood and grabbed the back of his neck, using her body to push him backward to the wooden chair by the table. His calves hit the front of the chair and she nudged him downward to sit.

His hands clasped onto her hips and she spun around before he could pull her onto him.

"I know you like this." She backed up, her wet thighs straddling him, slipping along his legs until her backside hit his chest. Leaning back into him, she lifted her left arm over her shoulder to wrap her hand around the back of his neck.

Her right hand found his wrist and she wrapped her fingers around the back of his hand. Controlling his movement, she dragged his fingers up along her stomach, her ribs, and then set his palm on her breast, squeezing it. "I know you like this."

He exhaled, ragged and conquered.

Her left hand came down from his neck and she found his left arm, capturing his fingers and flattening them on her stomach. "And I know you like this." Her fingers tight on his knuckles, she sent his hand lower, caressing her abdomen before dipping down, her hand setting his fingers deep into her folds.

Her hands stayed tight over his on her body as she leaned back against his chest, his face aligned with hers, and she turned until the edge of her lips met his. "This is me parting for you, Logan. Me trusting you with everything I am."

She slid downward.

A rumble from deep in his chest shook her, shook the chair as his right hand clenched fully onto her breast, his mouth dipping to ravage her neck.

He shifted his hips upward, his cock piercing her.

A gasp flew from her mouth at the sudden pulsating filling her full and hard. Even with these past three days, her body was still getting used to the size of him. Of how he stretched her in ways her body remembered, but her mind did not.

His lips clasped hard onto her neck as his fingers rolled her nipples into hard nubs, sending pangs of fire from her breast to her core. It stole her breath, stole the gasps from her mouth.

She lifted herself along his cock, and his left hand dropped, spreading her wider to him, his fingers sliding along her slick folds. Her body losing control, her right hand flew up, gripping the back of his neck as ballast.

His mastery of her body sent her gasping, curling as she plunged down on him, the crux of her trembling, her nerves recklessly firing in every direction. The length of him drove deep into her in rhythm with the strokes of his fingers. Her thighs clenching at the exertion, she couldn't stop the thrusts, couldn't bear to break the motion.

He shook behind her, shook almost to loss of control, but then he grabbed her hips, lifting her and bringing her down, speeding the pace until all she could do was grip the back of his neck, holding on as he forced her to her explosion.

"Hell, Sienna." His hands went back to her breasts, gripping her, pleasure that bordered on pain as he thrust upward, her body taking him deeper than she thought possible.

His muscles roared around her, his growl into her neck savage as his seed exploded into her and sent her already racing heart to pounding in her chest.

Her fingernails dug into his neck, holding on as throbbing waves encompassed them, his chest and breath furious along her backside.

His head dropped forward, his lips on her shoulder as his hot breath filled her pores.

"Hell to heaven, Sienna." The words were cracked, breathless. "You do know me. And you won't let me forget it."

She smiled.

{ CHAPTER 9 }

Logan carried her over to the wide tester bed, his body falling ragged against her as he collapsed forward on the bed, crushing her for only a moment before he spun so she could sprawl on top of him.

Splayed wide on the bed, she could have stayed like that all night, riding each and every one of his breaths coming and going from his chest, his skin hot and damp and salty and stirring her core, ready for him to catch his breath and give her more.

Then her stomach rumbled.

"Was that your stomach or mine?" His deep voice vibrated his chest, tickling her breasts.

"Mine. All mine." She extracted her limbs from his, unsticking her still-damp skin from his. Sitting up, she patted his chest. "Get into your cold tub. I still have clothes to dunk."

"Are you sure your clothes will dry by tomorrow?"

She stood and walked over to the table, picking up a chunk of bread and pulling it apart as she watched Logan heave himself from the bed and trudge toward the bathing tub. A dry bite of bread stuck in her throat as she watched him walk. He was beautiful. A sculpture straight from Michelangelo's workshop.

How had it even been possible that she had forgotten this man? That he was hers?

She filled a tea cup and picked it up, washing the bread down her throat with the now-cold floral-infused brew.

"No. But wet skirts are preferable to the mud that is caked on every fiber."

Logan eased himself into the cold water without flinching. Admirable. She sat on the chair next to the table, not bothering to put her shift back on. She wanted to wash it as well, and all she could hope for was that temperatures weren't too chilly in the morning when they left and she would be in damp clothes.

After several bites of bread as she ogled her husband, he ducked his head under the water to rinse his hair. By the time he popped back up, a question had formed on her tongue. "I know you want my brain to remember things on its own timeline, but why are you so impossibly stubborn about not telling me anything about our past?"

He looked to her, water dripping off his dark eyebrows. His steel grey eyes turned guarded and he shrugged.

"You shrug like it's nothing, but you aren't the one with years of missing memories." She tore another bite-size chunk from the bread, staring for a long moment at the blue sapphires in her ring that she had rewrapped with a snippet of blue ribbon and set back upon her ring finger where it belonged. "But maybe you have it wrong, Logan—maybe if you tell me something—anything of our youth, maybe it will spark a memory. Maybe it will spark all my memories."

His forehead furrowed and he grabbed a washcloth and soap to start scrubbing his arms. "I have always admired your tenacity, Sienna, but on this score, I wish you weren't so determined."

She popped the bread into her mouth, chewing as she contemplated him. She just wanted something from the past—anything tangible she could plant herself in and hope it would inspire more memories. "Then tell me how I knew what to do with that knife I stabbed you with. I have never in my life stabbed anything, but I knew where to stick it into you to drive you back. My arm—my hand—they knew the motion without thinking."

His left eyebrow arched as he looked to her, a sure denial on his lips. But then a smile spread across his face. "That, I can tell you. You already know that we grew up in a whorehouse, so you can imagine why knowing how to wield a knife may come in handy?"

"I had surmised as much."

"Granted, you were Bournestein's only child, and he forbid anyone to touch you—but there were too many patrons coming and going that didn't know that rule." He bent his knee up in the tub to scour his leg. "So you needed to know how to protect yourself and I was the one to teach you. You and Robby both."

"How old was I?"

"When we started practicing, you were six, maybe seven. I had gotten one of Bournestein's men to carve us some wooden daggers to practice with. You pouted about that. You wanted a real blade." He switched legs. "The top rooms of the Joker's Roost were where we spent much of our time—so that's where we practiced. And it was hot, much like this room was before we opened the window— hot all the time because the chimneys converged around the rooms."

"Was I good with the blade?"

He chuckled, his eyes lifting to her under hooded eyebrows. "Not so much. Not at first. Robby was better—

quicker because he had such long arms and yours were so short by comparison. He'd beat you every time you had practice bouts with him."

"I don't believe it." She set the chunk of bread down and picked up her fork and knife, cutting into the beef on her platter. "I feel like I was really good at wielding a dagger for how natural it was when I stabbed you."

He laughed. "It's true. You were awkward. But you got better, and quicker, and then Robby's long arms didn't mean as much. He was still a bit clumsy, but you grew into grace fairly quickly."

"So I bested him often?"

"As often as he would best you." Logan shook his head, a wry smile on his face. "And you two would fight—quibble for hours on end and I would constantly be trying to keep the peace between you two."

"How did you manage that?"

"It usually ended up with me putting Robby in a chokehold."

"You'd hurt him?"

"Not so much hurt as restrain him." Logan tossed the washcloth into the water and stood from the tub, water slicking down his naked skin. If her stomach was not still grumbling she would have tackled him from across the room in that moment.

He reached for a towel as he stepped out of the tub and began to dry off. "Remember, you were off-limits. The only person that could lash you was Bournestein after your mother died, and he never did—even though you probably deserved it now and again."

The memories, so wrong and yet so fond, reflected in his steel grey eyes. So much so that she was taken aback at how precious a memory like that could be.

A memory she didn't have.

She took a bite of the beef, chewing it slowly as she tried to rein in her emotions—tried to rein in her demands that he tell her everything of her childhood. Futile, for she already knew he wouldn't answer her thousand questions.

She swallowed the beef and it sat in her throat, slow to move downward. "Where is Robby now?"

Logan immediately spun away from her, the towel rubbing furiously across his back. Silence.

"Another thing you won't tell me."

He turned around to her, his eyes pained. "Sienna—"

"So then tell me something happy." She plastered a bright smile on her face. "Tell me of a time when we were so happy you couldn't stand it."

He stood for a long moment, his skin still damp, staring at her. Clearly wanting to say more, but holding himself back. He drew a deep breath and wrapped the towel around his waist, then nodded, moving across the room to her.

"After our wedding, we had time before I had to report to my regiment and we went to visit the high cliffs off the Yorkshire coast."

"By Scarborough?"

"Yes. It was a sight to behold, the waves crashing against the cliffs. And it was cold so there were very few people about. And you decided you needed to follow the skinniest path down the side of the cliffs to the sea so you could see the view from below of a cliff that jutted into the sea. Granted, it was a sight to behold with the rock worn down underneath creating a precarious archway. You were almost to the bottom and you were looking up at the rock formation."

She blinked as a flash flickered across her mind of catching a face full of frothing, freezing water. She cringed. "Did I slip into the sea?"

"Not quite. A rogue wave caught you—caught us— blasting us with icy water. You slipped and I just barely caught your wrist before the wave took you with it."

Her shoulders shook as shivers ran down her back.

"Exactly. It was cold, and I was furious with you and all you could do was laugh through the shivers. You were freezing, but you were happy. You were happy because we were free of everything—there was just us and that stupid sea." The smile on his face went distant and he was clearly living in those moments again. "So we followed the trail the rest of the way down and found a nearby sea cave. It was empty, but it must have been a smugglers' cove because there were lanterns and logs for making a fire in it. We got the fire going and I peeled your wet clothes off and then mine and I wrapped you next to my skin and we sat there for hours."

A grin slid onto her face. "We did more than just sit there, didn't we?"

"Maybe—yes." He moved to her, bending down to set his lips on the tiny dip behind her ear. "I believe I did this." His tongue traced a lazy circle on her skin.

Sienna closed her eyes, fighting her way back to the memory.

"And this." His lips went downward, trailing along her collarbone as his thumb slid along the side of her left breast, finding the nipple and rolling it between his fingers.

Her eyes still closed, she smiled. "And then you tried to stop—not finish what you started."

"I didn't want anyone to find us. We had been there too long as it was." His mouth still on her shoulder, his words mumbled into her skin.

She reached forward and slid her hand up his inner thigh. "And then I did this and you didn't care about anyone finding us." She went higher, cupping his sack, her fingers dancing along his already hard member.

"I feel the same today. Be damned anyone seeing or hearing us."

She chuckled. "You're trying to occupy me with sex again to curb my questions, aren't you?"

"Possibly. You don't seem to mind."

She reached up with her free hand, her thumb under his chin as she cupped his face with her fingers to draw his attention to her. His silver eyes on her, her breath caught in her throat. "I want that freedom again, Logan. Freedom with you. I can almost feel it. Feel it like it was."

"So let's have it, Sienna." He dropped to his knees, his hands sliding behind her lower back to pull her body toward him, her legs wide on either side of him. He kissed the center of her chest, looking up at her. "I only have to attend to some matters in London at the Revelry's Tempest, and then we can be free. No entanglements with anyone but each other."

Her hand went into his dark wet hair, running through it. "Yes, except I feel as though there is still this unfinished business—the weight of my lost memories haunting me."

His head shook, his eyes vehement. "The memories aren't worth it, Sienna—aren't worth trading our chance at happiness for it."

"But what if I never remember, Logan?"

His arms tightened around her back. "Then I hold the memories for both of us."

His lips went to her right breast, teasing the nipple until he was satisfied and she was mewing. Downward, along her skin, his mouth trailed until he was at the crux of her. And all thoughts of memories too difficult to remember left her, the moment at hand consuming her.

He would remember for them both. She had to trust that.

{ CHAPTER 10 }

"Logan, you are back in London early." Cassandra, one of the three proprietresses of the Revelry's Tempest, stood from the table she sat at in the ballroom of the gaming hall. Card and hazard tables punctuated the ballroom, the copper edges of the felt-lined tables gleaming.

Sitting with her back to him, Violet, one of the other proprietresses, was quick to turn around and come to her feet at Cassandra's exclamation. Violet's movements were slowed by the mound of her belly preceding the rest of her body upward. Her latest babe would be coming soon and she was well past due for confinement.

A pang of guilt sliced through Logan's chest. Violet hadn't been this large when he'd left a month and a half ago. She'd insisted that she would spend very little time here at the Revelry's Tempest helping to manage it while he was away in Northumberland, yet here she was, helping prepare for a gaming night. He wondered how many days she'd spent here at the Revelry's Tempest in the past fortnight. He should've known she'd stretch her promise.

No one was better with the books than Violet, yet still, she shouldn't be here, not when she should be at home resting. He never should have believed her promise to limit herself. Though he imagined her husband, Lord Alton, was irate enough with his wife for the both of them.

Cassandra smoothed the front of her functional yellow day dress and stepped quickly to him. "We didn't expect your arrival for at least another month."

"I had a change of plans," he said, a scolding look still centered on Violet's expanded womb.

Cassandra looked past him, eyeing Sienna as she trailed a step behind him. "Who is this?"

His look jerked to Cassandra, noting her honey brown eyes had narrowed. There was no bandying about this announcement. Not with these two. Logan stepped to the side, setting his hand along the back of Sienna's shoulder and prodding her forward. "This is my wife, Sienna."

Violet choked, coughing, as she moved next to Cassandra, her look flying between Sienna and him. "Your wife? You left for two months and instead, you come back weeks early with a wife? How?" A second round of coughing captured her throat.

He had to wait for Violet's hand to flatten against her chest, tapping it until her fit of coughing dwindled. "Sienna, this is Lady Alton, and Lady Vandestile, Violet and Cassandra respectively."

Sienna conjured a bright smile even though Logan knew she didn't feel it. While he only saw her beauty—rumpled, yes, from four days riding—she had shied back in the mews wanting to wait with the horses because her riding habit was muddy from the journey. He wouldn't let her. This place, these women, his guards—all of it had been his life for the last ten years, and his pride bursting, he couldn't wait to introduce his wife to the lot of them.

Her smile steadfast, Sienna looked between the two women and opened her mouth. "I am del—"

"But why? How?" Violet's gaze continued to flicker back and forth from Logan to Sienna until she shook her head suddenly, seemingly remembering her manners and realizing she had just rudely cut off Sienna. She stepped forward, grabbing Sienna's hand and clasping it. "Oh, I apologize, Sienna. I did not mean to cut your words."

Stepping to her left, Violet swung her arm wide, ushering them into the drawing room attached to the ballroom of the Revelry's Tempest. "Please, forgive my rudeness and let us sit. This...this was just an unexpected shock." She looked to Logan. "I had no idea there was the possibility you would be getting married, Logan. Did you, Cass?" Her gaze travelled to her friend.

Cassandra's manners had not fully returned to her, as her wary look was centered solely on Sienna, calculating. Her eyes didn't veer to Violet. "No. No idea, Violet. None at all." The hesitant coolness in her voice told Logan all he needed to know.

Cassandra's guard was fully up. She was protecting him. Protecting him, just as she'd been protecting him from her husband since the couple had returned to England from America six months ago. It was innate in her nature. She was fiercely protective of those she loved.

Logan moved to slide his hand to the small of Sienna's back and nudged her forward with him into the drawing room. "Cassandra, Violet, I apologize at the unexpectedness of this sudden introduction. I know it is a gaming night."

Violet waved her hand in the air, sitting on a wingback chair as Logan and Sienna sat on the settee. A wide smile filled her face. "Posh on that. Gaming is hours away and your guards have had everything under control—Greyson, specifically, has been a godsend. You were right to leave him in charge. I daresay he manages this place better than any of us." Her hands clasped together. "Now you must tell us how this wedding came to be."

Logan glanced at Cassandra. Refusing to sit, she remained standing next to an empty wingback chair, her arms crossed in front of her. Her dark hair and flawless face combined with her utter stillness made her look like a painting come alive. He looked back to Violet, finding her friendly, though confused, smile. "The wedding was actually about eleven years ago, Violet."

Violet's smile froze in place, her words escaping past her frozen jaw. "You have been married this entire time, Logan? This entire time we have known you? But you—you never once thought to mention you had a wife? Truly?"

"I didn't think it necessary." He glanced at his wife, grabbing her right hand that she had clenched on her lap. "I thought Sienna was dead. I believed I had lost her during the war in Spain."

"But she was alive?" Cassandra finally spoke, her left eyebrow arched in disbelief.

Just when Logan opened his mouth, Sienna cleared her throat, drawing Cassandra's scrutinizing look. "I was. I was in the village of Sandfell in Yorkshire and I had no memory of Logan, no memories of anything other than waking up there. I have been with a woman that claimed she was my grandmother since then. She also claimed that I fell off a horse and hit my head and forgot everything of my life."

"But that is not what happened?" Violet leaned forward, her smile having faded and her attention rapt.

"No, I don't believe so. Not so far as the few memories I have regained tell me. I believe I was tossed into a wall and hit my head, but I am not sure as to why. Most things I don't exactly remember."

"What do you mean, you don't remember?" Cassandra asked.

Sienna looked up at Cassandra, meeting her piercing gaze. "Some of my memories have returned—some of Logan, some of what happened in Spain, small flashes of people here and there—but most memories have not. All I have seen so far are snippets, disparate memories that are jumbled and make no sense."

"How can your memories make no sense?" Cassandra shifted on her feet, her arms tightening around her middle as her look bored into Sienna.

"They…the memories are like a story without a narrative, without context…slivers here and there of people and places and feelings and emotions. But I cannot figure out who everyone is and what they mean to me." Sienna looked at Logan and her eyes softened. "Except for Logan. Him I remember."

"How did you find him?" Cassandra asked.

"I didn't," Sienna said. "He found me in Sandfell. He followed me from the baker's shop."

Cassandra's look finally lifted from Sienna, shifting to Logan. Both of her eyebrows were now raised, stretched high on her forehead.

Logan nodded at her. "I did. I saw her and then I nearly accosted her, for which she stuck a knife into my belly for my troubles," he said.

A laugh spurted from Violet and she covered her mouth. "I am sorry, Logan. But you appear to have recovered well enough and she seems like exactly the wife I would expect you to have." She chuckled, leaning forward over the mound of her belly to pat Sienna on the knee. "This is remarkable, truly remarkable. And the duchess is going to love you, my dear."

"The duchess?" Sienna looked to Logan.

"The original proprietress of the Revelry's Tempest, Adalia, the Duchess of Dellon," Logan said. "She is in residence at Dellon Castle at the moment. She was the one that started the gaming house and the one that hired me. Which in turn, let me create my guard."

"Men which are the envy of every gaming house in London, I might add," Violet said. Her gaze landed on Sienna. "So you must have remembered something if you went from sinking a knife into his gut, to what I now see before me?"

"I did." She nodded. "Just as he was leaving town, I remembered." Sienna looked at Logan, a soft smile on her face. "Remembered enough."

Hell. The heat in his wife's blue eyes when she looked at him was beyond anything. She'd always had this softness under the fire about her. If he could shove Violet and Cassandra from the room, he would damn well take his wife on the settee in that instant.

Instead, he shifted uncomfortably on the cushion. "And we came straight from Sandfell to here. Sienna didn't want to go back to her house. So we've been traveling by horse on muddy roads for five days."

He tore his attention away from his wife and looked at Violet. He wasn't about to venture a glance at Cassandra just yet—she was still glaring at Sienna with far too much suspicion in her brown eyes. "So this is where we need your help."

"Of course—anything, Logan," Violet said.

"Sienna needs clothes, and I don't have a clue as to how to procure women's clothing."

~ ~ ~

"This is far too generous."

Sienna stood next to the bed in Logan's chamber in his townhouse—now hers as well—and stared at the mounds of clothing piled high on the bed. Dresses and chemises and stockings and stays and slippers and riding habits and boots and gloves and hats.

All of it of the finest quality.

Stoking to life a fire across the room, Logan looked back to her over his shoulder. "I should have limited them—started with Violet, as she is most similar to your size, or at least was before her belly swelled." His eyes swept across the piles upon his bed. "This is ridiculous—we won't have to visit a seamstress for years with this horde." He turned back to the fire.

It was nightfall by the time they'd left the Revelry's Tempest. They had eaten the most sumptuous roast sirloin with potatoes and Chateaubriand sauce, spinach herb quiche, and flummery with raspberries at the gaming house, and she'd been fortunate to spend time alone with Violet and Cassandra when Logan had disappeared to speak with his guards.

Sienna liked both women immensely, even if Cassandra's skeptical gaze did little to waver—Sienna knew

Cassandra was only suspicious of her because she cared deeply about Logan. That was obvious. And for that, Sienna admired the woman all the more.

She'd also had the good fortune to meet a number of Logan's men. Sienna instantly recognized why they were so sought after as guards—each was almost as handsome as her husband and each looked like they could easily crush anyone that crossed something they were to be protecting.

When guests had started to arrive at the Revelry's Tempest for the evening's gaming, Logan had excused them and they'd travelled on to his townhouse several streets away.

His home sat on a nondescript cobblestone lane, large, but simple, just as she'd hoped for when Logan said he owned a house in London. It stood four stories high, built of the smoothest white Portland stone with nondescript black door and trim. Quietly elegant. A calm street with nothing but a stray rooster confused about the time of day upsetting the peace. Logan hadn't been expected back in London for another two weeks, so the house hadn't been readied for them and they'd had to fumble about in the darkness until he lit some sconces on the main level and then several lanterns, sparking the house alive.

Candles had been lit for only fifteen minutes before footmen were knocking at the door, delivering bundle after bundle of clothing.

Violet and Cassandra had given them the names of their dressmakers and promised to take Sienna shopping at their favorite linen-draper in a few days, but both had still found it necessary to rush home and have extras of their

ready-made clothing delivered so Sienna could change out
of her muddy riding habit.

Sienna's hands went onto her upper arms, rubbing
her bare skin as she stood in her chemise. She didn't know
where to start with the piles of clothing on the bed. She
stepped forward, fingering the soft blue fabric of a muslin
dress that Cassandra had sent. Cassandra's piles stretched
even higher than Violet's.

She glanced at the back of Logan's head. "That one—
Cassandra—it surprises me that she sent over as much
as she did, as I don't believe she cares for me." Sienna
couldn't help the note of insecurity ringing in her voice.
Both Violet and Cassandra were beautiful—and kind—
even if Cassandra looked at her with a wary eye. Not to
mention that both were ladies. And both clearly adored her
husband—too much for her liking, if she let her jealousy
get the best of her.

Logan leaned the fire iron against the black marble
that lined the fireplace and turned to her, a reassuring smile
on his face. He had stripped down to his trousers, the scars
along his torso reflecting the light from the fire. She still
didn't like seeing the scars—didn't like that he'd suffered
them without her near to help him heal. Her look dipped to
the scab where she had sunk a blade into him. At least she'd
been able to tend to that wound, though it couldn't heal fast
enough for her.

He moved across the room to her, standing next to
her to assess the piles on the bed. "Cass doesn't know you,
that is all." He reached out, his fingers dragging along the
wool skirt of a deep plum riding habit. "Think on it from
her perspective—she has known me for ten years, and then

one day I randomly show up with a long dead wife? I would shine much suspicion upon it as well."

She looked up at him. "You never talked about me? Never once told them that you'd been married?"

Logan paused and turned fully to her, his voice near to cracking. "My fractured heart was mine alone, Sienna. I wasn't about to share it with anyone."

A lump swelled in her throat. The reality of how he must have suffered—not only from his wounds, but also from thinking her dead—striking her brutally hard. She couldn't imagine—didn't dare to imagine—his dying on her. How that would destroy her.

A bright smile suddenly took over his face.

Bright.

Too bright.

Fine if he didn't want to dwell on the past, but this was too suspicious.

Her eyebrow lifted at him.

"Now that we're in London, there is something else I need to tell you." He reached out, grabbing her bare upper arms, his fingers rubbing them, sending warmth along her skin. "I had hoped to leave this unspoken until you remembered more—at a time when all of this wasn't so overwhelming—but I fear I cannot do so any longer. But what you need to know is that it is something I never wanted any part of."

She braced herself, her mind racing with horrors. Was he married? Going to prison? Dying? "What?" Her voice came out in a squeak.

"I inherited my father's duchy."

She froze in place. "Duchy? What? What duchy? You never said your father—he was a duke? A real duke?" Her head started to swing wildly back and forth. "You're a...a duke?"

Logan shrugged, unfazed by her skepticism. "It never, never should have happened. My three older half-brothers should have been plenty. But not one of them had sons, and they have all died."

Her head flailing back and forth slowed but didn't stop as she tried to comprehend what he was telling her. "But—but you didn't have the title when we married—I haven't forgotten that vital fact? Even though I clearly have no memory of who your father was."

"No, all of my brothers were alive at the point in time when we wed. You met them in Northumberland just before we married." A hard glint flashed in his silver eyes and his voice turned brutal. His hands dropped from her arms. "I never wanted the title, and they certainly never wanted me to have it."

Her head snapped backward with a heavy blink at how vicious his words formed. "Logan, you're furious—why?"

"They were despicable humans, horrid to the core, Sienna."

She lifted her fingers, setting them gently along his upper arm. "What did they do to you?"

"Aside from casting my mother, Robby and me out of the ducal estate after my father died?"

"You told me that, but I didn't realize they were titled—you are right in your anger, as that is beyond all behavior becoming of a duke. How did they even think to get away with casting you and your mother and brother out?"

The vicious glint hadn't left his eyes. "Their hatred ran deep, Sienna, and it knew no bounds of propriety."

"Then it appears as though they received their due comeuppance." Her hand dropped from his arm. "It also seems as though the best vengeance was you inheriting the title."

"Except I never wanted it. I vowed when I was five to never have anything to do with the estate after watching the castle—our home—disappear as our carriage rolled away. So when the youngest of my three half-brothers died, I planned to never take possession of the title. I planned to let the estate wither away without care. But then I was persuaded otherwise."

"How?"

"My hand was…encouraged to do so. One of my men needed a favor cast his way, and that was the price. I needed to take possession of the title for a mutual agreement to be reached."

Her head cocked to the side. "That is odd. Why would anyone care if you took on the title?"

"They care because there are some lucrative travel routes through the ducal lands that needed to be protected."

"Why?"

He shrugged. "I don't ask and I don't involve myself. I took on the title, and that was what I agreed to do. Beyond that, I rarely participate with the estate. I tell no one of the title. I have one of my guards—a trusted friend—handle the lands in Northumberland, and I do everything necessary of me through proxies."

Her hands went to her temples as her head dropped forward for a long moment. She still could not place all this in her mind just yet. Her shadowed eyes lifted to him. "So you're a duke, and no one knows? Not Violet, not Cassandra, not the duchess—Adalia?"

He shook his head. "No. I haven't told anyone. Especially those three. There are a few that need to know me in parliament. Adalia's husband, the Duke of Dellon knows, even though Adalia does not. Anything I need a proxy for, he delivers. And the estate is small compared to some and is so far north in Northumberland that to anyone that even cares enough to think on it, I am a recluse duke, at most."

Her head snapped up, her wide eyes pinning him. "If you're a duke, that means…"

"You're a duchess. Yes." He chuckled and stepped forward, wrapping his hands around her lower back.

"What?"

"Your face right now is priceless, Sienna—perfectly priceless."

Her hand swatted his chest, landing to press into the muscle. "Not fair to laugh—it isn't every day one learns she is a duchess." Her other hand lifted, swatting onto his chest as well. "And you kept this from me? Why didn't you tell me this earlier?"

"As I said, I didn't want to overwhelm. It truly has no bearing upon my life, and shouldn't upon yours either, Sienna." His brow furrowed. "Unless you want it to? If you want it, if you want to live the life of a peer with London society and the balls and dinners and opera and foxhunts and horse racing and gaming—I can make that happen. I will give it to you without question. But I will warn you, from everything I've seen at the Revelry's Tempest, it is much the life of frivolity."

"Why would I want that? I want you, Logan, not the pressure of being a duchess." Her hands lifted from his chest to cup his chin. "I can be the recluse duchess—just like you. That will suit me fine."

A smile, wide and heated, spread across his face and he lifted her up to him. "That will suit me very well." He kissed her nose, then tossed her onto the mounds of clothing on the bed with a wicked grin. "But I might start calling you duchess in bed for fun."

She laughed, sinking between the piles of silk and muslin and lace. "Does that mean I get to order you about?"

"Please do."

She swatted the jumble of clothing next to her. "Then you better get in here and start doing my bidding, husband."

His fingers went to the fall front of his trousers, unbuttoning.

A knock, loud and echoing up the stairs and down the hallway, stopped his motion.

His face instantly shifted to irritated annoyance, a groan breaching his lips.

Sienna chuckled. "Now that is a look that's priceless."

"Damn those women—how much clothing do they think you could possible need?"

Another knock echoed up to them.

"Blast it all."

She shooed him with her hand. "Go and take the bundles so the footman can go away—I swear I won't move from this spot."

"Move enough to get your shift off and we have a deal."

"Done." She sat up, already wiggling her chemise up her thighs.

Another primal groan at the sight of her bare legs and Logan turned from her, tugging on his boots and grabbing his white linen shirt from the chair by the fire. He exited out into the hallway, his boots clunking along the wooden floor.

She heard the door open just as she tugged her shift over her head.

Crash.

Her arms froze above her head.

Thunk. Crash. Shatter.

She tugged her shift down and scrambled from the bed, running out the door. She was down the steps in seconds, flying around the newel post at the base of the stairs as she searched for her husband. "Logan?"

Thunk.

Something hit the wall in the drawing room next to her so hard it made the floor vibrate under her feet.

She rushed into the room.

All air left her lungs.

Three huge brutes held Logan against a wall in the dark shadows of the drawing room.

His arms straining, his body convulsing against their power, Logan struggled against them. One on each arm pinned him to the wainscoting. One in the middle of him, shoving hard against Logan's neck with his forearm.

A fourth brute with a club pointed at Logan's forehead, pushing his skull back onto the wall while he stuffed a rag against the raging scream in Logan's mouth.

A flash of purple caught her eye, and Sienna spun toward the door and the light from the sconces in the hallway.

Purple coat. An orange swath trimming the lapel.

Purple coat.

The bottom dropped out of her gut.

Purple coat.

The man in the purple coat stepped toward her, his rotund belly leading the way, gold-tipped cane tapping the floor. Beady eyes. Pockmarked nose. Strands of greasy hair strung across his balding head.

His tiny dark eyes sparked when he saw her, glowing with what appeared to be genuine happiness, but below them, his mouth had pulled back into a smile that reminded her of a snake's.

Her look darted to Logan straining, his legs swinging against the four men that held him back. Fear skewered her heart.

Haltingly—her breath not her own, not giving her any support—her gaze travelled back to the man in purple. Four more brutes moved into the drawing room, flanking him. Blocking the entrance.

Instinctively, she threw her shoulders back, straining the straps of her chemise as she pulled herself as tall as she could in her bare feet. "Father."

{ CHAPTER 11 }

"Aye. Ye remember," Bournestein said, thumping the cane he clutched in his meaty paw on the floor. "I suspected as much once I heard ye disappeared."

She could hear Logan struggling behind her, but she kept her gaze riveted on her father. Her mind recognized him as such. Her father. But she could pull no memories as to what he was like—other than she intuitively knew she couldn't turn her back to him.

She did, and he was likely to strike.

"You knew I left Yorkshire?"

"Aye. I know every step ye've taken these past ten years, child."

"It was you—you were the one that kept me there? Kept me at Roselawn?" She shook her head, trying to shake free her memories of this man. Without memories, without knowing what he was capable of, she was severely disadvantaged. "Who was that woman—grandmother? Who was she?"

Bournestein blinked, surprised. "You don't recall?"

Her eyes narrowed at him. "Recall what? Does this have to do with the whorehouse?"

He grunted as his head tilted to the side. "What do you remember, Sienna? It isn't much if you don't recall Miss Johnson. But you seem to know about the Joker's Roost."

Blast it. She'd already revealed too much. She bit her tongue, her chin jutting out in stubborn refusal to answer.

Bournestein let out a wicked chuckle. "Not much, then. But just as bull-headed as always." He lifted his cane slightly to point at her. "Miss Johnson worked for me for a number of years. Then she was too old to service the customers. I thought she'd make ye a good grandmother."

A growl roared through the rag in Logan's mouth and Sienna spun back to see him twisting, freeing his arm. The club slammed into his gut, his arm recaptured before he could do damage with his swinging fist.

Bournestein lifted the cane to point past her shoulder to Logan struggling against the wall. "Do ye even remember this one, child?"

"Enough." She turned back to her father, her lip curling. "I know Logan's my husband. I know that he's my lifeblood. I know that he hasn't been lying to me for the past ten years."

"Lying?" Instant red splotches mottled Bournestein's balding head. "I been keeping you safe, girl. Keeping you in peace like yer mother wanted. Out of the city. That's where she wanted to go with ye, so that's where I stuck ye."

"I had a life." Without taking her eyes off of her father, her arm flew back, her fingers motioning to Logan. "A life with this man and you ripped that away from me. And now this? What is this? You come into our house with these… these…brutes and you attack him? What kind of a monster are you?"

Bournestein jabbed his cane at Logan. "Knock him."

Before Sienna could fully swivel around and stop it, the club was blasting down on Logan's head.

Her heart stopped.

Logan's head fell forward, limp.

"Logan—"

"Don't wail, child. They just knocked his eyes out."

She couldn't take her look off of the top of Logan's dark hair. Willing him to move. Willing his eyes to open and his head to pop up.

One of the brutes shifted and Logan's head rolled to the side, unresponsive. A thin trail of blood snaked down his temple.

She started to rush them, but Bournestein snatched her arm and jerked her to a stop.

"For the devil's sake, child." He pushed her aside and moved toward Logan and his men. "Check him. He alive?"

One man set his ear to Logan's chest. He nodded.

"See. A bump on the boy, that all it be." He thumbed toward the door. "Take him out the back."

Sienna considered grabbing the man closest to her that held Logan's arm. Grab him and then what? Get knocked down and be no closer to getting them to let Logan go? There were too many of them.

She spun to Bournestein. "What are you going to do with him?"

Her father's lips pursed for a long moment before he exhaled a malevolent breath. "I'll let him live, that should be courtesy enough." He looked to his man holding the club. "Dump him by the docks."

The brute lifted his club, his eyebrows raised. "Or I could kill him right now, sir?"

Bournestein shook his head. "No. Deliver him to the docks. He can find his way home, or off English soil if he's wise on his next move."

The ruffians moved in unison as they dragged Logan from the room, his feet trailing behind him and his body limp as jelly. Their footsteps echoed down the hallway toward the back of the townhouse. In the cover of darkness they could get Logan out past the mews without anyone noticing.

Full panic seized Sienna. Logan was out of the room, being dragged to the docks. And she was alone with this man that she could only remember in flashes of terror mixed with begrudging respect.

Her look darted about the room, desperate for escape, desperate to follow her father's men and Logan. She was half naked and without boots, but if she could follow them, she could get Logan to safety once they dumped him.

"Don't be thinking yer going to escape me just yet, child. Wherever ye try to get to, my men will be on yer tail and Logan will be the one to suffer for it."

She stilled, her forehead tilting down as she looked up at her father, her eyes skewering him.

He smiled. The snake smile. "That's the fire I remember. There be things we need to discuss, daughter."

"I have nothing to discuss with you."

"But ye do."

"Why do you hate him?"

"Who says I hate him, child?"

"You just knocked him into darkness and you're dumping him by the docks. I would hate to see how you treat someone you truly despise."

He chuckled. "Ye really don't remember much, do ye child? Deliverance to the docks was generosity I don't usually bestow upon those that wronged me."

"He wronged you?"

Bournestein turned to his four men still flanking the front wall of the drawing room. "Light the sconce and leave us."

The brutes silently filed out of the room, one coming back with a lit candle from the sconces in the foyer. He quickly lit the two sconces that flanked the entrance and exited, closing the door behind him.

Bournestein's beady dark eyes followed the man until the door closed. He turned to Sienna, his voice taking on a kinder tone. "It's clear ye don't remember much, child, but if ye did—"

"If I did—what—you wouldn't have barged in here and nearly killed my husband?"

"I wouldn't have needed to." The tip of his cane smashed onto the floor. "I loved that boy like a son and he betrayed me, child. Betrayed me like no one who has lived to tell the tale."

"Betrayed you how?"

"He took ye from me, child. Just like he always took his mother away from me."

"He took me?" She took a step backward, understanding dawning on her. "You drove me away, didn't you? Logan didn't take me away—I wanted to escape— escape you."

His cane lifted, smashing into the wall next to him. "I did no such thing, girl." He took a step toward her, spittle starting to form in the corner of his mouth as his voice spiked. "Ye be grateful, child. I gave ye everything yer mother wanted for ye. And then when I got ye back, I gave ye Roselawn. I gave ye peace."

"But I didn't want that—I wanted Logan and you took me from him." Her arm swung out, her finger pointing at the closed door. "Which one of them was it that came after me in Spain? Which one was it? Which one threw me into a wall so hard that I lost everything—every memory of who I was? Is that giving me everything, Father? Because the only thing I've ever wanted was Logan. And you ripped me away from him and locked me into a life at Roselawn that I didn't even realize was a cage."

Bournestein stilled, the snake smile that always danced on his lips fading away. "Take care, child, on what ye say next."

"Why did you even come here—come after me? What do you think I'm going to say, Father? That I will happily go back and live with you at the whorehouse? You can't possibly be that deranged."

His cane smashed into the wall again, and this time plaster flew, chunks stinging her face. "Ye watch yer mouth, girl." He advanced on her.

Sienna locked her feet in place, meeting his fury and his cane poised to strike her straight on. "I will never give Logan up. And if you kill him, you lose me, Father. You lose me forever."

His feet stopped, the raised cane dropping to his side.

Slowly, the snake smile curled back onto his lips as his look bored into her. "But without yer memories, child, ye don't know what ye're talking about."

"But I do know what I'm talking about." Her arms crossed over her chest, her voice vibrating with vehemence. "I know there is nothing you can say, nothing you can do that will tear Logan and me apart."

"No?"

"No."

Bournestein stared at her, his head nodding.

Nodding for far too long in silence.

He opened his mouth, words curling around his snake smile. "Logan killed yer mother, child. Maybe that might make ye rethink yer vow."

~ ~ ~

"Next week, Sienna."

Sienna's blue eyes went wide, a smile spreading across her face so striking it could turn the moon. "Next week? Truly?"

Logan nodded, beaming under her glow. "I have enough. Enough to get us passage—to last us until I can find work."

Sienna squealed, jumping and wrapping her arms around his neck, her lips on his cheek, working down to his mouth. Her body pressed into his, all her curves fitting against his muscles.

She was too close. Far too close for him to continue to curb himself. He'd sworn to himself—to her—that he'd wait until they were married on the ship to take her. But every day that passed he was finding it harder and harder to control himself. To keep his hands off of her.

He could hardly kiss her anymore—not without restraint that left him in pain, near to breaking his vow.

Not that she wanted him to keep it.

But this was sacred to him. For how they grew up. For the things they were witness to at such an early age—every carnal act imaginable—whether they wanted to or not. They had seen it all, and because of it, this was sacred. Her body and his. Together after all these years. Sacred.

Logan drew a deep breath just as her lips met his.

Out of London. Onto a ship. And Sienna would be his.

One week to go.

He stepped back abruptly, grabbing her wrists at his neck and untwining her from his body.

The pout on her face turned her full lips into a sulking frown so quickly he had to chuckle.

"I know, Sienna—but we have to remain norm—"

The door to his room blasted open, missing his head by an inch and slamming into the wall.

Bournestein charged into the room, breathing fire, rage mottling his forehead and an ax swinging in his hand.

Shit.

"Bastard boy." He shoved Logan into the wall, took a step, and shoved Sienna into the opposite wall. "Little fuckin bastard boy." The yell thundered in the room, shaking the floor.

Bournestein went to the left bed—Logan's bed—and flipped it up with one hand, slamming it up and over Robby's bed.

"Father, stop—stop." Sienna pushed off of the wall and ran at her father, grabbing his arm before Logan could reach her and intercede.

Bournestein didn't glance at her. Didn't acknowledge her. Just swatted her away like a fly. She went flying, hitting the wall hard.

The ax lifted and Bournestein swung it down, chopping into the worn floorboards. Screaming, swearing, he swung at the floor again and again, shreds of wood flying in all directions.

Logan couldn't get a clear line to tackle him, not with the wild ax hacking away wood.

Robby ran into the room, slipping to a stop when the backswing of the raging ax came at his head.

Sienna reacted before Logan could, pushing off the wall and attacking Robby. "You bastard—how could you?" Fists swinging, she cut Robby across the cheek.

Logan looked from Bournestein to his brother. Robby's eyes were slow to track Sienna attacking. Hell, Robby was drunk—barely standing drunk.

"You told him—you told him, Robby. How could you?" Sienna's second fist against Robby's jaw snapped him out of his drunken stupor and Robby finally reacted, catching her around the waist and twisting her around. She turned into a hellcat, kicking, scratching every bit of Robby she could reach.

Just as Logan was about to leap, tackling Robby away from Sienna, the hacking of the ax against wood ceased and Logan spun around to Bournestein.

Bournestein heaved himself to the ground, his arm diving, fishing into the hole he'd hacked into the floor.

No. Hell no. Not their way out.

Everything.

Everything was under those boards. Their future. Their freedom.

Throwing the ax to the floor, Bournestein stood, yanking the snuff box from the floor in his hand. He cracked it open and coins spilled everywhere.

Bournestein whipped the box at Logan's head. Logan dodged, but the corner of the steel box cut along his temple.

Spit flew with Bournestein's rage. "Everything was yers and ye think to leave me, boy? Ye think ye can escape me, ye stupid brat?"

Logan turned back to Robby. "You told him?"

"Ye were gonna leave, Logan—leave me," Robby's words slurred, barely coherent. "I heard ye makin' plans with Sienna. Ye were gonna leave, Logan—leave me."

Bournestein's men rushed into the room, the brutes pushing aside Robby and Sienna and attacking Logan.

Arms swinging, Logan held them off for a minute before Bournestein kicked him from behind and Freddie Joe caught his right arm. Flesh met fist three more times before Tommy caught his left arm. They slammed him against the wall.

Wiping his mouth, Bournestein pointed out the door. "Get her out of here."

Ignoring her scream, Robby picked up Sienna, tossing her over his shoulder.

It slammed the air out of her and she gasped for breath, arms swinging at his back.

Robby hauled her out of the room, his steps swaying.

Logan twisted, kicking, trying to break the holds on his arms. The brutes only lifted him forward and slammed him into the wall again in unison.

Air flew from his lungs, pain crashing through his body.

Logan taught them that trick long ago.

Asses.

Bournestein walked to the door, grabbing the handle and slowly, quietly, closing the door. He didn't turn back to Logan. "Ye were never going to leave Robby behind, were ye, boy?"

Logan caught breath enough in his lungs to speak. "No, you bastard—just you, you and your fucking depravity."

Bournestein spun and punched Logan square in the face. Blackness. Stars.

Logan shook his head, trying to right his vision.

Another fist at his head.

Sienna screamed from down the hall. Screamed and screamed.

Rage that he'd never felt fired through Logan's veins and he dodged Bournestein's next fist at his face, sinking to the ground.

His weight downward loosened the grips the brutes—his friends—had on his arms.

Sienna's scream pitched high. Desperate.

Logan rolled on the floor.

A foot smashed down on his ribcage.

He reached for the ax.

Logan jerked awake—his head pounding, his stomach churning—and he wasn't sure if he was twenty and living that moment in time again or he was dreaming. Remembering.

His eyes blinked.

No. Not twenty.

His cheek dragged against splinters of rough wood. Darkness smothered him. Water lapped. His head exploded with every breath.

The docks. He was face down on the docks.

Heaving a groan, he flipped over onto his back, his hands going limply to his stomach. Bare skin. Cold air snaked around his toes. His boots were gone along with the coins in the inside slit. He'd been rolled. Everything of value stolen off his body. Even his shirt.

At least he hadn't been crimped. No broken bones. Trousers in place.

He angled his body to the side, pushing himself upright, trying to focus his blurry eyes.

His mind raced—already a thousand steps ahead of his bruised body. The hovels and holes he needed to search. The beating he needed to deliver unto Bournestein so he would tell him where he stuck Sienna this time—for he already knew she wouldn't be waiting patiently for him in his townhouse. He had to find her before Bournestein forced her so far away she was lost to him forever.

Bournestein had always underestimated Logan's capacity for savagery. Always. His advantage, for his capacity had just swelled a hundred fold.

But first, he needed a shirt. Boots.

It was time to light up Bournestein's empire.

{ CHAPTER 12 }

Logan took a long swallow of the cognac in his hand. Ridiculously smooth with fruity hints, it slid down his throat and he suddenly regretted his long ago decision to never drink in front of his men.

He looked down at the glass of amber liquid. He'd been supplying the guards of the Revelry's Tempest this Courvoisier cognac for the past ten years. No wonder they were so loyal—this brandy alone could move mountains.

His gaze lifted to his men sitting and standing two, three deep around the long rough-hewn table centering the guards' room at the Revelry's Tempest. It had taken half the morning to round the guards up from their haunts about town, this band of twenty-five of the most coveted guards in London.

The silence in the room was deafening.

He had stood before them and offered them the truth, as much of it as he could afford to—the crux of it being that Bournestein had his wife. The men knew Bournestein well. Some had tangled with him, some had been rescued from his harsh, choking grasp. Far too many of them harbored deep-seated animosity for the man.

But going after Bournestein was something Logan was going to do alone. *Had* to do alone.

This meeting with his men was about succession. About keeping the band of Revelry's Tempest guards intact after he was gone.

Logan cleared his throat. "Bournestein threatens everything here because of me. It is me he has always been after." He set his glass onto the end of the table. "I refuse to give up my men to my mistakes, so I do this alone."

A bear of a man, Greyson shifted in his chair, the wood creaking as he leaned forward to the middle of the table to grab the decanter of brandy. His movements precise, he poured himself a healthy swallow. Logan hadn't seen Greyson touch the bottle since he yanked him out of Bournestein's clutches nine years ago.

Greyson took a sip, savoring it before he leaned back in his chair. "You aren't giving us up, Logan. You go into Bournestein's lair alone and you will fail."

Logan's mouth tightened. Greyson would point out the obvious.

"I plan on hiring men in St. Giles. Bournestein controls them, yes, but there are plenty that wish to see him sink—that will gleefully help him sink."

"No, Lipinstein. Those bastards aren't loyal to anything." Greyson took another quick sip. "We are. We met your wife yesterday and it was more than clear that she is a part of you." He looked around the room at his fellow guards, meeting their eyes, and then his gaze travelled back to Logan. "She is a part of you. So she is a part of us. We all go."

"Willingly." Thomas, the guard Logan had snatched from a press gang at the docks six years past, nodded.

"Willingly." At the far end of the table, Anthony echoed the vow.

"Willingly." Directly at his left, Simmons's meaty fist landed on the table.

Again and again, the word echoed throughout the room until every man had his say.

Logan looked about the chamber at his men, his chest tightening.

All soldiers. All injured during the war—both in body and spirit. Men that were whole again, or at least on their way to becoming so.

This penance he had served for his actions in the war—for marching his men toward the Spanish village by Arapiles—had healed these men, and a number more that had moved on from the Revelry's Tempest.

But he hadn't expected this.

He opened his mouth, words not manifesting.

"Before you deny us this, Lipinstein…" Fredrick, the quietest of the guards, spoke up from the middle of the table on the right. "We are warriors. We were born that way. Trained that way. We haven't lost that. We've repurposed it, yes, but it is still deep in our bones. You gave us that. You gave us our lives back. And now it is time for us to return the favor. There is no one better than us to have your backside." He paused, his head tilting down as his look pierced Logan. "Plus, you must know we'll just follow you into St. Giles, regardless of what you want."

The denial on Logan's tongue stuck and he swallowed it back. It was madness to even consider it, but he needed them. Each and every one of them.

His stomach flipped in self-loathing.

That he would even consider this again. Consider marching his men into what could easily be death.

It meant taking them into a battle he needed to win—one he couldn't win alone—one he wasn't sure he could even win.

But he would do it for Sienna. Do it again. Sacrifice his men.

He unclenched his clamped jaw, his knuckles landing on the edge of the table in front of him as he leaned forward. "Some of you have been here since the start. Victor, Wallton, Pinkers—you started this guard with me ten years ago and you trusted me when there was no reason in hell to do so."

Victor, Wallton, and Pinkers nodded from their spots at the table.

"But you came. And you were loyal. And we built something." His look travelled around the table, meeting the eyes of each of his men. "We built something with each and every one of you. But it isn't over here. We only do this if the guard goes on—no matter what happens to me or to any of us when we walk into Bournestein's lair."

Twenty-five heads nodded in unison.

His heart thundering in his chest, Logan heaved a breath, his voice fierce. "Then it's time to start a war."

~ ~ ~

Logan tightened his grip on the lapels—the fistful of Bournestein's purple tailcoat he clutched. His right hand pulled back, fingers curling under his thumb.

Another blow fired from the depths of his hell and Bournestein's lip busted open, blood splattering up Logan's arm.

"Where is she?" Logan's voice had lost its initial rage. He'd asked the question thirty times now, and the beating that Bournestein was taking only worked to cool his rage into relentless resolve. She wasn't in the Joker's Roost. She wasn't in the three other brothels Bournestein owned in the surrounding streets.

So now Logan would beat the man until he gave up Sienna.

Both of his eyes bloodied, swollen, Bournestein stretched his right eye open far enough to catch the glimmer of light from the lantern hanging from the back door of the Joker's Roost. "Same answer, boy."

A fresh shot of rage flashed through his limbs, and he slammed Bournestein back against a crumbling brick wall, then jerked him forward with his grip on his coat.

Logan set his nose right to the mangled mess of Bournestein's face. "Where is she?"

It wasn't the first time someone had been bloodied in the alleyway behind Bournestein's main gaming and whorehouse. It *was* the first time Bournestein had ever been subjected to the pain of it. Pain Logan needed him to feel a thousandfold more.

Four of Logan's guards stood watch on either side of him, each with a torch. The rest of his guards had already cleared Bournestein's men out of the gaming hell, sending them to the streets in front of the building along with all the drunks and whores inside.

Bournestein chuckled, blood and spittle spewing from his mouth.

Logan lifted his fist again. He would beat him until he got an answer. And beat him. And beat him. And beat him.

"She doesn't want ye, boy." A bloody dribble sprayed down Bournestein's chin. "She told me herself."

Logan's fist lowered and he slammed Bournestein against the wall again. He was rewarded with a satisfying grunt exploding from Bournestein's chest at the blow. "You're mad, old man."

A rancid chuckle left Bournestein's throat. "And yer bitter because it was me that saved her in the war—not ye, boy."

Logan stilled, both of his hands gripping the front of Bournestein's coat. "What?"

Bournestein's torn lip managed to stretch into his snake smile, his broken hand lifting to grab Logan's wrist, but only flopping uselessly to the side. "Who do ye think saved her from those French troops—cause it sure as hell wasn't ye, boy."

"What do you know of it?"

"It was my man that dragged her away from that village. I sent him there to follow her, make sure no harm come to her cause I knew ye weren't up to the task."

"Bastard." Logan's fist flew fast, connecting with Bornstein's jowl, again and again, sending his head smashing into the wall with every blow.

Bournestein's legs collapsed and he slumped down against the brick, the only thing holding him from sinking into a crumpled heap was Logan's grip on his coat.

Still, Bournestein twisted his head, scowling up at Logan with a sneer on his lips. "Ye never even knew my man was there. But he was watching the whole time." He coughed, hacking up blood. "Reporting back. Ye were playing at war while I was busy protecting her."

Logan jerked him up to his feet. "Protecting her, you madman? You took away her life, her memories."

"No," Bournestein yelled, strength that should have long been beaten out of him bursting forth. "I took her away from ye, boy. Just as ye took her away from me. Quid pro quo, my boy."

Logan's hand crept up, curling around the front of Bournestein's neck. "I'm not your boy."

"No, yer not. Ye lost that title long ago. Ye could have had everything one day. My empire. My daughter. But ye left." He sneered. "Good thing yer brother was handy."

Logan's fingers jerked, crushing his neck. "My brother was off-limits—always—you swore it to my mother."

Bournestein squirmed as Logan's grip on his throat tightened. "I swore a lot of things to yer mother. I loved the lass."

"Loved her?" Logan's lips pulled back, his teeth gritting. "You made her your whore." He slammed Bournestein into the wall, his fingers not moving from his neck.

"And she never loved me—not with ye brats around. Ye took her from me and then ye took my Sienna from me. Yer brother was what little was left to scrounge—second pickins at best."

Logan brought him forward only to crack him back into the wall again. "We were never yours, Bournestein— never—none of us. Now tell me where the hell my wife is." With a savage growl, Logan yanked his hand away from Bournestein's throat, his arm pulling back in a wild coil.

Just as his fist descended toward Bournestein's skull, his forearm was snatched to a stop in its swing.

"Stop, Logan, stop."

A voice. A voice he hadn't heard in years.

He turned his head. "Robby?"

"Hello, Logan." Robby released Logan's arm as his words drifted into the alleyway, the low drawl his brother had always spoken with filling the stale air.

Logan twisted his grip on Bournestein's coat, making sure the bastard didn't move a muscle as he looked at his brother. "I thought you were in Newgate."

Robby motioned with his head to Bournestein's slumped body. "Bournestein got me out."

"How?"

Robby shrugged his shoulders. "Didn't ask and he didn't tell."

Before Logan could even reconcile the fact that his brother was standing, alive and healthy right before him, Greyson slammed open the back door of the Joker's Roost and ran to Logan. "The place is cleared, Logan. Checked over thrice. His men scattered or face down in the street." He looked at Bournestein and then sized up Robby. "You need me to take care of this one?"

The question jarred Logan, snapping his attention back to Bournestein and what he was actually doing in this alleyway. "No." He glanced at Robby. He had grown. A man. The same size now as Logan. His frame thinner, but then, he'd been in Newgate for years. *Survived* Newgate for years.

His look narrowed at his brother. "No, Greyson, this one is going to let what happens here, happen."

Robby's eyebrow cocked, but he made no motion to stop Logan, no rebuttal.

Still gripping Bournestein in place, Logan turned to Greyson. "Good. Then hand me a torch. This place needs to burn."

Bournestein's feet slipped, scurrying in place as he pushed himself upright against the wall. He struggled against Logan's fist holding him in place as his beady eyes, nearly swollen shut, pierced Logan. "No—ye won't do it, boy."

"You think I won't?"

Greyson handed him a lit torch and Logan held it out from his body, the flames licking high, hungry for more fuel. He turned back to Bournestein, his voice callous. "Last chance, Bournestein. Tell me where she is."

Bournestein managed to lift his unbroken hand, his weak grip landing on Logan's fist clutching his coat. "Ye ain't got the guts, boy. Ye never did."

Logan paused, a caustic chuckle bubbling up his throat to escape. His look centered on Bournestein as he released Bournestein's purple coat from his grip, shaking his hand free. "On the contrary, you bastard, I learned from the best."

Logan moved to the back doorway of the Joker's Roost and tossed the torch into the building.

It took minutes before the fire caught, and then it lit fast, burning the squalor and decay of the building in flames licked with scorching redress.

Whorehouse. Gaming hell.

Home.

The third floor bedroom he'd shared with his mother and brother. The hidden cubbies under the false floors on the fourth level where Sienna liked to hide from him during hide and seek. The secret staircase to the roof where he'd first kissed Sienna. The bed his mother died in. The bed Sienna's mother died in.

It burned.

Quickly. Mercilessly. Irrevocably.

{ CHAPTER 13 }

"Kill 'im. Ye know that be what Bournestein wanted."
Freddie Joe grabbed his hand with his meaty paw and shoved a
blade into it.

Where Freddie Joe got the blade, Logan didn't know.
Lifted it, most likely. Or probably Bournestein slipped it to
him. "Kill 'im, Logan."

The hazy glow from the street lamps snaked down through
the fog and Logan looked at the limp body at his feet crumpled
next to the railing of the bridge over the Thames. Blood slid
down in a stream on Logan's face, dripping off his chin and
onto the top of Gregor's head.

A vile retch blasted up his throat and he swallowed it
back.

He couldn't vomit now. Not in front of the boys.

"Kill 'im, Logan." Freddie Joe poked him in the back.
"Only one of ye is comin' back. That's what Bournestein said."

Logan reached down, grabbing the back of Gregor's ragged
shirt and lifting him up. Without a doubt, Gregor would have
killed him by now if their spots were reversed.

Which was all the more reason Logan had needed to win.

He bent, setting his eyes in front of his friend's mangled
face. Gregor's head bobbed, rolling about on his neck, only
slightly on this side of consciousness. "You can jump in the river
now and end it, or you can run, Gregor. It's your choice. Run
and never set foot in St. Giles again, or it'll be the river for
you."

Logan released his hold on his shirt, and Gregor fell to the bridge. It took a long moment for Gregor to flop his limbs about, his broken hand slipping again and again on the railing as he tried to pull himself to standing. On his feet, Gregor leaned his side against the top of the railing, his arm flopping over the side.

For one second, Logan thought he was about to flip himself over the edge. Instinct stepped him forward, ready to yank his friend back from death.

But then Gregor's feet started moving, running, slipping every other step on his broken ankle, his weak hold against the railing the only thing keeping him upright.

He ran. Ran off the bridge. Ran away from St. Giles. Ran from Bournestein.

Lucky bastard.

Logan coughed. The metallic twinge of blood flooded his tongue. His head swiveled in a circle, looking to each of the faces of the boys surrounding him.

His look went pointedly to the sight of Gregor at the end of the bridge, floundering into the fog.

"Watch him run, boys, but know we're no better than him." Logan coughed again, blood filling his mouth. His voice had recently changed, lowering into a rumble he couldn't always control. A voice he didn't always recognize. "We're Nowheres Boys, through and through. We don't belong nowhere. And we fight to keep what's ours."

A chorus of squeaky-pitched "Ayes" surrounded him.

It was done. He was the undisputed leader of the Nowheres Boys. Just as Bournestein wanted.

Fifteen minutes later, Logan left the boys in the alley behind the Joker's Roost and went up to the back card room above the main level of the gaming hell whorehouse.

Smoke, thick, rushed at him as he opened the door. Thick cheroots glowed in the smoke around the table and Bournestein sat in the middle slapping cards onto the table, his booming laughter filling the dingy room.

The smoke made Logan gag, near to upending the vomit he was still forcing back.

He stepped into the room and Bournestein, barrel-chested and huge, laughed and looked up at him.

"I didn't know which one of ye boys was gonna be walking back through the door, boy." Bournestein sucked in a long drag of his cigar.

Logan nodded. "Gregor is taken care of."

"'Bout time ye started earning yer keep 'round here, boy."

"Yes, sir."

Bournestein eyed him through the haze of smoke and the room grew quiet.

Blast it. Logan needed to get out of here. Out of here before he retched all over the floor. And Bournestein was working up his latest pontificating. He must be six brandies in.

"Boy, ye gotta toughen up if yer gonna survive here." Bournestein's hand swept around the table at his men. "The one thing these brutes about me understand is pain. Pain is power, boy. Master it and the world is yours. Master taking it. Master giving it. And this empire be yers, boy."

Logan nodded. "Yes, sir."

"Be gone with ye." Bournestein waved his hand, dismissing Logan, and went back to the cards on the table.

Logan exhaled a breath of relief. He must be ten brandies in if his pontificating was that short.

Logan's feet couldn't carry him up the stairs to his and Robby's room fast enough. He stumbled into the far corner of the tiny space, sliding to his knees in front of the chamber pot. Curled over it, he heaved, over and over, everything emptying from his stomach.

His guts empty to the core, he sank back onto his butt, untangling his legs to stick out straight as he leaned against the wall.

The curtain next to him moved, and Sienna popped out from behind the torn, faded red velvet. Damn that she was still so small she could hide there without being seen.

Her blue eyes were huge, fear shining in them. "Was it awful, Logan?"

Logan lifted his right hand and dragged it across his face. Fresh blood smeared across his palm. He met her eyes. "You watched it, didn't you, Sienny?"

Her lips drew inward, her mouth clamping shut.

"You watched, didn't you, Sienny?"

She nodded, the red-blond braids on either side of her head swinging against her shoulders.

"Dammit, you were supposed to stay here."

She shrugged, not in the slightest apologetic and walked over to stand in front of him. Even sitting, he was almost now eye level with her. He grew too much in the last six months.

"I couldn't, Logan."

He shook his head and clunked it onto the wall behind him, his eyes closing to her. "Yea. You couldn't listen."

"You didn't kill him."

His eyes flew open, his look narrowing at her. "I was never gonna kill him, Sienny, no matter what Bournestein said. You know that."

She went over to the cracked basin of water in between the two beds and dunked a cloth into it, wringing it out before she brought it to Logan. She went to her knees and started dabbing at the blood on his forehead and temple.

The cloth quickly turning red, she was more shuffling about the blood than removing it. She sighed. "I will miss Gregor."

"Yea, I know. Me, too." He reached up with his right hand and grabbed her dabbing fingers, moving them so he could see her eyes. His voice turned hard. "But you are too young for how he was looking at you. You gotta understand that now, Sienny. That's gonna happen and the Nowheres Boys are sworn to make sure it doesn't. But you gotta watch out for boys like him."

She nodded, a deep frown dragging down her face. She didn't want to be the cause of Gregor's banishment. "I'm the cause so I gotta be the reaction. It's what you always say, Logan. So we need to find Gregor and help him. He's got nowhere, no one, now."

"No, we don't." He squeezed her wrist. "It had to happen, Sienny, not just for that. For all of our sakes. If that had been Robby that had taken Gregor on, he would've killed Robby, and I would've had to stop him." He paused, shaking his head. "And I don't know if I could've let him walk if he hurt you or Robby."

"Robby never should've crossed him. Gregor just wanted to be the leader—the boss of all of us. And Robby don't like to be bossed by anyone."

Logan chuckled. "Especially by me. But you know how he's been since our mama died." Logan shrugged. "But that's how it is now. Nothing we can do on it."

She let loose an exaggerated exhale and got to her feet, going back to the basin to rinse out the rag. "Robby will get over it."

"I'm not so sure, Sienny."

She looked over her shoulder at him and her eyes dipped downward, then went wide. "Logan, your wrist. It's weird."

Logan looked down at his left arm, his hand dangling at an odd angle.

She ran across the room and tried to grab his left hand.

He snatched it out of her grasp. "No—don't touch it. It's broken."

"Oh." Her hands fell to her skirts. "Well, we should fix that."

"Yea." Logan nodded. "We should fix a lot of things around here, Sienny."

~ ~ ~

Logan slammed his fist into the wall. Already raw and split from the beating he gave Bournestein, a thin scab broke free and blood stained the plaster wall in his changing room.

After leaving the Joker's Roost in flames, he and his men had been to every single one of Bournestein's brothels, ale rooms, and gaming hells, searching for his wife. All night. All day. And into the darkness again.

She was nowhere to be found.

His men, ragged and soot-stained, had all needed rest. He needed rest.

He needed to clean the soot and dirt from his skin and come up with a clear thought. A clear thought would lead to a clear plan.

He had just laid a bitter swath of destruction and he was no closer to finding Sienna than when he started. Not only that, he had dragged his men deep into the fray. By the graces, his men had only suffered two broken bones and five gashes that needed stitches. The bruises and cuts were numerous.

Logan looked down at his fingers, exhaling a low whistle as he shook his hand, the sting in the sharp bones of his knuckles going deep.

Clear thoughts.

Bath. Sleep. Clear thoughts.

Logan yanked down his trousers and stepped gingerly into the cool water of his copper-lined bathing tub. He'd been lucky that one of his guards had sent over a maid with food from the Revelry's Tempest and she'd happily filled his tub for an extra crown while he ate in stony silence.

He hadn't been in the tub for ten minutes—just barely scrubbed the blood from underneath his fingernails—when he heard a floorboard creak in his hallway.

Blast it. How had anyone gotten into his house? Greyson had insisted on staying watch in front of his house with another two of his guards watching the mews.

Logan looked to his left to see a ragamuffin boy of maybe eight years old standing in the doorway, staring at him. Dirty and scrawny, the boy nervously twisted his fingers together in front of him.

"How did you get in here, boy?"

"I followed ye. I followed ye all night, sir. And when yer maid left the door open to get water from the well and chatted with that monster of a man in front, I snuck in by them. I followed ye from the Joker's Roost, I did, sir."

"You were at the Joker's Roost?"

"I was, sir. I saw ye in the alley with Mr. Bournestein. And ye be a hero, sir. A true hero. I saw what ye did to 'im. I know plenty in his streets that would want to be ye getting to hit 'im." The boy paused, his fingers lifting to tuck the dirty strands of his too-long hair behind his ears. "And I heard what ye want. Ye want the pretty lady. The one with the strawberry hair and sweet skin."

Logan sat straight up in the tub. "You saw her? The woman with the red-blond hair?"

"Kinda red, kinda blond, sir? She was with Mr. Bournestein's men yesterday. She didn't look none happy, sir. Looked like she done got caught in one of his traps, sir, and was headed for the whorehouse. Angry sad. He had lots of men 'round her—more than normal—that's why I noticed."

"You know of Bournestein's brothels?"

"I do, sir. My mama lives in one."

A pang cut across his chest. He could very well be that little boy. "Where did you see her?"

"By the whorehouse on Wild Street. That's where my mama lives."

"The Canary brothel?" He had checked there. Checked there thoroughly. Or had he? His mind was still muddled. He eyed the scamp. "You are sure on that, boy?"

"I am, sir."

"Are you more sure if there's a sovereign involved?"

"A sovereign, sir?" The boy's eyes went wide, his words tumbling out.

"A sovereign for your honest answer. Or two. I would hope several gold pieces would override anything you were sent here to say."

His wide eyes expanded and he looked like he was about to run from the room. But the boy held his ground. "You know, sir?"

"That you came here to send me into a trap?"

The boy's jaw dropped. He nodded.

"It isn't hard to figure out, boy. You're nervous as hell."

A small smile lifted the corners of the lad's mouth. "I never been a good liar, sir. Never. Mama always said so."

Logan nodded. "So did you actually see the blond woman?"

"That I did, sir, but she ain't at Wild Street." He stopped, his head tilting to the side as he eyed Logan. "Ye sure ye got those gold pieces, sir?"

"I am. They are yours."

"Then yer lady be at the Risky Hen gaming hall. She didn't go to no whorehouse." He shoved his thumbs under the waistband of his trousers, his feet tapping with unspent energy. "Mr. Bournestein showed up there too, last night after ye let him go. Showed up there a bloody mess, wat with ye made of 'im."

Logan nodded. For all he knew of Bournestein's holdings, he hadn't known Bournestein had taken over the Risky Hen gaming hall. They hadn't checked there. There'd been no reason to. "Let me get dressed and I'll get you your sovereigns, boy."

"Or ye could just tell me where they be and I be helpin' meself."

Logan had to stifle a chuckle. He would have asked the exact same thing twenty-odd years ago. "I'll get you your coin, plus three, if you can be patient about it."

He coughed, choking, his head bobbing up and down. "I can, sir. I rightly can."

"Then wait downstairs in the drawing room—the room off the front door." He gave the boy a stern look. "And know anything you pilfer from there won't be worth as much as what I give you."

The boy nodded, turning to exit out the door.

"Oh, and lad, be far, far away when I show up at the Risky Hen. You were sent here with a mission and I don't see Bournestein looking to take a double cross lightly upon you."

"Yes, sir. Me mama too, sir?"

"I'll give you ten more pieces so you can take her with you. That should be enough for her to set up trade in another part of town, or look for a different position if that is her choice."

The boy nodded, a wide smile bursting across his face. "Yes, sir, most kind, sir." He disappeared down the hall, his excited steps clambering down the stairs.

Logan's head clunked back against the rolled copper edge of the tub.

His mind revived with the boy's news, clear thoughts sped through his brain. He ran through what he knew of the Risky Hen from years ago. Five stories high and brick, the building was more structurally sound than most of Bournestein's rickety holdings. It was night and that would help him. Bournestein was surely busy attempting to cobble back together his empire after the terror Logan and his guards had brought upon his brutes and his establishments during the last twenty-four hours.

He would go alone. It would give him the best chance to slip in and find Sienna unnoticed. And his men needed a break. Needed to sleep. They were as battered and bruised as he was—several of the men mending broken bones.

But he hadn't lost any of them. A fortunate gift.

Logan glanced at the mixture of blood and dirt still on his arm—he'd never gotten to scrubbing it off. May as well leave it now. He'd go in dirty and unkempt, all the better to blend in to the masses of St. Giles.

He stood, water sloshing everywhere as he stepped from the tub.

~ ~ ~

Logan pulled the rough cap down over his brow, slipping along the edge of the main gambling room at the Risky Hen. The place was alive with raucous games of loo, vingt-et-un and hazard. Plenty of women mixed in with the men, draped on laps, delivering tankards of beer. It was as jolly as he'd ever guessed this place had been.

He shook his head. Burn one gaming hell down, and the bird-wits all just moved onto the next. A cycle he had long ago accepted as fact of life in St. Giles. The only thing that mattered was who owned the gaming hell still standing.

Bournestein was an expert at that.

Logan sidled near the entrance to the rear stairs, watching closely for guards and surprised to find none.

He waited until a half-staggering man with two women fawning about him walked past and into the stairwell. Logan followed them closely, as though he were part of the group as they walked up the steps and onto the second level.

Apparently, the displaced whores from the Joker's Roost had moved in here.

The threesome dipped into a room in front of him and closed the door. Logan glanced about.

He breathed a sigh of relief. No guards were waiting in the hallway of this floor. This was one of the four main levels above the gaming room and Logan quickly went down the corridor, discreetly checking in the rooms. Half were busy with women and customers. Half were empty.

No Sienna.

He made his way up to the next level. No guard on this level as well.

His gut began to sink.

Nonetheless, he moved along the rooms, level after level, cracking doors and peeking inside.

No Sienna.

On the top level he stopped at the end of the hallway, staring at the red peeling paint on the door in front of him that he'd just closed. The last door. And his wife was not here.

His sinking gut turned into a jagged rock.

A fool's errand.

He'd just been sent on a fool's errand.

The floorboards creaked at the end of the hallway and Logan's head swiveled to see a boy dive into the shadows of the stairwell.

Blasted boy.

Logan ran down the hall, catching the boy that had sent him here by the scruff of his neck halfway down the stairs.

"She was never here, was she, boy?"

"Please, sir." The boy's hands flailed in front of him.

Logan shook the boy, lifting him off his feet. "Was she ever here?"

"No...no...no, sir." He wiggled, trying to squirm away.

He lifted the boy higher, looking at him straight in the eye. "Bournestein sent you to bring me here?"

The boy nodded, defiant in being caught in his lie. "He did."

Logan resisted smashing the boy into the wall. Instead, he dropped him. The boy stumbled to his knees. "Why do it? You know how Bournestein is—you'll not live long, boy."

The boy scrambled to his feet, looking up at Logan with curiosity in that he didn't just get blasted with the back of Logan's hand. "Maybe, sir. Maybe. But I be living under Bournestein's watch, not yours, sir. I had to do it."

As much as he wanted to fault the boy, Logan understood. He understood too well how life was when one was trying to keep his family safe from Bournestein's wrath. It was hard to think past what was directly in front of one's eyes. Food. Warmth. Survival. It was impossible to imagine a different life.

Logan pointed down the stairwell with a sigh. "Go. Out of my sight, boy."

Arms and legs floundering about, the boy scrambled, flying down the stairs.

Logan stared down the dark stairwell, the cacophony of hoots and jeers from the main level drifting up to him.

Bournestein had lured him here, but not for an ambush.

If that was his plan, he would have had a stack of men waiting for him.

Bournestein didn't underestimate. He especially didn't underestimate Logan.

But why?

What was his game?

Bournestein always had a game. Always had a next move. And he never stopped. Never.

Hell.

Logan broke into a run, tearing down the stairs and out to the street. Rain had started, the muck on the street sucking at his feet. The first horse he saw, he ripped the reins from the rider and mounted it, sending it into a thundering gallop down the street.

He needed to get to the Revelry's Tempest.

{ CHAPTER 14 }

The top floor had already collapsed by the time he arrived on Brook Street.

Flames licking high. Embers drifting upward into the sky.

In a daze, Logan dropped from the horse he'd stolen, staggering toward the building. Staggering so close the heat licked his face, smoke singeing his eyes.

No.

Not the Revelry's Tempest. Not the one thing that had mattered to him since losing Sienna. His salvation. His men's salvation. His purpose. It didn't deserve this end. They—Cassandra and Violet and Adalia and his guards— didn't deserve this end.

His look flew around and he spun in a circle, searching the people in the street, the fire brigade shooting water at the flames skirting out from the street level windows.

He spun and spun, the rain and the mayhem blurring in front of his eyes.

His people. Where were his people?

He froze in place, frantically searching his mind. It wasn't a gaming night. That had happened days ago. His men were at their homes, resting after tearing up St. Giles. Cook would have retired for the day back to her townhouse by now—as would the maids. Violet and Cass and Adalia would be home with their families.

No one should have been inside. No one.

Please let there be no one inside.

Whereas he'd cleared the Joker's Roost, Bournestein wouldn't take such a care.

A thunderous crash exploded behind him and a blast of heat scorched his neck. He reeled around to the building. The third level had just crashed down, bringing the second floor with it. Stone and bricks tumbled and a sparking whirlwind of searing heat overtook him.

His hand lifted to shield his eyes and he stumbled a step backward, crashing into a carriage.

The window of the coach he staggered into opened up next to his temple and a head popped out. A balding, greasy head set upon a palate of purple and orange glistening brilliantly in the glow of the fire.

"That is uncomfortably hot, wouldn't ye agree?" Through his blackened, swollen eyes, Bournestein's look focused on the burning building, a devil's glow dancing about his face.

"I'll kill you." Logan twisted, grabbing Bournestein around the neck and yanking him through the tiny window.

Two pistols pressed into either side of Logan's head.

Bournestein's brutes were quick to surround him. Quick to make sure they inflicted as much pain as possible as they dug their barrels into his temples.

Logan released Bournestein, his hands going up and fingers spreading wide as his lip curled. "You've gone too far with this, Bournestein. This will never end. Not now. You don't come back from this. Coming into this part of town. You don't know what you've done, what will rain down upon you. You have just lost everything with this."

"Did I? Oh, I don't think so, boy." His words slurring with his broken jaw, Bournestein pulled his portly form back in from the window, smoothing the lapels of his orange-trimmed purple tailcoat and sloughing off the rain from his forehead and balding head. "In fact, I do believe it is ye that has just lost everything." His snake smile slinked onto his lips, though the left side of his mangled mouth drooped from the beating he took. "Ye lost her. And I didn't even have to convince her to abandon ye."

Logan twitched, ready to strangle him, and the gun barrels dug viscously into his temples, ready to explode his head. He froze. "It'll never happen. Sienna would never leave me."

"Never?" Bournestein chuckled. "Well then, I give ye this one last gift, boy, and then I be done with ye—I tell ye she's safe."

"She'll never be safe near you."

Bournestein nodded and flicked his fingers to his guards. They lowered their pistols from Logan's skull. "I agree, boy. And that's why she's gone back to Roselawn."

Hope flared in Logan's chest.

The countryside. Of course he would send her there. Far away from Logan. Far away from the squalor of London. He always knew she was too good for St. Giles. He would protect her from this life. For all of the evil in Bournestein, he loved his daughter.

Loved her too much.

Bournestein's snake smile stretched wider, grotesquely distorting his face. "It shouldn't spark hope in ye, boy. After I told her what ye done, she left on her own accord. It was her idea." He rubbed the side of his busted jaw. "Ye be dead to her, boy."

Logan stilled, his words escaping through gritted teeth. "What did you tell her?"

"The one thing ye wouldn't. I told her what ye did to her mother. That ye killed the fine lady."

"Bastard. You swore." Logan started to lunge at him, but was instantly held back by the brutes flanking him. "You swore you'd never tell her, you bastard."

Bournestein chuckled, long and slurred from his askew jaw. "That I am, boy. That I am."

He reached under the orange lapel of his purple coat with his unbroken hand and pulled out a gold ring, embedded with blue sapphires the color of Sienna's eyes and wrapped on one side with matching blue ribbon. He held it up and out the window to Logan, the sapphires glittering with the flames of the fire, droplets of rain soaking the ribbon. "She said to deliver this to ye. She won't be needing it any longer. She said to leave the ribbon on, or ye won't be believin' she gave it willingly to me."

His fingers shaking, Logan reached out and snatched the ring from Bournestein's grasp. That the man had even touched the ring, defiled it with his meaty paws, made his stomach roll.

Another triumphant chuckle left Bournestein's crooked mouth and he slapped the side of the carriage. His brutes released Logan and ruthlessly went to clear a path for the carriage through the throngs of people gawking at the fire.

The coach rolled away.

Logan stood in the street, watching it disappear down the street.

Sheets of rain drowning him.

Flames licking hot at his back.

~ ~ ~

"Get out, boy, I don't want you in here." The words spat from Sienna's mother as her palm lifted to him, her fingers bending and stretching manically in his direction. "You're death, boy. Death is about you, it always 'as been. It follows you everywhere. I can see it about you. Get out."

"Please just don't hit her no more, Miss Vivian." Logan glanced over his shoulder. He hated this room, hated the stench of the thick French perfume. The door was so close. Just three steps and he could escape her. It'd be easy. His feet started to shuffle backward, then stopped. He took a deep breath. Sienny needed this. "Please, Miss Vivian. No more. She's hurt so much from earlier."

"Don't tell me what to do, boy. If your bitch of a mother 'adn't shown up here—I'd be happy—happy—and Bournestein would still be in my bed." Her red hair fanned out on the blue pillows behind her. She looked like an angry sun. "You know, boy, he 'asn't visited my bed once since your whore of a mother showed up here? Pathetic she is—shows up with nothing. Except you two brats. What are you now, boy? Seven? Eight? How long 'as your bitch mother been here?"

"I'm seven, Miss Vivian." Logan braved five steps forward and clutched the side of her bed. "Please, just don't hit Sienny when you see her. We didn't mean to be late. If you need someone to hit, hit me. Just not Sienny no more. Please."

She slapped him. "I said don't tell me what to do, boy."

The sting of the ruby ring she always turned inward on her finger drew blood. He could taste it on the corner of his lip. No matter. It was nothing compared to the beating there would be *if she saw that they had accidently dyed Sienny's arm purple at the textile factory. He wasn't sure how much more Sienny could take.*

Her head jerked to the side, looking out the door. "Where's my girl? She was supposed to be with you, boy—where is she?"

"She's coming up, soon, Miss Vivian. She's in the kitchens with Robby, then she'll be up."

"Good." She flipped her fingers out, her long nails motioning toward the variety of jars atop her bureau. "Be a dear and get my medicine for me, boy."

Logan went to the jars, pulling open the stopper on the pink glass one that held the laudanum. He picked up a spoon and brought the jar to her.

She hadn't moved from the incline of her pillows. "Pour me my two spoonfuls, boy."

Logan did, and brought them carefully to her lips. He couldn't afford to spill any on her red silk chemise and rankle up her ire before Sienny showed up with her purple arm.

Miss Vivian's head fell back against her blue satin pillows. Her eyes closed. With any luck, she would be asleep before Sienny crawled into bed with her.

Logan started to shuffle his feet backward, but then tripped on a red slipper half stuck out from the bed. He stumbled, his feet thudding on the floorboards.

Miss Vivian's eyes popped open. "What are you doing in here, boy?" She spied the jar and spoon in his hands. "Oh, that, you're a good boy. Pour me my two spoonfuls and then be gone with you. Find Sienna and send her up—tell her quickly or I'll whip her."

Logan looked down at the pink bottle of laudanum. Sienny couldn't take another whipping. Not after her one this morning.

He looked at Miss Vivian, her eyes wide open and expectantly staring at him.

Another two spoonfuls and Sienna's mother would be asleep for certain—dead to the world until morning when Sienny could slip away before her mother saw her purple arm. Then they could scrub it more tomorrow—they'd had to stop earlier because the lye was rubbing her skin bloody and he couldn't watch her tears anymore.

His hands shaking, he poured Miss Vivian another spoonful. Then another.

Sienny needed her to sleep. So he would make sure of it.

They just needed more time to scrub the purple off Sienny's arm. They had been so stupid to go inside the textile factory— they should have just picked up the fabric for Bournestein's new purple coat and come home straight away.

He watched Miss Vivian for an hour. Watched to make sure she would stay asleep. And then he realized that he hadn't seen her chest move in some time.

His hand lifted to shake her, but he lost his nerve. He ran to fetch Bournestein.

Following him into Miss Vivian's room, Bournestein closed the door and pushed Logan to the side as he walked to the bed. He lifted Miss Vivian's arm.

It fell with a thud back to the bed.

He slapped her face. Nothing.

He set his ear to her chest.

Slowly, he lifted his head, looking to Logan. "She's dead, boy. What were you even doing in here?"

Horrified, his world imploding, Logan's words flew. Sienny would hate him. Hate him. "I—I gave her too much. She was confused and asked for more of the pink bottle and I gave her too much. I just wanted her to sleep. I didn't mean to, Mr. Bournestein. Honest. I didn't mean to. I have to tell Sienny. I have to go find Sienny, Mr. Bournestein." Logan stumbled toward the door.

"Wait, boy."

Logan spun around, his arms and limbs on fire, trying to escape his own body. How could he have killed her—how? Sienny would hate him. Hate him forever.

Bournestein turned from him, stepping back to Miss Vivian and drawing the sheet over her head. He leaned down, kissing her forehead through the sheet. "Sleep well, beautiful princess."

Logan's fingers pressed into his gut, grasping at the vomit churning in his stomach as tears started to stream down his face. "Sienny—Sienny, Mr. Bournestein. I was going to tell her but I don't think I can tell her, if she knows I—"

Bournestein moved to Logan and put his thick hand on Logan's shoulder, squeezing it. "Sienna doesn't need to know what ye did, boy. She loves ye too much for that. Her mother died. That is all she ever need know."

{ Chapter 15 }

"You look like a man that's lost everything, Logan."

Cassandra's gentle voice reached him through the pounding in his ears, though he couldn't look up at the sound.

"Logan."

Sitting on a charred beam of the collapsed building, he lifted his dazed eyes from the smoldering remains surrounding him.

Dawn had come—chased away the fiery darkness of the night to take over the land with an unusually bright sky. The rain had long since stopped, though without it, the whole street would've been engulfed in flames.

A peaceful morning, brutal in its beauty.

Cassandra stood on the top stone step of what used to be the entrance to the Revelry's Tempest, kicking aside charred chunks of stones with the toes of her boots. Portland Stones that had once glowed in whiteness, now blackened.

Bedecked in a functional deep blue walking gown with a matching Spencer jacket, Cassandra stared at him in the middle of the rubble. He couldn't meet her eyes.

His look dropped down to the pile of ash one of the gaming tables had been reduced to, only the twisted copper rim from the edge of the table recognizable.

He heard her exaggerated sigh and she muttered something incomprehensible as she started forth slowly, her toes testing her steps on the rubble for solid footing.

With her reticule swinging from her wrist, it took her an inordinate amount of time to pick her way through the destruction to the center of the building.

He didn't move, didn't look up in her direction until she had tiptoed her way through the debris to him. Silently, she drew her skirts together and moved to sit next to him, balancing herself on the thick, heavy timber that had once held up the structure, now askew in the stones and ash.

He glanced at her. "Where's Rorrick?"

"He's waiting for me in the carriage." She lifted her right kidskin-gloved hand and pointed to the end of the lane. The golden Vandestile coat of arms on the side of the coach gleamed in the gentle morning sunlight.

His eyes stayed riveted on the coach. "He saw me?"

"He did."

"And he let you come over here? Generous of him."

Her honey-brown eyes went to the sky and she sighed. "He saw you and chose to stay in the carriage. While he understands the severity of this situation, you cannot just expect for him to forget what happened to his brother—"

"I know, Cass." He kicked at a blackened stone brick by his boot. "I know."

She nodded, silent. For all that had happened between them in the past, Logan knew Cassandra's loyalty was torn. Her husband would always take precedence, as he should, yet Logan recognized what a fine line Cassandra balanced upon when it came to him and her husband.

She peeled off her gloves and she leaned forward, her fingers digging into the ashes. Picking up a handful, she let it sift away through her fingers. "It must have burned hot. Deeply hot. Did you see it collapse? When we heard, Rorrick wouldn't let me come. He thought it too dangerous."

"I did. No one was inside, thank the heavens."

"Indeed." She exhaled a long breath, almost as though she didn't know how to proceed. "We already sent word to Adalia at Dellon Castle. And Violet and I were together last night when we learned the news it had started. Violet heard word that it was intentional—Bournestein?"

Logan nodded. "Yes."

Her head shook, her bottom lip tightening. "Bastard."

"Exactly." His one word exhaled in a beaten sigh.

"Violet believed it right away, but I didn't want to even consider someone would do this intentionally." Her head still shaking, she leaned forward again, digging through the rubble with her fingers until she sat upright, a small prize in her hand. She flipped the small round clump in her hands, brushing away the soot and sludge of ash on it. A gold marker in the middle of the muck soon appeared—not charred—not marred—and the more she rubbed it clean, the more it glowed in the pink rays of dawn. She held it up. "Look, one of the third anniversary souvenir markers. This, I best keep for Violet."

Logan watched her tuck it away in her reticule, sadness like he'd never seen casting a shadow over her honey-brown eyes. "She'll like that."

Cassandra bent over once more, her fingers curling into the debris. She sat upright, staring down at her hand clamping around the ashes in her palm for a long moment, her knuckles turning white.

A long breath passed, and she unclenched her fingers, letting the ash fall next to her skirts.

Her look travelled about her, at the destruction, then her gaze travelled upward to where the upper floors used to be. "Do you remember, it was never meant to last more than the first months, then the first years, the Revelry's Tempest." She looked at Logan. "This place became so much more, to so many people, but it has served its purpose, and now we—you must find a new way, Logan."

His soot-blackened fingers lifted to rub his eyes before he could look at her. "Which is?"

"Well, for a start, I know you are beyond adept at running a gaming house. So you can rebuild the Revelry's Tempest—or a new house, call it something else entirely. Rebuild it for your men. And you will have Adalia's support and mine at your call. Violet's as much as she is able to with her babe due soon. And you will be more than successful at it. I know how important this place is for your men. For you. It has been their home, their salvation just as much as ours. You need this place, Logan."

His look veered from her to the open space between two townhouses across the street—the remnants of an abandoned building project. Early morning birds were flitting to and from their nests high in the eaves of the adjoining buildings. "Actually, I don't, Cass."

"What?" Her hands slapped onto her lap. "You don't need the Revelry's Tempest?"

His right cheek lifted in a slight cringe and he looked at her. "I have been waiting for the right moment to tell you."

"Tell me what?"

"I am a duke."

Her jaw dropped and she looked away from him for a long moment, the flabbergasted expression on her face the complete opposite of her usual porcelain poise. Comical, almost, if he could laugh at the moment.

Her gaze darted back to him, her jaw still gaping. "What? This is not the moment for comedy, Logan."

"It happened a number of years ago."

"A number of years ago? A duke? You're a true duke, and you were *waiting* for the right moment?" It was as close to a shriek as he'd ever heard her soft voice.

He shrugged, dutifully chided. "It was a bizarre set of circumstance. Three older half-brothers could not hold onto the title, all of them died, and so it fell to me. I'm the Duke of Culland."

Her hand flattened on the slope of her chest, her reticule swinging and hitting her stomach. "You're the recluse duke? The one that refused the title for years and then has never been seen in parliament—in London, for that matter?"

"I am."

Her still gaping jaw closed after a long moment of staring at him, her eyes searching his face. "But, why? Why did you not tell us?"

"I didn't want the title." He paused, sighing. "I didn't want to become something I wasn't sure I could control. You've seen them here at the Revelry's Tempest. The worst of the peerage."

She nodded, her jaw finally set firmly back in place as her look left him and searched the rubble around her. Her gaze landed on him, sharp. "Yes, and I have also seen the best of the *ton* here. Little old dowagers asking that all of their winnings be delivered to the asylum for orphans or the leper colony. People falling in love. People *staying* in love. Outcasts finding a place where they are welcome. We weren't always accepted by all in society, but for those that showed up, the Revelry's Tempest was a magical place. And the people, the ones that refused to make or take judgements—they were magical. And they loved it here."

A crooked smile came to Logan's face. "They did, didn't they?" His eyes turned dark. "And I ruined it. I ruined it all."

Her forehead furrowed. "Whatever Bournestein did—it was his choice to destroy this place, not yours, Logan."

"No, he did it to punish me. It was all about making me pay. Taking Sienna wasn't enough for him—he needed to make me suffer, and aside from Sienna, this was the only thing he could destroy that mattered to me and he knew it."

"Is it true she is back in Yorkshire?"

His eyebrows shot upward. "How do you know that?"

"Rorrick was here last night. He came directly when we heard and he said he was making his way to you when you bumped into Bournestein's carriage. There were pistols to your head, Logan?"

He nodded.

She visibly shivered, her eyes closing for a long breath. "By the time Rorrick pushed through the crowd and near you, he overheard what Bournestein said about Sienna."

"I didn't see him."

"I don't believe you would have seen much between hearing that and the Revelry's Tempest burning." Cassandra's gaze fell to her lap and she brushed some splotches of ash from her skirt. "So Sienna is in the north?"

"She is." His answer was curt, meant to cut Cassandra from a conversation on Sienna. He hoped she took the hint. He wasn't ready to talk about Sienna yet. Probably never.

"Is it true what Bournestein said? You are dead to her?"

She didn't take the hint.

He nodded, silent.

"She won't even see you again?"

He shook his head, his mouth clamped tight.

Nodding, she bent over and picked up a shard of charred stone. She turned it over and over in her hands as she stared at it. "Amazing it could crumble apart like this," she muttered to herself.

Taking a deep breath, she dropped the brick to the ground and her gaze locked onto him. "I just have one question for you, Logan."

He looked to her with his eyebrow cocked in question.

"If you're a duke, why on earth have I been paying you for these past five years?"

He burst out laughing.

She joined in, her soft laughter magical and light in the morning sun.

His belly straining against the laughter rolling through his body, he gasped a breath, holding his hand up. "I will have you know that you've been supporting the Cranesbill Hospital since it opened. It serves the women and children in St. Giles. And all those funds you've paid me during the years have been quite helpful in building and running the place."

"That is the hospital that Mr. Crawford's wife opened—the one they visit every year from Northumberland?"

"You knew about that?"

"The guards' room is directly next to the kitchens, Logan. Mr. Crawford always comes back to visit with his old friends in the guard when he is in town." She grinned. "I do tend to hear things while passing to talk to Cook."

He inclined his head to her astuteness. Cassandra was so quiet, he forgot sometimes that she saw and heard everything here at the Revelry's Tempest. "Well, know that the hospital is more than pleased with your patronage. You have a golden patron's plaque in the entrance."

She chuckled. "Then I will be happy to continue that patronage." Her laughter drifted off as she looked around her. Melancholy touched her eyes. "For all that this place was for all of us—it was just that—a place, a building, a means to an end. It filled our time, filled our coffers, gave us means for survival, gave us purpose. But it is the life beyond the Revelry's Tempest that is the important thing. The people we have become. And you have salvaged life for so many of us. Your men, me, Violet. For all you have helped others, Logan, you need to do the same now for yourself. You need to take your own life into control."

"And do what, Cass? What? Everything is gone." He motioned around him. "What's left?"

Her jaw shifted to the side. "Well, start by living your life in a way that makes you happy—or at least with as much grace as possible." She paused, her eyebrows drawing together as she studied him. "But I've only seen you happy once—truly happy—only once, Logan."

Logan drew away from her, shifting on the askew beam. "Don't say it, Cass."

"With Sienna. That one day she was at the Revelry's Tempest with you, it was as though you were an entirely different man with her. You were…complete. There wasn't that piece of you that has always been missing—for as long as I've known you—you have always been missing something. A silent darkness that had a hold of your soul. And it was her. She was what had been missing. It was so evident that day."

"There are things you don't know, Cass."

"Such as?"

His hand swung around him again. "Such as this. Such as I have spent my life sacrificing others for her—for us. It is the devil in me that I cannot deny. I love her too much, no matter what it destroys. And I do it—destroy things, people—again and again and again because I cannot stop. But this…"

His gaze left Cassandra and swept around him. His look landed on the bones of the fireplace in the lower drawing room, still half standing, poking up from the rubble. His hand lifted, his fingers rubbing his eyes, pinching the bridge of his nose. "This is too much. I need to be done. I need to let her go. I cannot keep destroying everything around me to have her."

"Bournestein did this, Logan, not you."

"He did it because I made him. I was the one that provoked him. I took my need to find her to such an extreme that he needed to bite me back." His hand dropped down and he snatched up a handful of ash, shaking it. "And just look—look at what I'll destroy for her. Anything. Everything. When is it enough?"

Cassandra shrugged, her answer almost immediate. "I guess it's enough when you have her back."

"It's not that simple, Cass."

"I think…" She paused, her mouth clamping shut for a moment before she nodded to herself and continued. "Sometimes I think we are made how we are made and one cannot truly deny one's nature. I would venture to guess that is the case between you two. After hearing the story of how you two were together, how she followed you into war. What you did to save her, the men that died."

"She told you that?"

"She did—when you went down to talk to the guards. I don't think she meant to betray confidence, but you must remember, what you told her was a shock, and added to the fact that she had just run off with a man she knew was her husband, but couldn't remember much of her life with. She was looking for reassurance that you were everything she believed you to be."

"So what did you say to her?"

"We reassured her." An easy smile came to Cassandra's face. "Logan, you are everything that a man should aspire to be. Loyal, strong, honorable, and with the ability for unspeakable kindness. And you love that woman. It is obvious she is your match. She knew all of that, but she was just worried that her own mind was failing her—playing tricks on her. She was worried that she wanted you so deeply she was lying to herself about who you truly are as a person."

Cassandra waved her hand. "But the crux of the matter is that you need each other, and neither one of you will

truly be happy—truly find some semblance of peace—
unless you are together."

"You have become a romantic, Cass."

"I have always been a romantic, Logan." She grabbed
his hand, unfurling his fingers and then carefully brushing
the ashes and charred remains from his skin before clasping
his hand between her palms.

Her look lifted from their hands and she met his eyes.
"And if you two being together means that you destroy
things to protect her, then you're going to destroy things."
She glanced around her, then patted his hand, a crooked
smile on her face. "Just be smart about it. Maybe try not to
burn any more buildings down."

He couldn't resist a meager smile. "So where does that
leave me?"

"Logan, for as long as I have known you, you have
been taking care of others—I would venture to guess you've
been doing that very thing since you could walk and talk.
And you're a master at it. Everyone around you is better
for crossing paths with you." She released his hand. "But I
think it's time for you to take care of yourself, for once."

"Meaning?"

"I believe it's time you give yourself leave to embrace
your nature. You need Sienna, and you need to do whatever
it takes to get her back. Whatever happened between you
two, you need to find a way back to her."

He shook his head. "But what I did, Cass—there is no
forgiveness."

"Well then, she needs to find a way back to you."
She set her hand lightly on his knee. "There is always

forgiveness. And my guess is that if she is worthy of you, she will find a way to forgive you."

"How can she find her way back to me if she won't even see me? She left London to escape me."

Cassandra's head dropped forward in consideration for a long moment. Then she gasped, looking up at him with a cringe. "I am channeling Adalia right now, what her answer to your question would be—not my own."

"Which is?"

"Have you considered kidnapping?"

{ CHAPTER 16 }

It wasn't a kidnapping, per se.

It was a very large sum of funds that had been transferred to the woman that had posed as Sienna's grandmother for her cooperation. As Roselawn was now under constant guard by Bournestein's men, it had taken a bit of trickery to extract Sienna from the estate.

A help to that end, Cassandra had managed to arrange the transfer of funds as she and her husband took an extended trip to the north and travelled through Sandfell. Cassandra and Rorrick had arranged a meeting with the grandmother through the neighboring baron, and Cassandra had delivered the proposal to the woman—assist with bringing Sienna north, and she would receive the funds and a new estate to live out her days far away from Bournestein's tentacles.

The elderly woman had gladly accepted the offer.

For extra assurance, Logan had managed to convince the one person that could ensure Sienna's unimpeded travel north to Northumberland. His brother.

The last person Logan had wanted to see, Robby had appeared at the carcass of the Revelry's Tempest hours after the last embers had sizzled to ash.

In the daylight, Logan could see the toll spending years in Newgate had taken on Robby. His grey eyes had aged a thousand years, his cheeks gaunt, sunken under the dark circles rimming his eyes. Even though he'd grown to nearly the same height as Logan, where muscle had once been prevalent, now his clothing hung limply on the sharp bones jutting from his skin.

Robby had stepped up to Logan in the middle of the debris of the building, alone, with no Bournestein brutes accompanying him. Odd, for Robby was still the heir to Bournestein's empire.

Logan had wondered how Robby managed the feat until Robby simply said four words, "How can I help?"

That had been a fortnight ago, and now Logan stood outside his castle in Northumberland, Shadowmoor, watching his brother walk down from the ancient structure to the stables where he waited.

Logan exhaled his breath in a long whistle, the dread he'd held in his chest for the past fortnight easing from his lungs. Not until that very moment did Logan know if his gamble on his brother would turn to his favor.

The last person he trusted to deliver Sienna to him just happened to be the only person he trusted.

Robby strode down the hillside and Logan was still unsettled at how his brother had grown—how the set of his shoulders had widened since the last time he'd seen him when they were young. Eleven years. Eleven years since he'd left with Sienna—left Robby behind in London.

Robby's frame now filled out his dark tailcoat and trousers well, his gait long and purposeful. His hair still long and unkempt—he hadn't bothered to get it cut since getting out of Newgate—dark strands fell into his eyes and he had to continually brush them back.

He'd put meat back onto his bones in the short time he'd been out of Newgate. His sunken cheeks had filled back in, the dark circles disappearing from his eyes. But the horrors that Robby had suffered in Newgate had scarred him.

Scarred him far more than their life in St. Giles ever had—scarred him deep in his soul.

Logan had seen it instantly the first time he talked to Robby at the remains of the Revelry's Tempest. And the two subsequent times after that they spoke, the haunted ghosts in his brother's eyes had not faded.

Foot tapping, Logan waited just inside the main entrance of the center stable out of direct view of the castle.

His brother stopped in front of him. "It is done. She is in her room."

"The travel here was uneventful?"

"It was. Bournestein's men didn't even question that I was sent there to bring her and Nan Rose to a new estate Bournestein had purchased."

"Nan Rose?" Logan started, his head shaking. "Nan Rose? As in our nanny, Rose? That's the woman that posed as Sienna's grandmother?" The image of the aging beauty, wrapped in her favorite yellow shawl, flashed in Logan's mind. Having aged out of Bournestein's stable of whores, Nan Rose had found new purpose under his roof raising Sienna, Logan, and Robby where their mothers could not.

"Yes. Sienna never told you her name?"

"No, and I just assumed she was a woman hired by Bournestein to keep Sienna at Roselawn." Logan rubbed the back of his neck. "Had I—is she—Nan Rose—has she left? Is she happy with moving to the coast?"

For all Nan Rose had done for them as children—actually showed them kindness, a rare commodity in their world—Logan wanted to make certain she was well taken care of. He would be sure to send an extra sum of funds to the solicitor he had set up for her on the coast of Norfolk so she would want for nothing. Her birthplace, it was where she requested to Cassandra to have a home purchased for her.

Robby glanced over his shoulder to the castle. "After she told Sienna she needed to rest, I snuck her down the back stairs and set her in the carriage myself, although I requested she not tell me her destination. The less I know, the better. She seemed pleased, a weight lifted from her shoulders." His hand lifted, fingers pushing back his long dark hair that hung in his eyes. A miniscule grin lifted the edges of his lips. "Nan Rose always wanted the three of us together—less trouble for her that way. So she left as content as I imagine she could be after the hardships of her life."

"Had I known…"

Robby's haunted eyes pierced him, the line of his mouth grim. "I thanked her enough for both of us, Logan."

"For everything?"

"Everything."

Logan inclined his head. He looked past Robby's shoulder to the southeast turret of the keep where he'd set Sienna's room to be. She was most likely in there, humming to herself as she unpacked, straying to the window to plot out the trails to ride upon.

Logan glanced at Robby, hedging his next question, afraid of the answer. "Does Sienna…remember anything more? Could you discern as much?"

"I don't think so. Not from what you told me." Robby shrugged. "There was a flicker of recognition when she saw me, but I could tell she couldn't quite place me other than I looked like you. Once Nan Rose introduced me, she was excited to learn we'd be traveling together. She didn't remember me, exactly, but she peppered me with questions about our childhood—how we grew up—the entire way."

"Did it spark any memories for her?"

"I don't believe so." A frown set on Robby's lips. "She is still desperate to have her memories return to her. She has not given up on that course."

"I don't imagine she would have. It is not in her nature to give up."

"Nor yours." Robby flashed him a quick smile. Logan couldn't remember the last time he'd seen a true smile from his brother. "Oh, and you should know, Logan, she did ask about her mother."

Logan stilled, his heart suddenly in his throat. "What did you tell her?"

"I think the question is what did you not tell me, Logan?" Robby's look strayed to the side, his head shaking for a long moment before he pinned Logan with his grey eyes. "You killed Sienna's mother?"

Logan winced.

"Why didn't you tell me what happened—if that even is what happened? I have a hard time believing it—did Bournestein lie to her? Or did you truly kill her mother?"

Logan nodded, bracing himself.

"Laudanum?"

Logan nodded again.

Robby sighed, his fingers running through his hair. "Blast it, why didn't you tell me, Logan? All this time—I'm your brother—you could have told me."

Logan drew a deep breath, his shoulders sagging on the exhale. "All I wanted to do was protect Sienna—just have her mother sleep through the night—it was that day we accidently turned Sienna's arm purple and I knew she would take a beating."

Logan paused, his chest rising as he drew strength into his lungs. There was nothing more he needed to hide from his brother at this point. "I didn't tell you because you were so young, Robby, just like Sienna. I didn't want you to know what I did. I didn't want anyone to know. I especially didn't want Sienna to know. And I didn't want either of you to have to bear the knowledge of what I did. It wasn't fair. We needed each other to survive and I could not break that."

His brother's eyebrow arched at him. "You were young too, Logan. What about you bearing it?"

"Young or not, I did it. And I knew it would destroy everything one day. Just as it has."

"Or not." Robby glanced back to the castle. "She has a sadness about her that I can only imagine is from the absence of you."

Logan glanced at the tower, his voice wistful. "I can only pray that is true. But she never tolerated lies from either of us. And there is nothing more grievous than what I did, who I took from her."

His brother's silver grey eyes narrowed at him. "I think you being taken away from her was more grievous, Logan. Bournestein did it while I was in the south, working the smuggling routes. Had I known that he'd taken her, hidden her away…" His voice trailed, his head shaking. He cleared his throat. "Plus, you have to remember, Sienna was always stubborn. The most of all of us. Perhaps she just needs time."

Logan's head tilted to the side and he offered a slight bow of his head.

His brother pointed past Logan. "You have a horse readied for me?"

"I do." Logan glanced over his shoulder. "Third stall on the left. Best one in the stable."

His brother nodded.

"Robby, I know what you've given up to help me."

Robby met his eyes, his look bitter remorse. "It's something I never should have wanted—to be Bournestein's chosen one. That bastard took the first half of my life. I'll not give him another year more."

And then the smallest glimmer sparked in his brother's eyes. A glimmer Logan recognized, just the same as he had felt on the day he and Sienna had escaped Bournestein's clutches.

A glimmer of hope.

"Where will you go?" Logan asked.

"I don't know." Robby shook his head. "Not back to London. Ever."

"How will I find you?"

A smile, genuine and wry lifted the corners of Robby's mouth. "I don't imagine you will."

Logan exhaled, his lips drawing to a tight line even as he accepted the answer. "You know where to find me."

"I do, brother." Robby moved past him, stopping in front of the third stall. He paused, turning back to Logan. "If she does remember everything...tell Sienna..."

He stopped, his eyes tilting upward to the sky as he shook his head, looking to the rafters of the stable. His gaze dropped to Logan. "Tell her I'm sorry. Tell her I know she belongs with you. I always did."

Logan couldn't force words past the lump in his throat. All he could offer was a nod.

There was much to forgive, much to reconcile from their childhood.

It was time to start.

~ ~ ~

In order to free his left hand, Logan balanced the silver tray of cold meats, cheese and pears on his forearm as he squeezed the decanter of brandy along the edge next to the teapot. Not that he expected Sienna to drink the brandy. But he might need it.

He fumbled a moment with the key in the lock, metal scraping against metal until the latch clinked.

Much louder than he had intended.

He knocked on the thick oak panel of the door.

"Yes? Enter." Sienna's voice sounded muffled, as though she was at the far edge of the room beyond the door.

Logan turned the knob, pushing the heavy door open slowly, peeking inside. He wouldn't put it past her to rush past him. Throw a chair. Stick him with a hairpin.

Instead, he found her standing by the south window, looking out the tall panes of glass. She glanced over her shoulder to him, her look only pausing for a second on his face before she turned back to the window, her fingers tapping on the lower rail.

Stepping into the room, he flipped a foot backward to kick the door closed.

"I should have guessed," she murmured to herself. Her breathing had turned rapid, her shoulders lifting faster and faster with every breath.

She stared out the window for a long moment before her breathing slowed. Settled, she turned from the glass, her head shaking, her lip curling in a sneer. "I thought this was another one of my father's tyrannical schemes, but I should have known this was you."

Logan went to the small round table on the opposite end of the room by the fireplace. The largest chamber at Shadowmoor, Logan had it refurnished in the last week. He set the tray on the table.

"I brought food, tea." He lifted the cloche covering the plate of meats, setting it on the table so she could see the selection.

No answer.

He turned fully to her. "Why did you think this was one of his tyrannical schemes?"

Her arms crossed over her ribcage as she glared at him. "You think the locked door escaped my notice?"

"I was hoping I could unlock it before you discovered it."

"So why unlock it now?" Her eyebrow arched. "Do you intend to leave it unlocked?"

"I only had to keep you in here for a few minutes until they left, Sienna."

"Who left?"

Logan eyed the decanter of brandy he'd set on the table. He'd need that sooner rather than later. He lifted one of the two glasses from the tray, pouring a dram which he promptly swallowed before looking at Sienna. "My brother. Nan Rose. They are gone."

"Gone?" Her eyes went wide and she spun to the window, looking out at the open land before it met the forest wall. She twisted back to him. "So you got rid of them and locked me in a tower? This is beyond despicable, even for you, Logan."

He winced.

She advanced on him from across the room. "Bournestein gave you the ring back, Logan, and that is all you need know from me. You're dead to me—dead."

"Except that I am very much alive."

Her hand flew out to the side. "Yes, and now you think to hold me hostage? For what purpose? You think I'll forgive you for what you did—for lying to me my whole life?"

"I was hoping for a moment to explain."

Her head snapped back. "Explain how you murdered my mother? You think that's explainable? You're deranged, Logan. Completely and utterly mad."

"Sienna, you don't know the whole story."

She jumped past him and grabbed the paring knife that sat next to the cheese on the tray. In the next breath, she rushed Logan, pressing the knife to his neck.

"You're not going to hold me captive, Logan. Never. I'm not your plaything to stick in a cage and twiddle with whenever the mood strikes you."

His mouth stretched to a thin line. "You've never been my toy, Sienna. You're my damn wife."

Rage at the very thought—that she would say those words—surged through his limbs. His fingers itched to grab her arm and twist the blade from her hand. It would be easy—she'd apparently never recalled how to hold a blade to someone's neck properly. The edge might nick him at most. But he kept his hands at his side, staring down at her.

She had a right to her anger. He'd abducted her and tossed her into a locked tower and if a blade on his neck was how her ire manifested, he'd take the blade on his neck.

He tried to simmer his rage—hard when he couldn't whistle, for he didn't dare do that and coax her fury any higher.

His voice low, just barely in control, his eyes cut into her. "Where are you going to go, Sienna? Nan Rose is gone. My brother is gone. We are in the middle of nowhere and you don't know where you are. You could take a horse from the stable, but then what? Travel to where? Back to London with no money? Back to your father? Or…"

"Or what?" Her hand fidgeted on the handle of the blade, yet her blue eyes still flung azure-tipped spears at him.

"Or you could kindly remove the blade from my neck and give me a week."

Her eyes narrowed at him, the fire in them not tempered at all by his words. But the pressure of the blade on his neck slightly eased. "A week for what?"

"Give me a week. A week where I won't touch you. Won't talk to you if you demand it. A week where you are here, near me, taking meals with me, and if at the end of that week you want to leave…I will let you go." As much as his words tore his gut in two, he forced them out. This was the gamble he had to take. "I will give you everything you need to live a life without me. Wherever you want. Back to London and your father. To the countryside. To Roselawn."

She eyed him, studying his face. "You won't touch me?"

"No."

She took a step backward, her hand on the blade falling to her side. "One week and I can leave?"

He nodded. "Yes."

She looked around the room, contemplating.

For as dank as some of the chambers were in the castle with the stone walls, these rooms with plaster walls were warmer and he'd had fresh furnishings and linens delivered from Leeds to appoint the room. He'd never thought to have it redecorated until this ill-advised plan to steal his wife away was concocted. But the room appeared to fit Sienna well, with its silks of soft yellows and blues draping the tester bed and matching curtains and coverlet. The furniture pieces, a desk with delicate lines of rosewood, several upholstered chairs of blue damask, and an armoire with elaborate carvings atop, finished the room. All of the choices courtesy of Cassandra's impeccable taste, as they had stopped in Leeds to order the linens and furniture after visiting Roselawn.

Sienna's wary gaze travelled back to him. "Where are we?"

"In my ancestral home."

"This is your castle in Northumberland?"

"It is. This is Shadowmoor."

She looked away and then glanced back to him. "A week?"

"A week."

"And you won't touch me?"

"I won't touch you."

Sienna moved to the table and set the knife down on the silver platter. "Fine. Agreed. I go in a week."

{ CHAPTER 17 }

Sienna looked upward along the rocky trail, inhaling the scent of wildflowers—rockroses, forget-me-nots, and mountain avens—tucked along the trail. Clouds dappled the sun, half of the bright summer rays bursting down upon the land.

"I almost feel guilty for sneaking away, but it is a glorious day." Bridget Crawford walked next to Sienna, her lively gait keeping Sienna from dawdling on the trail that stretched up to the craggy bluff.

Sienna looked past the line of hedgerow to her left, and she could see the castle in the distance, a mound of grey stone rising from the center of an emerald green earth circle ringed with oaks. Even from this distance the heavily fortified medieval castle with its four tall towers —a stark remnant from a long-ago time—stood coldly imposing. Desolate. But even as a captive to this place, she had to admit it had an odd, soothing calm about it. She glanced at Bridget. "You feel guilty?"

Bridget chuckled. "Almost. But I'm not that much of a martyr—I cannot quite manifest guilt for coming out here and enjoying this view. I've never been up into these ridges—I always travel around them. Hunter has been attempting to get me up here for some time, but there always seems to be too much to do."

Sienna smiled at her new friend. Bridget's husband, Hunter, was Logan's steward of the lands and clearly one of his most trusted men.

She and Logan had eaten with Hunter and Bridget and their three children at every meal since she'd arrived at Shadowmoor—a buffer that Logan graciously offered—or hid behind. She wasn't sure which.

She'd been quiet, sullen for the first two meals as Logan and Hunter and Bridget chatted on about the lands and the tenants as though she wasn't there. A former guard of the Revelry's Tempest, Hunter had moved here with Bridget at Logan's request to take care of the estate. Bridget was close to the same age as Sienna and was a remarkable woman—she'd been trained in surgery and medicine by her physician father, and now she served the area as their surgeon and healer.

Hunter and Bridget were a splendid match—finishing each other's sentences, they held an easy, teasing banter between the two of them that captured what a content life could look like. Though contentedness and three children had in no way mollified their marriage, if the scorching looks they gave each other was any indication—each had eyes that settled solely on the other.

Sienna had been determined to dislike everything about this place—but she was powerless against the Crawfords. They were delightful people. And they were obviously adored by the staff as well, as they enjoyed an easy rapport with everyone that worked at Shadowmoor.

Before Sienna had realized it, her sullenness at the meals had dissipated and she had engaged with Hunter and Bridget just as easily as Logan did.

Even with that, she did manage to remain distant to her husband, never speaking to him directly unless she needed the butter passed to her.

That was what he would get—cold detachment—and that was far more than he deserved.

She saw Logan at meals and that was it. He didn't approach her and she avoided any part of the castle that held the slightest whiff of him.

Four more days and she would be free of him. Free of the torture he brewed within her gut every time she saw him. Her love for him shrinking against a lifetime of lies. His most brutal betrayal.

Four more days.

Sienna and Bridget crested the top of the ridge and Bridget stopped, only slightly winded as opposed to Sienna's panting. Where the woman got her energy, Sienna wanted to know. Three children, a duchy full of tenants needing her healing services. It was a wonder Bridget managed the time away with Sienna today.

Bridget set her hands on her hips, looking outward as the breeze caught the light brown strands of hair framing her face. "The top. We walked faster than I thought we could."

They looked out upon a flawless pastoral scene from their vantage, the land rolling down below their feet, low rock walls zigzagging across the fields, hillsides jutting up behind hillsides in rolling composition. Gainsborough had never painted a more beautiful scene.

Sienna studied the land, her throat catching at the beauty of it. "It's breathtaking."

Bridget gave an odd smile, looking out to the vista. "It is that. It is a peculiar thing how quickly these lands become a part of one's bones. We have only been here for seven years and yet I feel as though this was where my bones always needed to be." Her head shook. "With the children and patients I rarely come this way, and never to this height, and it seems as if I have been remiss in doing so."

Sienna nodded. "I can see why this land would get into your soul. There is a peace here that is unusual. And nothing like London."

Bridget guffawed. "No. Nothing like London. And I am grateful for it." She stood for a long moment, taking in the sight, and then gasped and abruptly turned to Sienna. "I almost forgot—I said the word patients and that reminded me I promised Mrs. Landon I would check in on her and her gout today." She grabbed Sienna's hand and squeezed it between hers. "I must get back, but I insist you stay and enjoy the respite up here for the two of us. You will be able to find your way back to the castle? As long as you stay to the left on the trail downward, it will lead you directly to the stables."

Sienna's gaze drifted out to the panorama. She didn't want to leave this spot. Ever.

She nodded. "I will make my way back to the stables fine."

Bridget released her hand, a smile on her face. "Good. Just be sure to start down before sunset or Logan will have my head for taking you up here and leaving you alone."

Sienna chuckled. "I doubt it. I think your head is safe, as Logan is almost as enamored with you as your husband."

Bridget's eyes went to the sky. "Posh that. I just save him from the headache of keeping his staff and tenants healthy." Her head tilted to the side, a grin filling her face. "Which, I must say, he does appreciate. Maybe he is enamored with me."

"What?" Sienna's head snapped back.

Bridget's grin went wider. "Just making sure I could pique a spark of jealousy regarding your husband. That is a good sign." She inclined her head before Sienna could protest her reaction. "I shall see you tonight at dinner."

Bridget turned and walked down the rocky trail, disappearing quickly behind the trees with her springy gait.

Sienna looked out at the landscape, taking in the lines of the trees, how they broke, the hills of fields layered behind one another. The summer haze of the sky sweeping through the puffy clouds. The furthest hill, fuzzy in the distance, holding the promise of grandeur beyond it. There was something so familiar about the scene. Something that tugged at the bottom of her heart, waiting to be remembered.

The boots crunching on the rocks of the trail reached her long before he appeared around the bend in the trees.

Logan.

His steel grey eyes found her instantly as he crested the ridge, and he moved up the remaining trail to her, a leather satchel slung over his shoulder. Foregoing his overcoat, he was clad minimally in buckskin breeches, a dark waistcoat over a lawn shirt open at his neck, no cravat in sight. She watched him silently until he reached her, stopping in front of her, his eyes braced for her wrath.

Sienna looked past him and down the trail where Bridget disappeared. "Does everyone around me have ulterior motives?"

Logan followed her gaze, then shook his head. "Forgive Bridget—she didn't know I would be following you two." He let the satchel he carried slip from his shoulder and he set it on the ground beside his boots. "And she needed a break from the castle and all her responsibilities more than anyone. Hunter was glad to see her taking the walk with you. Plus, the look she gave me as we passed on the trail was all the scolding I needed."

"She doesn't approve of you kidnapping me and holding me hostage?"

He winced. "No, she didn't care for how you arrived here at Shadowmoor. Nor did Hunter. But as they can see you are not locked in a room against your will, they have promised to not interfere."

"Interfere with what?" Sienna's right eyebrow stretched high in suspicion.

"Interfere with the chance I am asking you to take, Sienna. Interfere with the week." He pointed with his thumb over his shoulder. "Bridget has threatened to saddle up two horses and take you back to London herself if she sees you distressed by me."

The thought was oddly comforting. She'd never had a true female friend. Only the Nowheres Boys when she was young if she was to believe the stories Robby told her on the way to Shadowmoor. And Nan Rose would never let her tax herself by becoming too friendly with the townsfolk in Sandfell. "Bridget seems utterly capable of that."

"She is."

Sienna nodded and her gaze moved from Logan to look out at the scenery. While her initial rage at him had tempered from when she'd first arrived at Shadowmoor, her anger still simmered just below the surface of her chest, threatening at any moment to explode again whenever she looked at Logan. His face—the face she loved—and the constant heat in his eyes when he looked at her made her forget everything.

And then she would remember. Remember the betrayal. What he did. And her anger would surge brutally through her veins.

A thousand daggers in her gut. Again and again.

She avoided his face and concentrated on the vista stretching out before them. If she didn't look at him, she wouldn't forget, and then she wouldn't have to remember. She needed benign thoughts, far away from Logan and what he had done—desperately needed them.

Her hand lifted to sweep the air in front of her. "This is magnificent—the perfect scene. Especially with the clouds dappling the sun. The casting shadows add such depth to the land. I wish I had my charcoals. Nan Rose had my things packed at Roselawn and we left just minutes after Robby arrived. She was remiss in packing them."

Logan leaned to his side to pick up the satchel he had set to the ground and held it up to her. "Actually, you do. I come bearing gifts."

Her eyes, but not her head shifted to him "Gifts will buy you no favors with me, Logan."

"No, but your happiness makes me happy, Sienna, and that is a favor to myself."

When she wouldn't take the bag from him, he set the leather satchel down and opened the top flap. He pulled free a rectangular mahogany box and flipped it in his hands. The deep grain of the wood shone in the sunlight, and as he turned the bottom of the box to rest on his hands she saw the fine lines of an orchid inlaid in white nacre on the top of the box.

"The lacquer on the top seals it so there are no seams with the inlay. It's completely flat and smooth." He stood straight, holding the box out to her. "Take it. It's yours. It would have already been in your room, but it was late and just arrived."

Her eyes wary on him, she stepped forward and wrapped her fingers along the edges of the box, taking it from him. Heavier than she anticipated, she balanced it on her forearm and then she flipped open the S latch that clasped the lid closed.

A gasp escaped her as she looked at the assortment of vine and compressed charcoal sticks, rubber erasers, and a thick stack of creamy vellum in the box. She couldn't hide the smile that spread on her face, not that she wanted to.

"You can use the top of the box to support the paper when you're drawing—that was important to have—but the whole thing should be light enough for you to carry anywhere," Logan said.

Her smile grew wider as she closed the cover and latched it, rubbing her thumb across the surface and tracing the inlaid orchid.

She couldn't be bought with gifts—but this…this was more than a gift and Logan knew it. This was peace. This was imagination. This was the fire within her.

"You could own the moon and the stars with that smile." His voice rumbled low, his words wrapping around her head and seeping into the crevices where she knew she could not defend against him.

Her eyes lifted to him. "Not fair."

"There were never any promises of fairness when you agreed to stay the week." A grin touched the corner of his mouth. "You should have bargained harder."

She nodded with her head to the rolling hills. "This spot, these charcoals, and I don't think you will see me the rest of the week."

"Then I will happily bring you food and carry you home when you fall asleep with blackened fingers."

She smiled, shaking her head at him.

Damn those crevices. Damn him.

Remember what he did.

Remember.

Logan motioned to the line of trees that held to the far crest of the ridge they stood on. "Come, there is a spot to sit."

She followed him across the grasses that sprouted up between the craggily rocks jutting out at her boots until he stopped in front of her and stepped to the side.

Perched along the crest of the hill sat a bench. A black, wrought iron bench with a lattice seat leading up to a back of intertwining scrolls reminiscent of butterflies courting. The outer edges of the soft lines were rusted, almost thinned away to breaking.

A bench she knew.

She staggered a step backward, her fingers struggling to hold onto the box in her palms, even as all feeling left her hands. Left her limbs. Left her body.

The box dropped to the ground.

The crash of it the last thing she heard before blackness overtook her.

~ ~ ~

"Are you sure this will work, Logan?" Sienna looked past him, her look creeping along the edge of the alley and then to the building across the street.

"We dress the part, no one will ask us anything, Sienny," Logan said. "We just say our father brought us and we lost him inside, so we looked outside for him. They won't even think on it."

Her fingers curled, clutching into themselves as she hopped from one foot to another—terrified and excited. She'd wanted to go into the building for so long. The only person she'd told about the place was Logan, and that was months ago when Miss Kitty had told her about the Royal Academy Summer Exhibition.

Sienna's drawings didn't have depth to them, and she needed to see what the world outside of London looked like. Except she'd never been out of the city, and even with the descriptions from the whores about what grand fields and rolling hills looked like, Sienna couldn't get it right. Miss Kitty had told her she needed to learn perspective, and Miss Kitty had been the one to teach her how to sketch with charcoals, so she knew what she talked about. Perspective was what Sienna needed, but she didn't know how to get it.

She had told Logan of this exhibition, and he had just nodded, running off like he didn't even care that she was desperate to see the art inside. But he'd also been secretive for months and then this morning he'd declared it her birthday, since they never knew when their birthdays actually were. Sometimes she had two or three in a year depending how Logan and Robby surprised her.

Logan took her hand, ready to cross the street when fast footsteps echoed down the alley behind them. "Wait—wait."

Logan dropped her hand and spun around.

Robby ran full speed at them, his hand waving, words flying fast. Robby always spoke fast, sometimes so fast she didn't understand him "Wait, Logan. I want to take her in. Why didn't ye tell me it was today? That it was open and this was it?" He looked at Logan's legs. "I was the one that found the trousers. I want to take her in."

"I'm already in the clothes, Robby," Logan said.

"But they're too small for ye."

"No, Robby. We're ready to go."

Robby pointed at the gap showing around Logan's ankles. "Just look at yer legs, they're too short and ye ain't got stockings."

Logan sighed. "Yes, but I don't want you to ruin this for her—do you even know how to act in there, Robby?"

"It's not like you do."

Robby bounced up and down, his legs never yielding springs. "Please, Logan, I just want to see inside, just let me go—let me go and I promise I won't knock nothin' down or nothin'."

Logan glanced at Sienna.

She looked at him with wide, pleading eyes.

Words she couldn't say in front of Robby pounded in desperation in her head. Please don't let him. Please. He'll ruin it. He can't be still. He'll ruin everything. Please, Logan, please.

Logan looked back to his little brother. "You're going to ruin everything, Robby."

"No, I won't. I swear it, Logan. I swear it. I'll be still. I can do it. I swear I can." He grabbed Logan's arm through the

rumpled overcoat he wore, tugging at him. "Please, Logan, please. You get to do everything and I don't get to do nothin'."

Logan sighed, his fingers running though his dark hair and mussing the carefully combed hairs he had set in place for the occasion. He'd even stolen a swipe of wax from her father's jar.

He was breaking. No. Please no.

She opened her mouth to protest just as Logan's hand flipped up in a wild swing. "Fine. You go in. But if you ruin this for Sienny I'm going to beat you, Robby."

Her heart sank, all her excited energy spinning into dread. This wasn't going to work. Not without Logan.

Robby jumped and the two of them moved deeper into the alley to a doorway they could partially hide in. Arms and legs flew as they changed clothes.

She watched them, glancing back over her shoulder at the exhibition hall again and again while biting her lip. She should have said something sooner. She knew Logan would get them in, but Robby—Robby was too quick to get bored, too quick to cause a fracas.

She needed this. She needed to get in there and study the paintings Miss Kitty told her about. If she didn't, she would never understand perspective and she would never get better. She needed this, and she needed it not ruined by Robby.

Logan and Robby came back to her, Robby almost skipping.

"Let's go, Sienny. Logan told me what to say." Robby grabbed Sienna's hand and started dragging her out of the alley. Bouncing in excitement, he tugged her around the horses and carriages as they cut across the street.

Sienna looked back over her shoulder, searching through the passing wagons and carriages until she found Logan.

He had settled himself on a bench in front of a milliner's shop. An odd bench, the metal on it scrolled along the back, almost is if two butterflies were dancing. Logan looked sad— sad deep in his grey eyes where he hid it. Hid it from Robby because he was always giving Robby everything and not keeping anything for himself. She wanted to push Robby down and run back to him. Run and dodge the traffic and make him come in with them.

She wanted Logan.

She wanted him to see this too. See it with her.

Robby pulled her hand, tugging her forward.

~ ~ ~

"Perspective."

Her eyes opened to slivers, the word on her lips.

Fingers stroked her hair, the gentle touch a tickle along her scalp that she never wanted to end. Her head was cradled by something soft. Soft but with a twitch. With a heartbeat. A lap?

She cracked her eyelids fully open, only to see the most beautiful man above her. His features so strong, so perfectly sculpted that Michelangelo couldn't have crafted a finer form.

Her husband.

Her husband held her head in his lap. His fingers in her hair. And for one fleeting moment, the world was perfect.

He looked down at her, his eyes concerned, but not frantic. "You fainted again."

"I seem to be doing that as of late." She shifted and a rock jabbed into her lower back just above her hipbone. The stab of pain was enough to spark her into action, to leave that moment of perfection behind as the memory of the current state of affairs between her and Logan flooded her mind. She sat up, scooting away from him even though it made her head swirl. "And you said you wouldn't touch me."

He shrugged, not the slightest bit apologetic. "I thought my leg a better pillow than the rocky soil."

She eyed him, unable to argue the point as her head still felt as though it was no longer tethered to her body.

"Perspective."

"What?" She blinked, confused.

"You said the word perspective just before your eyes opened." Though his face stayed nonchalant, there was a spark in his steel grey eyes, a spark that looked almost like hope.

She nodded, still trying to right her head. "I did, didn't I?" There was something she was supposed to remember. Something she had just grasped onto.

What was it?

She looked around her and spied the wrought iron bench. She gasped. "The bench, I remember it."

"You do?"

She moved to get to her knees, but Logan was to his feet in an instant, lifting her to standing. He kept a hand on the small of her back as she walked over with jelly legs to the bench.

But she didn't want to sit. She couldn't.

She reached out to touch the iron along the top scroll of the back, her fingers dragging softly along the rough, rusty edge.

"I remember you sitting on it. Except you were so much smaller. I was small." She looked up at him. "When you brought me to the Royal Academy Summer Exhibition so I could learn about perspective. There was a Miss...a Miss Kitty? She said I needed to learn perspective. And you were to sneak us in, except Robby showed up and made you change clothes so he could go in with me instead. I didn't want him to. I wanted you."

Logan nodded, a flash of sadness crossing his grey eyes.

"What happened?"

His brows lifted. "To the bench?"

"To us? Did Robby and I get in? I woke up before I remembered what happened—the last thing I saw was you on the bench." Her palm patted the top scroll. "This bench."

Logan's lips pursed for a long moment. He wasn't going to tell her.

But then he nodded. "You both got in and were in the building for ten minutes before Robby knocked over a statue of Mercury."

A chuckle bubbled up her throat. She could hold no ill will toward Robby when one, she couldn't remember how horrified she must have been, and two, one way or another, she'd obviously learned how to sketch with perspective throughout the years.

She met Logan's eyes. "He was gangly at that age, wasn't he?"

A hesitant smile lifted the corner of his mouth. "He was."

She motioned to the bench with her head. "Why is the bench here?"

"I bought it and brought it here when I discovered this spot a few years ago. It was still sitting in front of that milliner's shop." He reached out, setting his hand along the black iron scroll, the tips of his fingers almost touching hers. "I didn't come up to Shadowmoor at all for a long time. Not but once a year and for a day or two at most. And then I was held here by storms one year, so I took some time to explore the lands and I found this spot. It looked just like the oil painting by John Constable that you loved from the exhibition. The way the air moved into the lands." His free hand swept outward to the view.

Sienna's look followed to where his fingers pointed. "This is what the painting I was so desperate to see looks like?"

"To my eye. We got into another exhibition again six months later once there was a new guard hired there that watched the door. You sat and looked at that one oil—*Dedham Vale Evening*—for three hours. So it's imprinted into my mind."

A sad smile, full of melancholy, crossed his lips. "When I stumbled upon this ridge, the view mirrored it so, that all I could think of up here was you. I worked so hard in those days not to think of you constantly. You'd been dead for seven years at that point. But up here, I was powerless against it. It crushed me so—so much so that I couldn't leave this very spot on my own. Hunter had to drag me down the ridge in the middle of the night."

His palm patted the top of the bench. "So I bought the bench and had it transported and set here in this spot." His eyes lifted, looking around them. "It is the one place that I love in this land."

Her chest contracted, his pain sending ice through her bones. "Logan..."

His steel grey eyes pinned her. "You have always been my heart, Sienna. Always."

The vehemence in his eyes, the strain of muscles along his neck, his jaw flexing—he looked as though he wanted to grab her and crush her to him and was only barely holding himself back.

With a jerk, he brusquely stepped away, clearing his throat. He moved to pick up the box of charcoals, his strong fingers brushing off dust as he set it on the bench. "I will leave you to your sketching. The box survived the drop with but a small scratch on the bottom."

Without another word, his limbs stiff, he turned and walked down the side of the ridge.

She didn't move for long minutes after he left. She could only stare at the space he vacated.

This man had loved her her entire life.

He had loved her—he had told her that and she had felt that.

But she had no idea.

No idea as to the depths in which this man had always loved her.

When she could finally move again, she sank to the bench and her fingers found their way to open the box and pick up charcoal and a sheet of vellum.

Without thought, her thumb and forefinger immediately set to create an outline.

But not of the rolling hills. Not of the trees. Not of the clouds streaming long against the water-blue sky.

No, this vista held nothing against the only thing her fingers could create.

The only thing her fingers would allow her to create.

The outline of her husband's exceedingly handsome jaw.

{ CHAPTER 18 }

Sienna stood before the tall bookcase, her eyes glazed over as she tried again to read the titles of the leather-bound tomes in front of her under the glow of lit sconces positioned symmetrically along the wall.

She had come into the Shadowmoor library to find something to read. Something to take her mind off her husband—for he had already monopolized all of her thoughts that day.

Lifting her right hand, she traced with her forefinger the gold embossed words on the maroon leather of the book in front of her. If she pointed at each word specifically, maybe she could make her mind concentrate long enough to actually read the words.

Her gaze landed on the darkened color of her forefinger. The charcoal stain still tinged her skin from the day she'd just spent sketching.

She exhaled a long sigh. Sheet after sheet of vellum on the top of that ridge, and there had been only one thing could she draw. Logan's eyes. Logan's ear. Logan's chin. Logan's neck. Logan's torso.

Logan. Logan. Logan.

She'd wasted far too much of that precious vellum on her husband today.

But every time she had attempted to draw the panorama before her, she could only sit, staring at it, unable to start. And then her fingers would go rogue with a mind of their own and before she knew it, she'd be sketching some nuance of her husband's body again.

The door opened behind her, making her jump. Every ancient door in this castle was heavy, creaking with the weight of hundreds of years every time they moved. Her fingers snapped down to her stomach, curling into her peach muslin dress as if she needed to hide the evidence of what she had spent the day doing.

"Sienna—here you are." Logan closed the grinding door behind him. "You disappeared so quickly after dinner that I was worried when I didn't find you in your chambers."

She didn't turn around to him, her breath lodged in her chest as his footsteps on the wide-planked wooden floor echoed about the stone walls.

Her breath held until words she had no intention of ever saying escaped her mouth in the softest whisper.

"Did you kill her?"

Dammit. She hadn't meant to say the words—hadn't been able to.

She'd been refusing to speak the question out loud, paralyzed by the fear that Logan would validate everything she knew. Everything her father had told her.

She didn't want it to be true, even though she knew it was. Logan would have defended himself against it long ago if it was a lie.

"Sienna?" Logan's deep voice held caution, low and gentle as though he didn't want to frighten her.

There was no going back.

She had finally spoken the question—sent it into the air between them and she couldn't stop now.

Slowly, she turned around to face him, though she couldn't lift her eyes to meet his. She could only focus on his chest, staring at the deep V of the cut where his dark waistcoat overlapped in front of his white shirt.

"Did you kill her, Logan?" Her voice shook, the heft of the question sending a tremble she couldn't control through her body.

He didn't answer. But she could see his body tense, his muscles tighten under his lawn shirt, his shoulders pulling back.

Her gaze crept upward. Neck. Chin. Mouth. Nose.

His silver grey eyes. Eyes that reached into her soul every time he looked at her.

The second her eyes met his, he opened his mouth. "Yes."

Yes?

A pain shot through her stomach, hitting her with such force she doubled over, leaning back against the bookcase as her arms clenched to her belly.

She knew the answer. She knew he wouldn't deny it.

But to hear him actually admit to it. To admit it to her directly.

She gasped breath after breath, trying to force air into her lungs when her lungs only refused the air. Every gasp only made the next one harsher—air not reaching past her throat.

Choking—she was choking on her own air. On her own body.

A hand splayed wide on her back and Logan's boots appeared under her face.

A hand she didn't want—couldn't want.

Not now. Not now that it was no longer a possibility that it had all been a fabrication by her father. Not until that moment did she realize how desperately she wanted to believe it had all been a lie concocted to tear her away from Logan. How she'd lied to herself for weeks on it. How she'd refused to accept it.

No. No. No.

There had to be some explanation. She didn't understand something. Logan loved her—she knew that down to her bones. He couldn't have done it. He had to explain.

She latched onto a breath and forced it as hard as she could down her throat. Her lungs finally broke free, expanding with the breath.

Two more gulps of air and she was able to straighten slightly—enough to crane her neck to look up at him, her eyes skewering him. "You lied about it, Logan. You gave it to her, didn't you? Too much laudanum you told me—but you never said you were there. You never said…"

Her voice cut off, the horror of it collapsing her throat. She swallowed hard, standing straighter as she jumped away from him. Away from his hand on her back. Her brow furrowed as her eyes narrowed at him. "Did you always lie about it, Logan? My whole life? Or did you tell me what you did and I can't remember?"

"I always lied about it, Sienna." The stoicism on his face struck her. Did he not care? Not care at all that he had murdered her mother?

"You…you always lied about it?" Her arms retightened around her middle, protecting herself from the flat tone in his voice. "No. It had to have been an accident. It had to have been. Tell me it was. Why aren't you defending yourself, Logan?"

He shook his head, his face an immovable mask. "I cannot. I cannot defend my actions." His head flickered back and forth in a wince. "Your mother always saw it in me, and she told me it to my face. 'Death is about you, boy,' she said. And she was right, Sienna. She was right."

"But…but how could you keep this from me?" She took a step toward him, her voice rising. "You said you would remember for both of us. Remember everything for me. But your memories were a lie. You killed her, Logan. You killed my mother. And you never told me. Never admitted to it. You took her away from me."

He nodded, his emotionless mask securely back in place. "I did. I loved you too much to tell you the truth, Sienna."

She stared at him, his revelation reverberating through her body and setting her nerves on fire. Her lip curled. "Or not enough."

She ran around him, her muscles twinging as she yanked the heavy ancient door open. She escaped from the library, running up to her chambers.

He didn't follow.

~ ~ ~

He had left her alone for two days.

No gifts. No trying to catch her in the hallway. No surprise appearances at the top of the ridge.

Nor was he present at any of the meals.

Sienna was fine with it.

In her first few days at Shadowmoor, she had started to hope. Hope that it was all a lie. Hope that she had it wrong. That her husband hadn't betrayed her years ago, then lied about it their entire lives together.

But he had.

And she could tell herself no more lies on the matter. She could allow herself no more hope.

No matter how much she loved him.

Now she just needed to uphold the agreement. Two more days, and she could leave this place forever. Leave him forever.

Sienna looked out across the countryside, her fingers sending swoops of thin lines of charcoal to create the furthest hill away. Muted, fuzzy, so far from her eye she could barely see it, except for the unusual deep green it possessed—so very different than the slopes closer to her.

Footsteps crunched up the rocky trail. But they weren't heavy and painfully even as Logan's steps were—as they needed to be because of his foot. No, these steps were light, springy.

She watched the path, forcing a smile onto her face as Bridget appeared around the line of trees that flanked the pathway.

Several more quick steps, and Bridget's face lit up when she finally spied Sienna. She walked directly to her, stopping in front of her. A quick glance at the sketch on the vellum, and her gaze lifted to Sienna's face. "That, my dear, is one strained smile you just gave me." She moved to sit next to Sienna on the bench. "Is it because the hills aren't doing what you want them to do, or is it another matter entirely?"

Sienna gave her a look out of the corner of her eye.

Bridget chuckled. "So it is the other matter. I imagine it's the same reason Logan has been absent from anything and everything the past two days?"

Sienna shrugged. "I imagine."

Bridget patted her forearm. "Surely, though, it is something that can be mended?"

For a long breath Sienna looked straight ahead, far off into the distance. She slowly shook her head. "It cannot be fixed."

"I understand." Bridget's hand lifted from her arm and she looked out at the vista for a long moment. Her head tilted to the side. "Do you know that I see things all the time that cannot be fixed? But then they are. It is a surprise every time."

Sienna glanced at her. "With your patients?"

"Yes. There was one in particular, years ago, during the war on the continent." Bridget leaned back against the bench, her hands settling in her lap as she looked to Sienna. "I was there, helping my father hobble back together these men that had lost arms and legs and faces. It was heartbreaking every day. But there was one patient that was seared into my memory."

"Unfixable?"

"To say the least." A half-smile came to Bridget's face as she nodded. "It was in Spain, in a little village. We only had ten patients, but all of them were far too gravely injured to travel to the main hospital by the coast. So they found an abandoned traveler's inn and set us all in there. We were there for a month. My father saved each and every one of those soldiers' lives with his skill. But there was this one."

She paused, looking out to the rolling landscape. "He was under bandages from head to toe, it seemed. There were so many blade wounds on his body. Too many to count. Too many for him to survive the battlefield, but he did. He lost part of his foot to a bullet shattering his heel. His thigh was fractured. Left arm broken. Wounds on his scalp that swelled and sent him into madness time and again."

"I helped my father set all of his bones, and the man didn't scream, didn't even make a whimper."

Sienna cringed. "Men usually scream when their bones are set?"

"Absolutely—a bit of leather between the teeth and a few swallows of brandy can help, but there are still whimpers." Bridget glanced at Sienna, her green eyes haunted by memories Sienna couldn't even imagine. Bridget looked back out to the sloping hills. "At first, I did the minimum I needed to with that soldier. It sounds harsh, but I thought he was so far gone it wouldn't matter—and there was so little time to attend to all the wounds of all the men. So I changed his bandages, and I changed them quick."

"But after a week it was evident that his body was going to heal itself. He passed by a few days without a raging fever, so I started to tend to him better. That was when he started talking to me. His face was always covered with bandages because of the wounds and swelling. One of the worst I have ever seen—his broken face was bruised and swollen, his eyes were so enflamed he could barely open his eyelids. He was quite a mess. So all I could look at were these two lips peeking out of the white cloth."

"What did he talk about?"

"He talked about dying. About wanting to die and how his body wouldn't let him. He thought it terribly unfair.

Especially as he truly believed it was what he deserved for his sins."

"How awful."

"Exactly. He was unfixable, both in body and mind. But by the third day of his rantings, I finally figured out why he wanted death so badly. He had just lost his wife and quite simply, he wanted to die because she did."

Sienna blinked, her lips pulling inward.

"He kept talking of her, telling me all about her, all the while willing his body to give up. A body that refused to give in. So I started to talk to him. It took days, but I finally convinced him that if his wife's spirit was as beautiful as he said, then he would be failing her memory by giving up on life. That she wouldn't want him to follow her into death." Bridget shook her head, her eyes glazing over. "So he lived—against all odds—against a broken body. He lived to pay tribute to her. It was a heart-wrenching thing to witness. He was broken beyond all measure, yet he mended. The unfixable fixed."

Sienna let a long exhale breach her lips, her words breathless. "I know the man, don't I?"

Bridget smiled, her hand moving to clutch Sienna's forearm again and she squeezed it. "It was Logan—though I didn't know who he was then, nor how our lives would entwine again as they did years after the war. But I forever held his story close to my heart, because I always thought how lucky you two were to find each other. Even if it was for a short amount of time. Yours was the sort of love poets write about, dreamers dream about. And you had that."

"This isn't the same thing, Bridget. There are some things love cannot fix."

Bridget's right cheek lifted in a smile. "Actually, it can be quite the same thing, if you decide for it. I do think this can be the mending of the impossible."

Sienna's head swung back and forth, her fingers snapping the charcoal in her hand. "There is too much that cannot be erased."

Bridget squeezed her arm, then released it as she shrugged. "Maybe you don't need to erase anything. Maybe you just need to forgive and move on. Maybe that is all it takes."

"You don't know what I need to forgive—unless he told you?"

She shook her head. "Logan didn't tell me anything—hasn't told me a thing about what has transpired between you two. Clearly it is a grievous chasm that needs to be bridged. But as much as I despise his actions in kidnapping you and bringing you here, I do come down on the side of love above everything else."

Bridget paused, taking the sheet of vellum balanced on the box and looking at the sketch of the rolling landscape for a long moment. "You capture the land so well—this skill is in your soul, isn't it?"

Sienna shrugged.

Bridget set the vellum down onto the box on Sienna's lap, then her green eyes pinned her. "You are Logan's wife, you know his spirit better than anyone. But I think you should also know what has happened in the years you were missing."

"What?"

"I start with the fact that Logan saved my life. He saved Hunter. We would not have our life, our children, as we do now without him. He's saved countless other men—his guards at the Revelry's Tempest. Whether it has been saving them from bullets or their own demons, he's been a steadfast beacon to countless people that had nothing to hope for, nothing to live for. That was how he honored your spirit, Sienna. He did it by saving others, never setting himself and his own interests first."

"You're trying to convince me he's a good man?"

"I don't think I need to convince you of that." Bridget stood abruptly from the bench, looking down at Sienna. "But what I would like to see, for once, is for him to reach for happiness of his own and actually get it. Get it as he has helped so many others around him achieve it."

Bridget pointed over her shoulder to the trail, chuckling to herself. "I apologize if that sounded like a sermon. Why I actually came up here to find you was I wanted to let you know Hunter is taking me to the village of Peddington. It is a half-day's ride, and we'll be leaving when I get back down to the castle. I make it a point to get there every month, which helps combat the traveling apothecary that preys upon the town, doing more harm than good every time he comes through. The children will stay here with their nanny and we won't be back for a day or two, depending on how many patients I need to see there. I did not want to miss you if you should be gone when we return."

Sienna nodded. "Thank you for telling me—telling me everything." She lifted her box of charcoals off her lap and set them to the bench, then stood. "If I am gone by the time you arrive back, I do promise to write."

"I hope that is not the outcome, but if it is, do count upon me as a friend for life." Bridget pulled her into a hug.

Sienna had never been hugged by a female friend before and was discombobulated for a moment at how comforting the bond was. She managed to produce a true smile for Bridget. "Thank you."

Bridget nodded, and then moved her way down the path, her footsteps springing just as lightly as they had on the way up.

For long minutes, Sienna held her breath, half expecting Logan to appear after Bridget's disappearance.

He didn't.

And she wasn't sure if she was relieved or disheartened at the fact.

{ CHAPTER 19 }

"I've been here before." Her fork paused halfway to her mouth, Sienna's eyes went wide. She looked at the gaping hearth at the far end of the table from her, scenes flashing in her mind.

Even though they had eaten in that cavernous stone hall every evening with Hunter and Bridget, Sienna had never taken the time to truly look about her. She'd been too preoccupied with her anger at Logan, and then with the conversations with Bridget and Hunter.

But since Logan had sat down across the table from her a half hour ago—sans his overcoat and clearing the staff from the room as he had entered—Sienna had spent the entire meal in silence, looking everywhere but at her husband.

She wasn't ready to face him.

Not yet.

Maybe not ever.

Sensing it, Logan had remained silent as well. Though his agreeable silence didn't stop his steel grey eyes from scrutinizing her every movement.

She could have simply left the dining hall, but she was hungry after hiding up along the ridge all day and she didn't want to cause a commotion by having her meal delivered to her rooms when she was perfectly capable of eating in silence.

So instead, she'd passed away the minutes at the table, eating quickly while pointedly avoiding direct eye contact.

She watched the fire in the enormous curved fireplace, its low flames flicking high, attempting to stretch up into the chimney. Her gaze moved onto the wide ancient tapestries lining the coolness of the thick cut grey limestone wall across from her. Unicorns, maidens frolicking in the flowers, epic clashes of steel and horses—all of the scenes held the fantastical romanticism of the Middle Ages.

Far above Logan's head, her look had drifted to the circular stained glass window that reflected the light from the main wrought iron chandelier hanging high in the room. A heavy rain had started, a sheet of it slashing so viciously at the window it made her jump in her seat.

Her heart had started to thunder, her mind whirling.

"I've been here before." Sienna repeated the words, her fork clattering to her plate of roasted grouse.

Her head whipped around in a circle, her look frantic at her surroundings in the great hall. Her hands slammed onto the table, making her plate bounce. "This—this table wasn't here—it was over there." She pointed to the opposite end of the hall. "And it was a big table. Thick and heavy. Not this one. One for a lot of people. Old. Ancient."

Her gaze flew back to the hearth. "And there was a raging fire in there. Raging and I thought it would burn me with the popping from the wet wood."

She looked at Logan. He had frozen on the opposite side of the table, concern evident in his eyes. "Am I right? Do I remember this?"

His eyes narrowed at her and he gave a slight incline of his head. "What else?"

Pushing her chair back from the table, she stood, stumbling over to the hearth, needing to be in the spot where she could feel her skin singeing. "It…it was raining—a torrential rain just like now—and we were soaked. We were in the rain, and then in here." She pointed up. "And the rain slashed at that window above me, and I kept looking up, scared it would shatter and the glass would land on me."

Pain shot through her and her hand lifted to her breastbone, fingernails curling into her bare skin above the bodice of her dress. "And it was horrible—why—what was it—it's in my chest—and it was horrible—my chest squeezing the breath out of me."

Gulping air, she closed her eyes, the scene from years ago flashing in her mind.

Her eyes popped open and she found Logan.

He sat still at the table, watching her closely, his face not betraying what he knew of the event.

"And you. Oh hell, Logan." Her voice cracked as her eyes closed against the memory. "We were soaked, chilled to the bone and it was freezing and you—you were groveling. There was a man, and he looked like you except older and he told you to get to your knees."

She gasped, the pain in her chest exploding, sending furious shards to cut her insides to shreds. "And I didn't want you to. I wasn't worth it. We could go back—back to London. I wasn't worth it. And I wanted you to stand, I wanted to leave, but then you fell to your knees."

Her eyes flew open and she looked at her husband. He had stood from the table and moved toward her, stopping two arm lengths away.

"That was your brother—your half-brother, the duke—and he, he hated you—hated me—and he made you grovel—grovel for the scraps he was to give us—grovel for your commission in the army." Her words tumbled, furious. "You threatened to tell every one of his associates in society about how he cast out and ruined your mother and you and Robby. But still he demanded you sink—sink to the floor."

Her voice trailed as her jaw dropped. The agony in Logan's steel grey eyes told her this was true. Was real.

She choked back a sob. "He made you drop to your knees, Logan, and I wanted to kill him and you wouldn't let me. I had a knife in my hand and you grabbed my wrist and stopped me."

He nodded, his face tortured.

"And in the next instant you were sinking. Sinking to the ground. To your knees."

Logan flinched, but his voice was steady against the fury in her words. "For as much as we needed a way out, I would have given anything in that moment to keep us safe from Bournestein. To give us a way out. And my knees on this floor were our way out, Sienna. I needed that commission."

She shook her head, the fury she'd felt in that moment years ago still coursing through her. "You didn't need to do it, Logan."

"It wasn't a choice. We didn't have anything, Sienna. No money. No way out. And winter was descending."

"Why…" Her head shook for a moment, and she froze, her eyes going wide as she stared at him. "No way out because of my father—because of Robby—he told him." Her hands went to her head, clutching the sides of it as it rattled with a thousand stones rolling about in her skull. "Robby told him where the money was hidden. The money we were going to escape with. Father came into your room and cut it out of the floor with an ax, and Robby—he—he dragged me away, tossed me over his shoulder. And he was drunk and he shoved me into my room…and…"

She had to close her eyes against the fear in Logan's eyes—the fear she would remember everything.

She gasped a trembling breath. "And he shoved me into the room and he was so mad—furious—that we were going to leave—leave without him—and we weren't but he wouldn't listen and he…he…he said he was the one that deserved me…he…" She hiccupped a gasp.

"He tore your dress and you fought him." Logan's anguished voice echoed against the stone walls around them. "He thought we were leaving him behind and he was out of his mind."

She opened her eyes to him. "But I screamed and I hit him over the head with the pitcher and you came—you kicked in the door and your face was bloody and you ripped him off of me."

He nodded. "And we left. We ran out of there that night with your torn dress and my bloodied face and broken ribs. And we ran. We ran as far and as fast as we could."

"But this." Her hand swept around her. "This didn't need to happen, Logan. You didn't need to break, didn't need to drop to your knees. Not before that hideous man that called you a bastard."

Logan's chest lifted in a deep breath. His words came with his exhale, soft. "We had nothing, Sienna. We sold the horse I stole to leave London and then we had nothing. We had nowhere to go. I had no way to feed you other than what I could steal—and that was the one thing I swore I would never do again once we escaped Bournestein—never steal, lie or cheat again. I swore it to you. So something had to give, Sienna, and fighting was the only thing I was good at."

Her lips parted, her words deflated. "So you needed the commission. We needed it."

"I did. I needed it more than anything. Not giving you the life you deserved would have broken me, Sienna. Broken me a thousand-times over." His forefinger flipped out to point at the floor by her feet. "But this—my knees on this floor—this never broke me—it never could, because I would have done anything for you, Sienna."

He took three steps toward her, stopping in front of her, a foot away, his breath heavy with his words. "I still would. Anything."

"Anything?" The word hiccupped, stuck in her throat.

He nodded, his grey eyes piercing her.

"Including letting me go?"

His jaw clenched, but he forced his head up and then down.

"What if I don't want to be let go, Logan?"

His grey eyes widened, his jaw dropping as he drew in a sharp breath.

Her fingers at her sides twitched. She couldn't wait for him to break his vow not to touch her—she didn't want him to break his vow.

It was who he was to his core and she never wanted that to change in him. He made a vow, he kept it. And he made a vow to her long ago that she was his world—his always. He'd never broken that vow. Everything he'd ever done, he'd done for her—even without her memories, that one fact burned undeniably clear in her mind.

A fact she couldn't deny. Couldn't forget.

And she couldn't refuse any longer how much her body needed him. How much her soul needed him.

For good or bad, she was his. No matter the past. No matter what her mind was telling her. She was his—complications be damned.

She pounced forward, her arms wrapping about his neck, her fingers deep into his hair as she lifted herself to kiss him.

He reveled in her hungry lips for a moment before jerking his head away, his voice gravel. "Does this mean I can touch you, Sienna?"

A breathless chuckle left her. "If you don't I think I might gut you."

His laugh was cut off by his lips crashing down onto her, crushing her with purpose and promise, his arms wrapping around her as he backed her into the stone wall behind her.

The jagged edges of the ancient stone cut into her shoulder blades, but all she could feel was Logan's body against hers, hot and heaving, his hard muscles breaching their clothing to envelope her.

Her right leg lifted, her calf sliding up his thigh and backside before she hooked her leg along his hip.

He chuckled into her mouth, the laughter heating her from inside out. "Minx."

"Desperate, minx." Her breathless words sent another rumble upward from deep in his chest.

Dipping from her lips, his mouth attacked her neck, her collarbone, tasting her as though she was his last supper. His hand dropped, wrapping around her left thigh and he yanked her up, straddling her legs fully around his waist.

His fingers unsatisfied, he nudged her dress upward along her legs, diving under the fabric to trace along her stocking, past the ribbon about her thigh, and searching until he found the core of her.

His fingers delved forth, ripping the first shocks of pleasure into her body. His thumb found her nubbin, mastering it as his lips moved up her neck to the tender spot behind her ear.

She clasped her hands behind his neck, holding on for the wanton currents already racking her body at his touch.

He slipped his forefinger into her, exploring, readying her and then dragging out her slickness to her folds, swirling. It sent her over an edge she only thought she was nearing and her body tightened, jerking as the first brutal surges rolled from her core to her limbs. Rush after rush engulfed her, exploding and sending her gasping for air as he drew his fingers away.

Tremors wrenched her body and he spun them away from the wall, carrying her to the table and setting her backside on the edge. In one fell swoop with his forearm, he shoved all the plates to the far end of the table, several clattering to the floor.

In a blinding haze, her trembling fingers untangled from his neck, moving down to work the buttons on his trousers. His cock surged free, searching for her.

But a half smile curled his lips.

Not yet, it meant. He was going to go slow. Take his time. Relish her body.

She hated it.

She loved it.

Her skirts still high above her hips, her legs went tight around his waist, trying to pull him inward into her.

He held hard against her insistence.

"You're open and trusting me, Sienna." His words were low and thick, carnal honey in her veins. "But I want more."

His hand went to her belly, pressing her backward, lying her down long on top of the table until she was flat on her back. Her fingers couldn't reach him here, couldn't grasp his cock in her hands and caress him so hard he had no choice but to plunge into her.

No. He wanted more.

His fingers moved upward, slipping under the top of her bodice, stays and chemise, tugging them down. Buttons popped as he freed her breasts to the air, to him.

His steel grey eyes ravenous on her breasts, her nipples hardened under his gaze, desperate for him to take her into his mouth.

He leaned forward, the tip of his cock playing at her entrance as his mouth descended on her breasts. His hands trailed along her arms, taking her wrists and setting them high above her head. Smiling, he looked up at her from the breast he was feasting on. "So you don't entice me into going fast."

His attention went back to her left breast, his teeth capturing her nipple and teasing it between the sharp edges.

Edging to the borderline of pain, it sent wicked spikes of pleasure shooting down to her core.

He switched to her right breast, his tongue moving in gentle swirls about her peak. Just when he had lulled her nipple into stretching high for him, he nipped it. The shock of it sent her gasping, arching from the table.

She twisted her hands to free them and grab him, only to find he had clasped both of her wrists to the table with his left hand, freeing his right hand to move down her body.

His fingers dove down along the inside of her right thigh, caressing, tickling the skin with the lightest wanton touch. She sucked in a breath, her back arching even higher.

Damn him for knowing that spot. Damn him for using that spot.

He chuckled, his breath warming her slick nipple.

"Higher, Sienna?"

"Higher." The word escaped so cracked, she wasn't sure it made a sound.

He swirled his fingers along her skin, trailing only a touch closer to her folds.

"Higher."

His hand moved upward.

"Higher, dammit."

He chuckled again, looking up at her, his lips soft with the juice on her skin. "I just needed to hear you swear. I know you're going to hurt me now."

His fingers shifted up along her body in that moment, his thumb diving down the center of her folds just as his engorged member breached her, filling her to the hilt in one long stroke.

She didn't think her body could take more tortured pleasure. She was wrong.

He kept her arms clasped above her head, her breasts high to him, her body writhing under him. Every stroke he would end with a slash against her nubbin. Frenzy. Her body flew into nothing but a frenzy, her legs clasping him as tight as she could to her body.

Withdraw. Plunge. Swirl. Lick.

"Hell, Logan." *Blasted man.* She wanted him coming with her. Needed him coming with her.

There was only one thing to do.

She opened her blurry eyes, finding his steel grey irises and locking onto them. Her voice dipped guttural. "Go deep, Logan. Go so blasted deep you can't find yourself."

She licked her lips. "Deep into me. Hard. Pounding into me. Ripping into me."

His control snapped and a growl tore through his chest. He released her wrists, his hands whipping to her hips to clench her in place.

He tore into her, grinding, losing himself in her body. Again and again. So deep, so rock hard, she couldn't tell where her body ended and his started.

It built in his chest, his eyes, the roar that catapulted him over the edge, taking her with him.

Their bodies jolted against each other, his cock expanding with everything he was. Her body greedy, ripping every wave from him and making it her own.

She kept her eyes on his, locked, never letting go.

Never letting go again.

He collapsed on her, and for one delicious moment, the full weight of him was on her, their trembling bodies heaving against each other. He wedged a hand under her lower back and flipped them, splaying her on top of him. It took long minutes before their gasps quelled, their rippled breathing moved halfway to normal.

An inordinate amount of time passed before Sienna realized that they were on the dining table. That servants were around. That they still had most of their clothes intact.

Her head popped up from the nest she had created along the V of his waistcoat. She looked around the room. Rain still slashed at the window above. The doors were closed. No servants peeking in on them. At least not at the moment.

Logan's hand lifted, curling an errant lock of hair away from her forehead. His grey eyes pinned her, solemn. "Sienna, your mother."

Her hand whipped up, her fingers on his lips. "No. Not now, Logan. That…" She closed her eyes as a long exhale left her. "I still need time."

Silent, he nodded, sitting up and wrapping her in his arms, tucking her head under his chin.

She settled in.

"Do I get to carry you upstairs?" His voice was oddly rough.

She nodded into his lawn shirt. "I have been curious what your rooms look like."

"They're in the opposite tower from yours, and they are not nearly as warm or as pretty as yours."

She wedged her head to look up at him. "Why so far away?"

He shrugged. "I couldn't trust myself to be near to you in the middle of the night. And the cold helps."

With a chuckle, she wrapped her arms around him, squeezing his chest. "Then you best figure out a way to keep me warm."

"That, I can do, Sienna."

{ CHAPTER 20 }

Logan had hoped, but wasn't positive Sienna would come with him on the ride, but she sat on her white speckled mare next to him, her focus straight ahead on the lane that separated the river from the forest.

Early this morning in his bed, she'd stirred in his arms and he'd wanted nothing more than for her to fall asleep again. Fall asleep where she was still in is arms. Still his to hold.

For he knew once her eyes opened and her mind straightened, she would push away.

Push away from him.

For all that their bodies reconciled last night, he knew she was still holding back. Her head couldn't fully forgive him, even if her body could.

He just wondered where her heart stood on the matter.

He wanted his wife back. All of her.

He glanced at her, the deep blue riding habit fitted tight to her torso, her skirts long on the horse, and her red-blond hair was pulled back, though hanging free from under her crisp blue bonnet. Her blue eyes were slightly squinted and a deep-set frown dragged her face downward.

She was struggling, desperately trying to remember more. She had been since last night, tossing and turning in his arms for hours, even in her sleep. He couldn't fault her for it—to be doled out snippets of memories without the full context of them had to be exasperating, in the least.

Even with last night, even with the way she'd screamed under him, shuddered beneath his touch, Sienna had made no promises to stay past this last day at Shadowmoor.

Nor did he demand promises. He couldn't. He knew their bodies meeting had never been a problem—their bodies meeting was fire almost too hard to control.

But forgiveness—that he couldn't demand from her. Couldn't even bring himself to ask of her.

As she stirred in his arms, he'd had to hold himself back from shaking her. Shaking free all the memories from that blasted mind of hers.

If only she could remember.

He wanted—needed her to remember everything. If she did—maybe—maybe there would be a chance of absolution.

But on the flip of the same token, he never wanted her to remember everything—never wanted her to have to feel the pain of the memories.

He swallowed the lump in his throat, looking away from Sienna's frown to the swaying of the tree branches along the trail. If she didn't remember, he'd already decided he would never force the past upon her, as much as he needed it for himself. Once spoken, the damage the past would do to her would be irrevocable.

And he wouldn't do that to her. No matter what.

He stared ahead on the trail, the morning sun dappling the dirt path through the quaking leaves of the woods to their right.

One day left.

"Where are we headed?"

Her words cut into the soft cacophony of the forest—birds chirping and busy in flight, trees rustling in the breeze, squirrels in mad chases leaping from branch to branch.

He looked at her. The frown had eased from her face. "A bridge that crosses this river. It's not too far ahead."

She chuckled. "A bridge? Why would that be our destination?"

"It is an interesting sight to see, that is all."

"Ah," she said, nodding as her eyebrows lifted in confusion.

"It's interesting because it's the whole reason I agreed to take on the title."

"A bridge was your reason for not letting the duchy rot?" She craned her neck to look around the upcoming bend. "This must be one fantastical bridge ahead."

He chuckled. "It wasn't, at least when I took on the title, it wasn't."

"No?"

"No. Do you remember when I said there are lucrative travel routes through my lands?"

She nodded. "Yes."

He pointed forward on the path. "This bridge is on the edge of my estate and in the path of the most direct route from the seaport at Alnmouth to Yorkshire and then London. A ferry has operated here for ages, but ferries can take time, and there wasn't always a ferryman around. Not to forget it was dangerous to cross the river after heavy rains. It adds a day, at the least, of travel to get to the next closest bridge." He adjusted the straps of the leather reins around his palm. "My last half-brother refused to finish the building of the bridge because he knew that trade along his lands would explode to annoying proportions."

"Why annoying?"

"There are plenty of honest traders making way through here, but this is also a favorite route of smugglers. He knew there'd be even more so if the bridge were in place and he didn't want to have to deal with them."

"Smugglers?" Her eyes flashed understanding. "Ah, hence the lucrative travel routes you spoke of." Her head tilted to the side as confusion took over her face. "Why would you allow that? Why did you finish the bridge?"

"It was part of the deal I made."

"A deal with who?" Her blue eyes went to slits.

"With Bournestein."

"You made a deal with my father?" Her voice nearly screeched.

He lifted his hand to calm her. "I avoided it for as long as I could. After my last half-brother died, I didn't acknowledge the title for two years. I told you I planned to never take it on. But then I had to make the deal—my part of the bargain was I take on the title and finish the bridge. Your father needed the route for his smuggling partners."

Sienna's face twisted in disgust. "And his end of the bargain?"

"Was to let two people that deserved to be free of his insatiable need for revenge, be free of his revenge. It was an even trade, one I would do again."

Her head snapped backward. "And so you let smugglers traipse all over your lands?"

"They have been…*requested* to travel along the edges of my land until they get to the bridge. Soon after they cross, they are off my land and someone else's problem."

"Requested?" Her forehead tilted forward as she eyed him through her dark lashes. "As in threatened?"

"As in it behooves their interest to spend as little time as possible on my lands."

Sienna's head half nodded, half shook as she took in his words. Her look snapped to him. "Who were the people?"

"The smugglers?"

"The people you freed from my father's cold hands."

He studied her, his tongue stuck to the roof of his mouth, debating on telling her. This had happened in the years he'd thought she'd been dead, so it wasn't a memory he'd be giving her. "Hunter and Bridget."

Her mouth flew open for a moment, her thick lips forming a circle. She clucked her tongue, then smiled at him. "I think you made a good deal."

He grinned. "I do too."

Their horses rounded the last corner before the crossing and Logan pointed to the bridge ahead. Their trail led up to the side of the bridge and the main road, so they had an excellent view of the graceful arch of iron supporting the weight of the bridge, the river rushing along below from the recent rains.

Logan stopped his horse and Sienna followed suit. He dismounted, tying his horse to a nearby branch, and then went to help Sienna from her mare.

Her gaze stayed riveted on the bridge as he slid his hands around her ribcage and lifted her to the ground. She removed her hat and gloves, hooking them on her sidesaddle, then stepped around him without looking at him.

"Why does this look so familiar?" Her head swung back and forth from the bridge to him, yet her look wouldn't tear away from the arch of the bridge. Finally, she forced her head to turn fully to him, and he could see the panic in the azure streaks of her blue eyes.

"You said this wasn't completed until a few years ago, so why do I know this bridge?" She turned to the bridge, walking toward it.

Logan followed her. For as much as he wanted to tell her—tell her everything of it—he clamped down hard on his tongue.

She needed to remember this on her own.

It was his last chance.

Her footsteps sped, moving her closer to the bridge until she veered to the left off the path and into the grassy bank. She didn't stop until she was within a stone's throw of it, her neck craned upward as she looked up at the bridge from their low vantage spot by the river.

Logan studied her face as her eyes flew back and forth, searching the iron underside of the bridge.

She was so close to it—so close to the memory.

She kept her eyes on the bridge above. "I remember this bridge, Logan—I truly remember it. I remember walking down from the main road." Her look flickered to the roadway that led over the bridge. "I walked down from the roadway and you didn't want me to. But wait—this is different." Her head shook as her look dropped to him. "Why is this different?"

She remembered.

Remembered enough for him to speak. "Because it isn't the same bridge, Sienna. We visited the River Severn gorge where the first iron bridge stands in Herefordshire. This bridge is modelled after it, almost bolt by bolt." He pointed to the iron arch above them. "You found it such a wonder that you wanted to see the arch from below so you could lock the structure into memory and sketch it when we could afford charcoals."

Her blue eyes sparking, she smiled, her gaze lifting and running along the structure. "I did. I remember. Even though the sun was shining, it had rained that morning. And the air smelled just as it does now—wet dirt, crisp."

He inhaled. "Yes. But there are summer blooms in the air now."

"That's right—it was colder, the trees had changed colors." Her head bobbed. "And I ran ahead of you, didn't I?"

He chuckled. "You did. And you slipped."

Her eyes went wide and she smiled. "I slipped and I slid into the river."

"It was swollen and you almost sent me to my grave before I fished you out of the current."

She moved past him to walk closer to the bank of the river, her skirts sweeping along the rushes. She looked up at the bridge again, pointing at the far end of it. "This—this is different, though—three circles of iron on the outer edges of the arch instead of one giant one." She looked to him for confirmation.

His heart thudded hard in his chest. It truly was coming back to her. She wasn't just piecing together tidbits he offered. "Yes. Exactly."

She jumped, her hand waving at the river's edge. "And this was where—you dragged me out of the river, swearing at me, and you carried me up into the adjoining woods. You wouldn't set me down, you wouldn't let me go."

He shook his head.

Her pointed finger travelled up the river bank to the forest by the trail. "And you found this little private clearing in the woods—so private that you stripped me of my clothes and your clothes. And I was laughing the whole time and you were still swearing at me for scaring you. And then you—you started a fire. You wanted to warm me and all I wanted was your naked body."

"Yes."

She stilled for a moment, staring at the line of trees, and her voice dipped low, choking. "We had just gotten married at the Scottish border—a blacksmith wedding. It was directly after we stopped at Shadowmoor and secured your commission. We had the future and we had a month before you had to report to the crown for duty, and we went to visit the bridge because you thought I might like to draw it."

"Yes." His eyes began to water. He wanted to give her everything in this moment—every memory—everything of what they were and what they had been to each other. But he held himself like a rock, only offering a nod.

She spun to him and stepped close, her sparkling blue eyes lifting to him. "And it was perfect." Her words breathless, she lifted her hand, trembling, and she hesitantly set it on his cheek. "It was perfect. The one perfect moment in our lives where we could just exist. We didn't have anywhere to be. We didn't have anyone chasing us. We didn't have anything to answer to. We just were. You and me. And we just existed in peace. Together."

"You remember." He said the words softly, his voice echoing with reverence and disbelief.

"I do." Her eyes went wide. "I truly do."

He leaned down, finding her lips, opening her to him. She didn't resist, needing him just as much he needed her. Her lips soft under his, her sweet breath dusted his cheek, the tip of her tongue tangling with his. Kissing him with all the love she'd ever had for him. Her mouth on his, her body pressing into him.

Perfect.

Until she pulled away, her face contorting.

She staggered backward, her hands dropping from him as her feet stumbled away from him.

No.

Not more.

He wanted her to remember that moment. That one moment of perfection by the iron bridge. Just that one moment so her heart would win over her head's need to leave him.

Just that one moment. That was all he wanted. Not everything.

But it rushed her, waves of memories streaming across her face.

Pain. Tears. A smile. A smile torn away. More tears slicking down her face.

She reeled a step backward with every blow her mind delivered.

Up the bank, across the trail, and into the woods until her back hit a tree.

She doubled over.

Logan could only watch, horrified and helpless, his hands raised as he followed her, ready to catch her.

Her hunched-over body jerked, racked with sob after sob until she looked up at him. All he wanted was to scoop her into his arms, hold her tight against the pain, but every time he took a step forward, she flung a hand out, stopping his motion.

Minutes passed before she straightened slightly. Her arms stayed wrapped tight around her torso. She looked up at him, her tears no longer flowing. But accusation shone bright in her watery eyes.

"My mother…my mother was horrible." A tremble ran through her body. "She wasn't a good person, Logan, even at five years old I knew that. Why didn't you tell me that?"

His lips drew inward for a long moment, his heart tearing out at seeing her pain. "I couldn't tell you, Sienna. You didn't need to know what she was."

She straightened even more, her shoulder blades leaning back to the tree behind her for support. "But I did. I did need to know that. I thought you took away the only person that ever truly loved me—but she didn't. She never loved me. My mother…she never…she beat me…and that day she died…my arm was purple…and I thought…" She wiped away the tears that had started to stream down her face again. She slapped the tears away. She'd always hated crying. Hated how it made her look weak—especially when it was about her mother. He and Robby were the only people she'd ever cried in front of.

She remembered that now too.

She swallowed back a hiccup. "That day she died I wanted to eat those pies Cook made before I saw her, before

I went up to the room because I knew it was over if she saw
my purple arm. She would beat me till I was dead. I knew
that pie would be the last thing I ever ate and I wanted
something tasty on my lips."

Her face blanched, her limbs shaking. "I'm going to
be sick." She spun around the tree, hunching over as she
emptied the contents of her stomach.

Logan could stay back no more.

He stepped forward, his right fingers light onto her
back as he stroked her spine. She didn't push him away and
his chest tightened at her lack of resistance. His left hand
moved forward to brush back the loose strands of hair from
her forehead.

Hunched over, her body still convulsing, she shook her
head. "She was a monster, Logan. A monster."

His fingers curled along her back. "But you loved
her, Sienna, and that was what mattered." He took a deep
breath, his next words condemning himself as he always
needed to. "For as awful as your mother was, you loved her
and I took that away from you."

She twisted in a flurry, standing straight to look at him.
"No. You saved me from her. For as much as I loved her, I
knew she would kill me one day. I knew it. But I accepted
it because she was all I knew. I only loved her because she
was my mother and she insisted that I did so. Even though
she told me every day how she didn't want me. How father
made her keep me. Oh, hell, her ruby ring…she would
smack me…"

Sienna's eyes narrowed, skewering him. "Why? Why
didn't you tell me that you killed her?" She gasped, her eyes

startled. "You didn't mean to do it, did you? I know you, Logan and you would never."

He shook his head. "I just wanted her to sleep through the night before she saw your purple arm and beat you. That was all."

"And instead you killed her."

"Yes."

"Why didn't you tell me that?" She struck his chest with her palm. "Why didn't you defend yourself? I have been vilifying you for what happened and it wasn't true."

Her hand swung forward to hit him again and he caught her wrist, stopping the motion. "I couldn't defend myself against what I did, Sienna—you were either going to forgive me, or you wouldn't. Explanations wouldn't matter and I knew I could never convince you to forgive me if you didn't truly feel it. Only you could make that decision."

Her captured wrist jerked at him. "Yes, but you could have made the decision easier."

His grip on her wrist tightened, shaking. "Or not—I didn't want you to remember her—how she was to you—all of it."

"You could have told me I was unwanted, Logan. Unloved. It would have made more sense."

"No, I couldn't." He dropped her wrist and his hand ran over his eyes. How to explain the impossible? It took all his fortitude to make his eyes meet hers, and he pinned her with his look. "I know how you carried the wound of her hatred for you in your soul for years."

"Logan—"

He turned from her, his hands curling into fists, his voice rising. "I couldn't do that to you, Sienna—I couldn't inflict that wound onto your heart again. Not if it was in my power to keep it from you. And I couldn't defend myself against her death without you knowing that fact."

Silence echoed around them.

The forest stilled, birds quieted, squirrels frozen.

His heartbeat thundering in his ears, he couldn't turn back to her. Couldn't stand to see the scorn in her eyes one more time.

Then, mercy.

From behind him, her fingers wrapped around his upper arm. "You are more important than the past, Logan." Her voice was soft, calm, as though the weight of a thousand stones had been lifted from her chest.

She tugged at him, forcing him to turn to her. For a long breath he stood, his head bowed, gathering the courage he needed to lift his eyes and meet hers.

"No matter what has happened, Logan. No matter what you think you deserve for the way we were forced to grow up. The things we were forced to do." She stepped fully in front of him, her blue eyes glistening, the azure streaks in them sparking. "You, Logan. You are the one that has always refused to be controlled by your circumstances. Don't start now."

The boulder in his throat so constricting, he had to take an extra breath to force words to his tongue. "What are my circumstances, Sienna?"

Her look fixed upon him, her right cheek lifted in a slight smile. "Your circumstances are that you need to take me home."

His eyebrows lifted.

"Home to Shadowmoor."

{ CHAPTER 21 }

The sky had turned into a magnificent show of gold and violet streaks entwining, dancing in a mad fury over the warmth of the summer day blanketing the land.

They had taken their time in returning to Shadowmoor. Stopping to eat the bread and cheese Logan had brought. Walking the horses along the lane as she peppered him with memory after memory that filled her mind.

With every memory that was verified, relief flooded her.

Her mind was back, and she was still stunned to realize she'd forgotten so much for so long.

Halfway back she'd spied a glen nestled into a secluded clearing in the forest and she dragged Logan into it. Thick green grasses, so tall they bent over into haphazard mounds of sweet drifts, hid their naked bodies. She'd thought she could wait to get him alone and naked until they were back at Shadowmoor, but that was before she realized she was helpless against touching her husband. Not when her memories had returned and she could finally place the depth of her love for him.

Instead of just feeling it, taking on faith what was in her heart—she knew it again. Knew it from her first memory of him, when he had made her laugh with funny faces at the cook's table in the kitchen of the Joker's Roost, to the last memory she had of him in the cottage in Spain where he'd kissed her senseless, wanting—demanding more. "Always leave with a reason to return," he'd said with a wink, his dark silver grey eyes that she knew better than her own twinkling in the light of the hearth's fire.

Nothing but that—those moments with him—mattered. She knew again in her heart, in her soul, and in her mind that her love was unending and couldn't be broken. Not by the past. And never again by the future.

As long as she could avoid another knock to the head, that was. She would have to write herself some notes when she got back to the castle, just to guard against another unfortunate calamity taking her memories again and making her question her husband.

Sienna glanced up at the sky.

Dusk was quickly settling, and across a wide field she spied the ancient castle with its four imposing towers as they emerged from the trail that led to the river. Their time in the glen had done little to satiate her need of Logan's touch—it had truly just aggravated her urgency to get him to his chambers.

She set her horse into a gallop across the open land and Logan's laugh followed her as he nudged his horse next to hers.

It wasn't until they were almost at the stables that she realized something was wrong ahead. Deathly wrong.

Frantic, she pushed her mare to its limit the last hundred paces.

She yanked on her reins, and the horse's front legs reared up at the sudden stop. Grabbing the pommel, Sienna's heart dropped into her stomach as she scoured the scene in front of the stables.

Hunter stood in an open air phaeton, a rifle jutted against his shoulder, his head cocked down as he aimed. He was still. Deathly still.

The line of his rifle's barrel was aimed at three men by the center stable's entrance. Four huge men flanked a slightly shorter, rotund man bedecked in a purple coat.

Her father.

Her father, here at Shadowmoor.

A cloud of dust swirled by her as Logan jerked his horse to a stop slightly in front of her.

She glanced at the four brutes on either side of her father. She didn't recognize any of them. No loyalty there.

All the Nowheres Boys she'd grown up with, except for Logan and Robby, were probably dead or in Newgate.

Her gaze flew back to Hunter.

Bridget stood behind him with a second rifle in her hands. Cocked and ready for her husband, she presumed. Sienna squinted, tracing the line of Hunter's rifle to the target. Hunter had it aimed at Bournestein instead of at the fool to the left of her father waving a pistol at Hunter and Bridget.

Without moving a muscle, Hunter's voice cut across the eerie silence to Logan and Sienna. "We just arrived back from Peddington as our guests here were dismounting. I was just encouraging them to leave."

"The three?" Logan asked from atop his dark steed. Sienna knew instantly Logan was asking about their children, but didn't name them as such. Given the chance, if her father knew there were children here, he wouldn't hesitate to use them to his advantage.

"In the castle," Hunter answered.

She pulled her stare from her father and his brutes to look at Logan as he nodded. She guessed there was enough staff inside that would give their lives for those three children, they were so beloved. Her father would never get to them. The relief at that fact did little to ease the angry stones that had settled into the pit of her belly.

"What are you doing here, Bournestein?" Logan slid off his horse and took two steps toward the line of men.

"What do ye think I'm doing here, boy?" Bournestein looked to Sienna, then back to Logan. "Ye think that double-crossin' bastard brother of yers went unnoticed? Taking me only daughter from her safe and secure home."

"What do you want, Bournestein?" Logan asked again, his voice hard. Lethal. Vibrating with contempt.

Sienna had never heard him like this. Logan was always in control. Always. But his voice alone told her he wasn't in control of himself. Not by far. And control was what one needed when facing off with her father.

She remembered that. Remembered it well.

Swinging his gold-tipped cane, Bournestein stepped toward Logan, his men moving in flank with him. "I come to retrieve what's mine."

Instinct sent Sienna flying off her horse, striding past Logan and planting herself in front of her father with a screech escaping her lips.

With her memories came the knowledge of how ruthlessly brutal her father could be and she'd not have Logan or Hunter or Bridget hurt because of her. "No. I'm not your property, Father. I never have been. You need to leave."

He slapped her quick, the sting of it sending her cheek tingling. "Hush. Ye'll stay out of this if ye know what's good fer ye, lass." He flipped his head toward Logan. "This is between yer husband and me."

"You mean you and your four brutes," Sienna spat out.

Bournestein's beady eyes flickered to her, then settled back on Logan. "Just evening the odds, lass."

She grabbed her father's forearm, the purple velvet crushing under her fingers. "No. You need to leave—leave us in peace, Father."

"Sienna—"

Her name came from Logan's lips, full of raging fury. Without turning back to him she tossed her free hand up behind her, spreading her fingers wide to stop him. Stop him from advancing. Stop him from saying another word.

For a long moment, her father appeared to actually consider her demand. Then the snake smile spread across his lips. "I don't think so, lass. I think I just be taking ye."

Bournestein motioned to the brute at his left and the man snatched Sienna's arm, spinning and pinning her, crushing her into his chest. She started to fight, swinging at anything her fists and feet could reach. Then she heard a distinctive click and the barrel of a pistol set hard against her temple.

She froze.

"Father." Her yelp came out strangled.

Bournestein waved his hand in her direction. "It'll keep ye still for this, lass. Don't want to jostle Blue Bob's arm now, do ye?"

Logan had already closed in the distance to Bournestein and his men, stopping far enough away to not be an immediate threat, but also past the distance her father's cane would reach. Her father used his cane mercilessly, and he was quick with it, the iron rod running through the middle shaft of the wood making every blow brutal.

"Get that pistol off of my wife's temple, Bournestein." Logan's tone had shifted. A tone she recognized. Still deadly. But now cold as well. Cold and controlled. Cold to the point that he was going to win. Win no matter what.

It was exactly what she needed to hear.

He was going to be fine, no matter what happened next.

The brute's arm around her belly tightened, clasping her hard to the stench of him. If she didn't have the barrel of a pistol aimed at her head by a twitchy hand, Logan's voice would have done even more to bolster her confidence.

Bournestein lifted his cane, circling it as he pointed it to the castle behind them. "Ye think this fancy hunk of stones gives ye right to order me about, boy?"

"It'll give me the power to tear you down, whorehouse, by whorehouse, gaming hell by gaming hell, if you don't let Sienna go."

A caustic chuckle left Bournestein and he spit toward Logan's feet. "Ye reach too far, boy. Ye always have. Those presumptuous airs about ye." He swung his cane in front of Logan, cutting it with a whistle through the air. "Yer me, boy. Ye've always been me. Born in the wrong station. The only difference is I know where I belong and I've never fought it. I embraced it and that has given me the world." He jabbed his cane into the granite gravel next to his foot. "The money. The people. I control everyone in St. Giles."

Logan's glare skewered him. "Not everyone."

"No. Not everyone." Bournestein chuckled, the snake smile curling the outer edges of his lips into his portly cheeks. "Ye were the only one to ever defy me and live. And still ye fight it. I told yer mother ye were the heir—ye would have me empire. That was how she let me into her bed, boy, did ye know it? She whored herself out fer ye."

"You bastard, I never wanted your empire—your blood money." Logan's voice lost the note of cool detachment and he took a step forward, fists clenched, then stopped himself, withdrawing his gained step.

He wasn't ready to strike. Not yet.

He was waiting. Waiting for something. Sienna's muscles coiled. Whatever it was, Sienna had to be ready.

Bournestein whipped his cane through the air, jabbing it at the castle. "Ye think the riches of yer duchy are clean? Built on the end of a blade—just the same as mine—the only difference being it was hundreds of years ago."

"Yet we don't live in that world anymore, Bournestein." Logan's voice had tempered, back in control again.

"We always live in that world, boy. That's what ye never could accept." Bournestein guffawed, shaking his head. "I never should have kept ye for Sienna after yer mother died. I figured on ye being her best protector, but I should've kicked ye and yer brat brother out of the Joker's Roost the second they took her body away."

"And I should have left." Logan's reply was instant and cold, juxtaposed to the rage starting to mottle on Bournestein's forehead. Logan glanced up at the sky. Sienna's eyes followed his look. Darkness was settling. Whatever was going to happen, needed to happen fast. Her father's men excelled in the dark—it was where they lived and breathed, in the darkest shadows.

Logan's gaze fell to Bournestein. "But I stayed because I couldn't leave Sienna to your mercy. I was her best protector. You're not wrong on that score. Only she needed to be protected from you." Logan took a cautious step toward him, within striking distance. "Bournestein, it's time. Let my wife go. Let your daughter go."

Bournestein swung his cane with the speed of a striking snake. Logan caught the end of the stick in midair, the cords of muscles on his forearm straining.

Bournestein tried to yank the cane away to no avail, and his face mottled fully, spittle forming on the edge of his mouth as his words flew. "Ye think yer so smart, boy, ye think reason will get ye out of this. That was what ye never understood. Folk like us, we decide things with blades and gunpowder. And I ain't seen none of that on ye, boy. So I think we'll be leaving now. And I'll be back fer me cane." His hand holding the cane flung open, releasing his grip on it. He turned and strolled lazily to his horse, grabbing the reins and bringing it alongside Sienna. "Try and stop us, boy, and it'll be the death of yer wife."

Logan's voice cut into the silence. One word.

"Hunter."

A shot blasted into the thick air.

The brute holding Sienna dropped behind her, sinking to the ground, his hand on the pistol falling from her temple. Sienna sank in unison, his dead arm tangled around her, dragging her down with him.

Another shot, the blast next to her ear as the man's hand hit the gravel, knocking the trigger.

She slammed into the ground and instinct sent her rolling. Rolling away from the brute, and when she landed on her back, she saw her father's horse rearing from the blasts of the guns.

Rearing directly above her.

Frantic hooves flailed high in the air over her face. White legs against the streaks of dark blues streaming across the sky. Hooves coming down at her face.

A mass of cloth and flesh landed over her eyes, her chest, suffocating her scream just as the hooves descended on her head.

She could feel the impact, hear the bones above her crushing.

One hoof. Two. Up, and then down again a second time. The weight of the horse crushed down upon her through the flesh. A convulsion ripped through the body atop her.

Everything went still. Everything except for the horse running, the ground trembling as heavy hooves darted to a frantic escape.

But the body on top of her face and torso—still.

Still and dead.

A mass so heavy she couldn't breathe.

She moved her arm, wedging it up next to her ribcage, pushing. Too heavy. She was quickly running out of air.

She shoved again.

And again. Then somehow freed her other hand to push up as well.

In one striking whoosh, the body lifted off of her, air and dust enveloping her. She flipped to her side, gasping. Gasping for air.

No. Hell. No.
No. No. No.
Not Logan. Not Logan.

Her eyes shut tight. She couldn't roll back to the body behind her. Couldn't see his crushed body. Blood on his face. On his skull. Couldn't see him not breathing. Not living.

"Sienna."

Logan's voice sank down to her, filtering into her ears between her gasps.

Her eyes flew open and she looked up.

Logan was crouched over her, his hand reaching to her face. Terror in his eyes.

A ghost. A ghost and this would be the last time she saw him.

No.
No.
No.

"Sienna." His hand touched her cheek.

A solid hand.

A hand made of flesh and bone.

Her fingers clasped onto the back of his, squeezing it, making sure it was real. "Logan?"

"Are you hurt? Sienna?" Panic had taken over his voice and he reached with his other hand to her shoulder, shaking her. "Sienna, talk to me. Talk to me."

"Logan? What? You're—if you're there—then what—who?" She pushed herself up slightly, craning her neck to see behind her.

Her father. His skull cracked. Blood seeping in blotchy spots into the purple velvet of his overcoat.

"Father?"

Logan wrapped his arms around her, pulling her upright. "Are you hurt?"

She couldn't tear her eyes off her father. His broken body. Always so big. Always so fearful. Now crumpled in a mangled mess.

The father she loved.

The father she hated.

Logan's hand went onto the back of her head, turning her away from the sight and tucking her face into his chest. His chin came down on the top of her head, cocooning her. "You don't need to witness it, Sienna."

She let him. Let him turn her from the man that had controlled so much of her life. She couldn't believe he was gone. Dead from the world.

She started to shake. Tremble after tremble racking her body.

Pulling back slightly, she looked up at Logan as unspent panic took a hold of her. "You—you ripped my heart out—I thought it was you on top of me and my world was collapsing into nothingness."

He didn't reply, only crushed her to him, holding her, refusing to let her go.

"Logan." Hunter's voice reached her ears.

Logan's chin lifted from her head and he twisted to the side to look at something.

"The other three?" Hunter's low words were deadly, ready for anything, ready for orders.

Sienna turned her head against Logan's chest, following the voice. Hunter stood next to them on the ground, the second rifle Bridget had readied in his hands and pointed at the three other brutes. One was flat on the ground, not awake, a bleeding gash across his head that could have only been caused by her father's cane. The second one sat next to him, holding his knee that was askew, his face grimacing in pain. The third stood behind the other two, his hands up in front of him, eyes begging for mercy.

Logan had worked quickly with her father's cane in his hand.

Her husband's muscles tensed under her cheek. Sienna shifted forward to look past Logan, only to see the brute that had held the pistol to her temple now in a pile on the ground, his forehead oozing blood.

"Go. They can go." Logan heaved a breath into his lungs. Sienna could feel how very against his instinct that command was. He wanted the brutes dead.

She wanted the brutes dead.

But that was not the world they lived in anymore.

"You are positive?" Hunter asked.

Logan nodded, his chin bumping into the top of her head. "There's already been too much bloodshed. But see them to the border of the land. Give them their horses and coin enough so they don't terrorize the countryside on their journey back to London." Logan's voice went brutal and he twisted to the brutes. "If I hear so much as a tulip was crumpled under your feet on your way south, I will come for you."

The two awake men nodded, quickly dragging their unconscious man back to the horses they had ridden into Shadowmoor. They heaved him on his belly over one of the horses and then mounted with haste.

His rifle still trained on the men, Hunter mounted Logan's horse and followed the men down the pathway to the main road.

Logan shifted, going to his feet and lifting Sienna up with him. He set her to her toes and Sienna looked around her at the carnage, her gaze averting past her father's lifeless eyes.

Her stare landed on the brute that had held her and she noted the bullet hole. Her look whipped to Bridget. "Hunter shot him? That was the first blast? He shot him with my head inches away?" Her mouth went dry at the thought of how very close that bullet had been to her skull.

Bridget nodded, a gleam of pride in her eye. "He's one of the crown's finest marksmen."

"*The* finest marksman. And the only one I would trust to take that shot—to hold your life in his trigger finger." Logan's arm tightened around her shoulders.

Bridget glanced at the two bodies, then looked to Logan. "I'm going to go check on the stable boy—we saw them hit him over the head and drag him into a stall when we pulled in. Then I'll gather up men to take care of the bodies and the horses."

Logan inclined his head to her. "Thank you."

Charging a wide swath around the bodies, Bridget disappeared into the center stable.

His arm moved down to an iron clasp around her back and Logan ushered Sienna up the path toward the castle. She didn't resist.

It wasn't until he'd led her up to her chambers and closed the door behind him that she could take a full, deep breath into her lungs.

His arm locked around her back slid off of her and he walked over to the table. He picked up the decanter of brandy on the table and set the crystal to the lip of a glass.

"He saved me, Logan." The words left her not as her own, small and breathless.

His hand paused in pouring the drink and he looked to her, the crinkles around his eyes deep in concern. "He did. In the end, he did."

He finished pouring the amber liquid into the glass and strode over to her, grabbing her wrist and lifting it. He set the glass in her hand.

Grateful, she took three healthy swallows.

She'd thought it odd that he'd left the full decanter in her room days ago and she hadn't touched it. But with her memories back about her, she realized how she actually liked the taste. Growing up in the Joker's Roost had done that for her. To her.

She took a fourth swallow.

Logan lifted the glass from her hand and drank the rest in one long gulp.

He set it on the side table by the door and moved back in front of her, his hands clasping her face between his palms. The tips of his fingers trembled against her skin. "Hell, Sienna, you don't know what those seconds when you were under that horse did to me."

"The same thing done to me when I thought it was you atop me, shielding me, bones cracking."

He nodded, his silver grey eyes solemn. "For everything your father was and wasn't to us—he saved your life. For that one action alone, I will honor his spirit and forgive the years before."

"Can you do that? Can *I* do that?"

His lips drew inward for a long moment. "I don't think we have a choice in the matter. He's gone. He cannot come after us ever again."

Tears sprung into her eyes, and for once, she didn't feel the need to wipe them away, to hide them from the world, from her husband. "We're free, aren't we?"

He nodded, the liberated look in his eyes simultaneously breaking and filling her heart. His fingers moved upward, curling into her hair. "Free. As long as I have you by my side."

She smiled through the tears streaming down her face. "You have all of me, Logan. You're my always."

{ EPILOGUE }

Sienna hadn't asked about it. Hadn't wanted to ask, for it had taken a month for her to even begin to think of her father's end. Of how his need for control caused his own demise.

That, she had finally settled in her mind.

There was just one thing more. Of everything of their childhood, of everything she had remembered in the last six weeks since her father's death, this was the one worry she could not shake.

But there, under the crook of her husband's arm long atop the back of the wrought iron bench high on the ridge, it was finally time to put to rest the last of the past.

Setting her thoughts in order, she watched the sun dipping low in the far-off sky, tinges of purple splendor starting to streak across the sky. Logan sat with ease, his right ankle propped atop his left knee, his fingers twiddling with a long lock of her hair, weaving it in and out of his fingers. The serenity about him struck her time and again— peace she'd never thought to see in his body or his eyes. Seeing it swelled her heart over and over.

So much so, she almost didn't want to ask the question and upset the tranquility. But she needed to know.

She twisted her head upward to see Logan's face, to see his reaction before he tried to cover up whatever he didn't want her to see. "About Robby—I never asked."

His grey eyes went guarded. "Never asked what?"

"What happened to your brother after he delivered me to Shadowmoor?"

"He left." Logan's look went off into the distance for a long moment before it dropped to her. "But he wanted you to know he was sorry."

"Sorry for that last night at the Joker's Roost before we escaped?"

"Sorry for everything."

She nodded, a deep breath settling into her chest. "Did he ever learn that we were never going to leave him behind?"

"I told him in London after the Revelry's Tempest burned down—and it was something he never knew. Bournestein certainly never told him. And all these years he lived with the belief that we were going to leave him behind."

"Did he believe you when you told him?"

Logan's right cheek pulled back. "I think—in so much as he wanted to believe me. I think he knows deep down I never would have abandoned him—*we* never would have abandoned him."

"I tried to tell him that night after he dragged me off, but he was too drunk to hear me."

"And he hurt you." Logan's voice went hard, remnants of long ago fury still tangible in his words.

Her lips pulled inward for a long moment. "I do not give him an excuse, but I know that was not the true him. He was drunk and in a rage, but even with that he would never hurt me. Scare me, yes, but never truly hurt me."

His arm tightened around her shoulders. "And I could never let him have you. Not when I needed you."

She lifted her fingers, touching the strong line of his chin that she loved to sketch. "I never wanted him, Logan, only you. Always you."

His head bent down to her, his lips finding hers in the longest, softest kiss that still managed to curl her toes.

She looked out at the last sliver of the sun disappearing beyond the rolling hills. "Tell me Robby escaped. Escaped to somewhere good after he left here. I want that for him, this peace we have found."

Logan shook his head. "I can't tell you where he has ended, for he didn't tell me where he was to disappear to. I hope to know someday."

She nodded and then pulled back suddenly to pin her husband with a look. "Oh, and I have one more item to set to rest with you."

His eyebrow cocked.

"What were you going to do if I had left after those first seven days here at Shadowmoor per our agreement? Would you have truly let me go?"

His mouth clamped shut, but the edges of his lips quivered, hiding a smile.

"Logan?"

"Do you want me to answer that?"

"Yes."

"Do you want me to answer truthfully?"

She swatted his chest.

"Then yes. And no." He exhaled a long sigh. "Yes, I would have delivered you to anywhere you wanted to be. And then no, I wouldn't have let you be. I would have set up camp at your front door."

"For how long?"

"For as long as it took, Sienna." He pulled her back against his body. "I was not about to be far from you when you forgave me. Or when your memories came back."

She swatted his chest again. "Part of me hates that answer, but mostly I love it."

He chuckled. "You've always been a complicated one, Sienna."

"Except in one thing." She had to crane her neck to look up at him he held her so close.

His eyebrows lifted.

"My love for you, Logan. That has never been complicated. Our lives, what was around us, yes. But you— my love for you was never complicated. Only right."

He set his lips to her forehead. "Always right, my love."

She nuzzled her head against his chest and looked out across the purples and pinks dancing in the sky above the vista. This was always her favorite time of day at Shadowmoor. "For as much as I always loved that Constable painting, this is so much better in person. Bridget was right about this place—it has gotten into my bones far faster than I imagined it could."

"Does that mean you're not looking forward to our trip to London next month?"

She grinned. "I do rather enjoy being the recluse duchess."

"Cass wrote to report the renovations on the house that will hold the new Revelry's Tempest are moving along nicely, so we may be able to postpone our trip by another month."

"Did the solicitor manage to buy that house directly next door to the old one?"

"He did."

"Did Cass mention if it was difficult to buy that townhouse? It would seem lucky to get it."

Logan chuckled. "She wrote that the owners were delighted to sell. Apparently, a house next to a gaming hall is not the most desirable thing to sell. They'd been trying to do so for years."

"Imagine that."

"Yes." He grinned. "Imagine that."

"And Greyson is doing well at managing it all?"

"Cass wrote that he is better than all of us at managing the construction and he has grand plans for the future. That, and he is holding the guard together well. He's even adding some men to the ranks as there have been plenty of special assignments rolling in."

She looked at him. "So we can just send the investment funds and not have to be there?"

"I see the twinkle in your eye." He smiled at her scheming. "So yes, hopefully. Greyson is doing so well our presence in London should only occasionally be required."

Her grin went wide, beaming. "Excellent."

Logan's bent leg shifted down and he stretched out his legs. "Though you do realize Cass and Violet and Adalia are all planning the next London season for you, duchess—one beyond all measure of restraint and good taste? A season to break all seasons."

"That sounds like fun," she said with a chuckle.

"Too much so, if you ask me. Not that they did."

She poked him in the chest. "As fun as I imagine it would be to make you suffer through balls and dinners and chitchat with the chortling peers chomping on cigars, I'm afraid the season to break all seasons will have to be placed on hold."

His eyebrows lifted in hope. "You're taking pity upon me?"

"Something akin to that." She reached across his chest and grabbed his hand, then clasped it to her belly, holding it flat against her skin.

He jerked upright, turning fully to her on the bench, his fingers curling over her belly, his silver grey eyes wide. "This? A babe?"

She smiled, nodding. "You work quickly, my husband."

He laughed, wrapping his arms around her and clutching her tight to his chest.

She had to wiggle her head backward to look up at him. "Our time was never before. But it is now."

"It is our time, isn't it?" His lips came down, meeting hers, the heady scent of him stealing her every thought. He lifted up slightly, his eyes intent on hers. "You are my heart, Sienna, and I thank the stars every night for bringing you back to me."

Her hand wedged upward to set her palm along his face, her favorite rough scruff of his beard tickling her skin. "The stars, I think, are finally our friends, my husband."

"That they are. May it always be so."

~ About the Author ~

K.J. Jackson is the author of the *Hold Your Breath,*
Lords of Fate, Lords of Action, Revelry's Tempest,
and *Flame Moon* series.

She specializes in historical and paranormal romance,
loves to travel (road trips are the best!), and is a sucker for a
good story in any genre. She lives in Minnesota with
her husband, two children, and a dog who
has taken the sport of bed-hogging
to new heights.

Visit her at www.kjjackson.com

~ Author's Note ~

Thank you for allowing my stories into your life
and time—it is an honor!

Be sure to check out all my historical romances
(each is a stand-alone story):
Stone Devil Duke, *A Hold Your Breath Novel*
Unmasking the Marquess, *A Hold Your Breath Novel*
My Captain, My Earl, *A Hold Your Breath Novel*
Worth of a Duke, *A Lords of Fate Novel*
Earl of Destiny, *A Lords of Fate Novel*
Marquess of Fortune, *A Lords of Fate Novel*
Vow, *A Lords of Action Novel*
Promise, *A Lords of Action Novel*
Oath, *A Lords of Action Novel*
Of Valor & Vice, *A Revelry's Tempest Novel*
Of Sin & Sanctuary, *A Revelry's Tempest Novel*
Of Risk & Redemption, *A Revelry's Tempest Novel*
To Capture a Rogue, *Logan's Legends, A Revelry's Tempest Novel*
To Capture a Warrior, *Logan's Legends, A Revelry's Tempest Novel*
The Devil in the Duke, *A Revelry's Tempest Novel*

Never miss a new release or sale!
Be sure to sign up for my VIP Email List at
www.KJJackson.com

Interested in Paranormal Romance?
In the meantime, if you want to switch genres and check out my Flame
Moon paranormal romance series, ***Flame Moon #1***, the first book
in the series, is currently free (ebook) at all stores. ***Flame Moon*** is a
stand-alone story, so no worries on getting sucked into a cliffhanger.
But number two in the series, ***Triple Infinity***, ends with a fun cliff, so
be forewarned. Number three in the series, ***Flux Flame***, ties up that
portion of the series.

Connect with me!
www.KJJackson.com
kjk19jackson@gmail.com

A man accustomed to hiding secrets. A woman with a lost past.
Love that cannot be denied.

A MAN ACCUSTOMED TO HIDING SECRETS.

His dark silver eyes are haunted, and for good reason. Logan Lipinstein lost his wife years ago in the war and has been a living shell of a man ever since, attempting to atone for past sins. Until one fateful day, when she walks past him carrying a basket of bread.

A WOMAN WITH A LOST PAST.

Sienna Ponstance lives in the comfort of her grandmother's estate, having long ago put herself on the shelf as a spinster. She has her charcoals, the village that she loves, and peaceful days—even if something has always been missing from her life. Until the day her tranquility is shattered when a strange man accosts her as she is walking home from the village.

LOVE REUNITED.

His wife—dead for ten years—walked along the path in front of Logan. Scarcely believing his eyes, he approaches her and is quickly rewarded wit a rebuff that includes the point of a knife. Sienna has no memory of him, thinking him only a ruffian.

Now he just has to convince her that he actually is her husband. And that their boundless love can conquer anything—including a past that threatens them at every turn.

ABOUT THE AUTHOR

K.J. Jackson is the *USA Today* bestselling author of the *Revelry's Tempest, Lords of Action, Lords of Fate, Hold Your Breath,* and *Flame Moon* series. She specializes in historical and paranormal romance, loves to travel, and is a sucker for a good story in any genre. She lives in Minnesota with her husband, two children, and a dog who has taken the sport of bed-hogging to new heights.

Visit her at www.kjjackson.com.

ISBN 978-1-940149-33-2

90000

9 781940 149332